THE LAST ASSI

GAVRIELLE GROVES-GIDNEY was born in Brooklyn in 1956. She has worked around the world as a geophysical consultant and now lives in the United Kingdom. This is her first novel.

THE LAST ASSIGNMENT

Gavrielle Groves-Gidney

Angela Royal Publishing

Published by ANGELA ROYAL PUBLISHING LTD
P.O. Box 138, Tunbridge Wells, Kent TN3 0ZT

First published 1997
1 3 5 7 9 10 8 6 4 2

A CIP catalogue for this book is available from the British Library
ISBN 1-899860-50-9

Typeset by Nick Awde/Desert♥Hearts
Cover design by Nick Awde & Emanuela Losi
Cover photograph by Steven Rothfeld (Tony Stone Images)
Printed by Biddles Ltd, Guildford

To Paul Bathurst
who gave me legs upon which to stand,
and to Jean McConnell
who graced me with wings to fly.

1

DHAKA AIRPORT WAS QUIETER than the clamour of its city streets, a refuge from the pandemonium, the gaudiness, the stench of its sewerless poverty and crowded filthy river. Carlton Ramsey leaned his ageing torso against a greying wall in the arrivals room, chewing impatiently on the end of an unlit cigar.

The damned plane was late. Well, what did he expect? Running on time wasn't a concept the Bangladeshis had ever bothered to grasp. He should have stayed in the Company house for a while longer. Done another hour's work.

What the hell.

He shifted angrily, trying to ignore the niggle of pain that sprang up in his chest. This wasn't the way to end a career. Not his anyway. He'd always expected to be carted out of the Company in a box. Not booted out the door when he was still full of energy, full of drive.

And it didn't matter what they called it. It was still the same: early retirement, another corporate euphemism.

That bastard Shumacker from Head Office, must have broken necks climbing to the top of the administrative heap just to have the pleasure of letting him know. "The Company's doing you a favour, Carlton. Letting you go early. I'd give my right arm for a chance to sit back and do nothing for a change."

Bullshit.

"And by the way, we're sending you someone to train up for us... A new boy from New York. A..." There was a pause on the line. "Wait a second, I've got a pile of papers on my desk three feet deep. Here it is. Let's see, a Jewish sounding name: Joshua Felstein. And Carlton... Try to get along with him."

Carlton wanted to smack the phone down but corporate instinct stopped him dead — Shumacker was the worst kind of enemy. He held his tongue.

"Try to get along with him."

Shumacker must have searched long and hard for a graduate like that just so he could get even. And the Company had played into his hands, expecting him to lie down and play dead to a know nothing snotty kid.

He grabbed the crumbling cigar out of his mouth and dropped it to the ground. There was a stir of beggars just behind him. He knew what they'd been waiting for. The moment he moved away the butt would be gone — one cigar could build half a family home the way some of these people lived.

He searched in his shirt pocket for another cigar — there was one left from the cache he'd bought from that little tobacconist on Mount Row in London. Should have asked the new boy to bring out some Havanas, at least then he would have served some purpose other than to cause irritation.

He wiped his forehead. The tropical climate was getting harder and harder to deal with. The heat that rolled up in waves from the melting tarmac, the smell of earth and sewage that pervaded every stitch of clothing or fold of skin was what Maribel had complained about. That and... Well, she of all people should have been able to adapt.

"Six months, Maribel," he griped aloud as if she were there. "Six months and then we're off to Connecticut. Retiring gracefully, like two old swans singing into the bloody sunset."

There was a tug on the leg of his trousers. Two scrawny children shoved their open palms upward.

"I've given you something already," he shooed them away. But as usual they refused to take no as an answer to their incessant scrounging.

Maribel and he had been tempted to take a few of the children into care when they'd first arrived in Dhaka. Not these urchins who begged at the airport. They were well fed, with sparkling bright eyes and mischievous grins. They earned a good living. No, he was thinking of the strays by the Government centre who lived, if that's what you could call it, in ramshackle straw and paper huts. Jesus, what a hell hole that was.

He shuddered. They had decided against. It would have been less than a drop in the bucket. Had they adopted a hundred children it would have been a useless effort, for a hundred more would have replaced them by the birth of another day.

Every thing about the place was a shock. Even to his hardened system. This had to be one of his toughest assignments. And it wasn't only the place that made it so. He understood only too well why Shumacker had picked an eager Jewish puppy to torment him.

The glint of plane flashed through the window before he heard the roar. Even if he had been blind, its arrival would have been obvious by the heightened chatter that filled the waiting room.

The craft breezed in. A good landing, followed by a louder squabble of excitement. Carlton also sensed it coursing through him. "Look on the bright side," he murmured to himself. "Someone new to talk to."

The waiting room burst into action: the bedlam of rickshaw drivers scrambling for a piece of the action, business men and relief workers needing transport. Rashid, the Company's man in Dhaka, was inside immigration and customs doing 'business' so that when Felstein came through loaded with bags and equipment he wouldn't have any trouble — not after Rashid used Company money discreetly.

Carlton checked his watch. Twenty minutes for the baggage, ten minutes for the rest. Right on cue Rashid came rushing out, he was getting better at his job every day. The Bangladeshi was followed closely by a tall wiry American with black wavy hair and thick dark glasses.

"Mr. Carlton," Rashid beamed with pride. "We have no trouble in Customs today. My cousin Jamal is on duty. No worries."

Carlton turned his attention to the newcomer whose facial features were close together, like a monkey's. He grasped the extended hand, expecting it to be limp. To his surprise it was firm and strong.

At least that was something.

"Mr. Ramsey, Josh Felstein. Hey, nice to meet you! Thanks for being here. What a great place!" He shouted breathlessly as if he'd just run off the plane. "This is amazing! Just amazing!"

"You travel much?" Carlton asked as they faced the exit, but the kid didn't pick up on his tone. They stepped out the doors, immediately bombarded by the expected battalion of young beggars, scratching and mewling like hungry cats.

"Bakshee, Bakshee," they cried incessantly, skilfully.

Carlton resisted the urge to press another coin into their upturned hands. He knew what happened when Baksheesh started flashing.

"Parents took us overseas once when I was a boy!" Felstein hollered over the beggars' cries. "Other than that I've just travelled around the States." He stopped and said, "Should I give them something?"

9

"Sure. You're probably the best thing they've seen this year."

Felstein dug through his pockets, started handing out US quarters.

'Now watch what happens,' Carlton mumbled to himself as a swarm of children, from nowhere, descended upon the gold mine. He wanted to see how the new-boy handled himself, see what he would do. He squinted in the hazy, heavy light. Felstein was emptying his pockets. Stupid kid. It would never satisfy them.

"No more Bakshee!"

The beggars didn't listen.

Carlton grumbled to himself, 'It's baksheesh, kid'. But he didn't bother to correct him. Let him find out for himself.

Felstein pulled the empty pockets out of his trousers. "Honest," he said, "I'm all out."

The kid's protests didn't make a dent in the cries for money, there was always something more you could give.

"All right, scram!" Carlton broke the scrimmage as a path appeared in the midst of squirming limbs. But as they hurried to the jeep, the beggars scurried around, knocking against their legs, tugging at the baggage, tripping them up.

"Welcome to Dhaka, Mr. Joshua." Rashid opened the doors of the vehicle despite the young rascals vying for attention. "My people are pleased to have you here. It is good progress for my country to have oil drilling."

Carlton had heard the same words on his arrival but since then it had become obvious that Rashid was a rare bird of welcome. Sure, he had something to gain from all this but he had a lot more to lose if events took a turn for the worse. Well he couldn't have asked much more from the man. He was reliable and consistent, an unusual quality in a people educated by the unpredictable ravages of nature and crooked politicians.

As they drove away the children hung on to the side of the vehicle, pressing their faces against the glass, their bright, earnest eyes searching for a hint of capitulation.

"You'd better ignore 'em or we'll never get out of here." Carlton turned from the pleading eyes.

They left the emptying airport. Felstein stared out of the window and it gave Carlton an opportunity to study him. The kid seemed to be absorbing every detail of the scenery: the flimsily clad brown bodies, the rickshaws, the tumult of the streets.

Carlton remembered the first time he'd been sent overseas, to

Jakarta. Sent out to work for old Hornsby, Maribel's dad. Damn, those were exciting days! Hornsby and he had got along so well, most people thought they were father and son. He glanced again at the Jew. There was a determination about the face, the jaw was strong and firm but stuck out a bit too much, making him look somewhat petulant. Like a child.

Carlton recalled the resume. The kid was only twenty four. Born April 1964. He had good reason to remember that date. That was the year his son, little Joe had been born and Maribel had almost turned tail and run away with that son of a bitch Shumacker. The memory jerked hard at his heart.

'Don't think about it,' he urged himself, returning his gaze to the trainee's face. He looked the thoughtful type. Not his kind of person. He liked doers, not thinkers. Sportsmen. Real men he could relate to.

Felstein met his eye, looking vulnerable and inexperienced. Too raw and exposed. Carlton hated the thought of having to deal with him. But if he didn't, Shumacker would have won. 'You didn't win the last round,' Carlton grumbled to himself. 'And you're not going to bloody well win this one.' But with Shumacker you never knew when he was going to let you have it.

And inevitably with the thought of Shumacker came ones of Maribel. He should have forgotten it long ago. But it stuck with him like a lingering poison every time he had anything to do with the man. His old friend, his college buddy, the bloke he helped get his first job when no one else wanted him. Another twinge in his chest made him clench his teeth hard on the cigar. The past should be forgotten, but Maribel's departure and Shumacker's sudden communication had brought it all back.

He let his gaze fall through the window: painted buses covered with images of deities made it impossible for any other vehicle to pass in the densely woven streets. It was sufficient to divert him from the thoughts of his wife as he pushed his back against the seat, relaxing his grip on the crumbling leaf.

Despite the difficulties and what Maribel did or didn't want, Carlton liked the scramble, the dive for space. It made him feel more alive, more vital.

They passed the waterfront: scores of fishing boats and ferries, hordes of people washing their clothing and bathing amidst the sewage and rubbish of the city drains. Burlap bags of food were heaved from muscular shoulders onto straw-covered boats, and sacks upon sacks of grain sat on ramshackle cement piers tilting into the river.

The river: their lifeblood and their executioner.

The stench was unbearable.

Felstein grimaced. The filth and the crowds were making their inevitable impression.

"Tell me about yourself, kid."

"What would you like to know?" he answered eagerly.

Carlton could see a film of perspiration lining the other's face.

"What kind of work do you see yourself doing ten years from now?"

Felstein scratched his head thoughtfully, his dark wavy hair just long enough to move under his fingertips.

"Gee, I haven't had any time to think about it. Ten years is a long time from now. I've just started in the business."

"Well, you just failed your first test."

"What?"

"Every manager wants to know his people are ambitious. Otherwise, it's a waste of time. Now, what are your goals?"

Felstein hesitated, his eyes startled. He stumbled over his words. "I suppose in that time I would make, maybe, middle manager." He shrugged and the gesture was irritating.

"So you're a one company career man are you?" Carlton edged his voice with antagonism.

"I'm not really sure. I don't know if it's possible to build a career with one company anymore. Loyalty doesn't seem to mean that much these days, does it?"

Carlton grunted but said nothing. Felstein was right. It was all business and no compassion. He shifted in his seat and searched hard for another question.

"Married?" he knew the answer.

"Yes sir. My wife, Bekah, is due with our first in three months time."

The older man nodded. Wife and babies. Nice traditional family. Just like his. He thought again of Maribel. That row they'd had just before she'd stormed out. He couldn't repress the resentment, though he'd acknowledged enough times how unreasonable it was. Why couldn't she tell that business had stopped taking first place in his life? Head office and Shumacker had seen to that.

Damn! He couldn't even remember what they'd been fighting about, but he still felt sore.

Rashid swung the jeep down a quiet side road away from the

ramshackle cement buildings and corrugated iron roofed huts; the hordes of staring faces; the carts tumbling with pineapples and bananas. They drove quickly down the hardened mud track where an occasional white washed villa or a palm graced the edge of the scrub lots. As they continued, the number of houses increased: they were well painted and comparatively large by native standards, surrounded by walls and enclosures and always accompanied by an armed guard or two.

"That's the Consulate's house," Carlton pointed to a walled mansion. Rows of palms separated the smooth green lawn from the concrete drive to the house. "Reminds me of the place where I was brought up, in Connecticut."

Josh glimpsed the house as they scooted by. Not the kind of place he'd ever seen the inside of. He didn't come from that kind of family. His was second generation immigrant. Start humble and work your way up. That's what he and his brothers were doing, except that he was the black sheep of the family and not performing as well. Not that his new job as a geologist didn't pay. It just wasn't the kind of work his mother could ever approve of.

"So, this is what you've decided to do for a living? Oh God! Don't you realise that you won't get anywhere in that kind of business. Why can't you be a doctor? That's so much safer. Look, you're smart enough. All those wonderful grades wasted! You can live in New York. Be close to your family. I can't understand why you're doing this to me!"

Josh blinked away the memory and sighed. If he hadn't looked so much like his elder brother, he would have sworn that he'd been switched at birth into the wrong family. He didn't seem to have the same desires as other members of his family. They were happy to conform. Happy to do anything their mother dictated, to keep the religion going. He just couldn't see the sense in it. It was too insular a life for him. He needed his freedom to experience the world, to be a part of it.

The jeep stopped. The building they pulled alongside was in keeping with the rest of what he'd seen of the wealthier part of town: a white painted villa of rectangles and square modules on different levels with terraces adorned by pots of shrubs and flowering plants. A large sign displaying the company name was tacked at the top of the building. Adjacent land was rough and coarsely grassed with half a dozen mangy cattle grazing, the road unpaved and half eroded, ruts filled with muddy water. On the opposite acres, straw huts, one virtually atop the other, were connected by strings of laundry.

"This is home, kid." Carlton jumped out grabbing a box of equipment as Josh and Rashid collected the bags.

"Hello Mr. Carlton." A young boy ran up to them as they entered the hall, dark eyes glistening, white teeth and smiles. He extended his hand to Josh, and Rashid said, "Habib, this is Mr. Joshua. He's come all the way from Houston, Texas to see our oil well."

The boy continued smiling, looking impressed. "Houston, Texas. Big cowboys. You cowboy, Mr. Joshua?"

"No, Habib, I'm not a cowboy. I'm really from New York. I just work in Texas."

"Oh, New York. Bad place. Everyone say — very bad place."

Josh shrugged. "It has its problems."

"Habib." Rashid indicated to Josh's cases. "Why don't you show Mr. Joshua his room. He is most tired."

"Sure, Mr. Joshua." Habib took one of the cases and Josh took the other.

"No, no, Mr. Joshua, you no carry cases. I carry them for you. I strong."

But Josh resisted. It wasn't right letting other people do his work for him, not when he was able. "Thanks Habib but I'll carry what I can."

The boy seemed hurt for a moment, then led the way up a long marble staircase. "This, Mr. Carlton's room." Habib pointed to a closed door.

"Where's Mrs. Ramsey?" Josh asked.

Habib shook his head. "Mrs. Carlton, very angry, she no stay here. No like food. No like Habib." The boy scowled and continued shaking his head.

"So she's not here?"

"No, she go to..." The boy paused and then smiled as if he had thought of something terribly clever. "Houston," he said brightly. "Play cowboy."

Habib unlocked another white painted door and pushed it open. "This your room, Mr. Josh. Is it nice?"

It was twice the size of his and Bekah's bedroom at home. He walked over to the windows, which were shaded by white net curtains. There was a view of the adjacent cow fields and a string of similar

14

company buildings interlaced with straw huts and corrugated roofed shacks.

"This good bathroom," Habib continued. "Running water. Very splendid."

Josh pushed his glasses further onto the bridge of his nose as a movement across the wall caught his eye. "Habib?"

"Yes?" The boy appeared beside him.

"That... thing!" He pointed to the shape.

"Gecko, Mr. Josh."

"But why is it in here?"

"Every room have gecko. Eats bad insects. Good lizard."

Josh sat on the bed. Snakes and lizards. He had an almost biblical fear. "Can you get rid of it?"

"No, no, Mr. Josh. You need gecko."

Josh stared at the green tinted creature tenaciously sprawled on the wall. He would get rid of it later, first he had to get Habib out of the room. He dug in his knapsack and handed the boy a dollar.

Habib backed away. "I house boy. Paid big salary. No take money."

"I'm sorry. I didn't mean to offend you."

The boy pondered a minute and then relaxed, putting back his bright smile and letting his eyes shine. "Okay, no problem. Anything you need, you ask Habib."

The boy left the room and Josh looked again at the gecko on the wall. Bekah would say that it was cute. That he should treat it like a hamster or a mouse. He shivered. How was he going to get rid of it? There was a knock on his door distracting him.

"Yes?"

Carlton stood on the threshold.

"Come in," Josh said but Carlton didn't move.

"Is the room all right?"

"I can't believe it's this luxurious. It seems weird."

"Well, don't get too comfortable," Carlton said. "We'll be going to the wellsite tomorrow and there are few creature comforts there."

Josh glanced again at the disturbing creature. "Mr. Ramsey, is there any way to get rid of the gecko?"

Carlton's eyes followed Josh's pointed finger.

"Better get used to 'em now, kid. They're all over the place."

The answer was no comfort and although Josh wanted to push the issue, he held himself in check.

"We're having dinner in an hour," Carlton said. "I suggest you get washed and changed then meet me in the staff room at about ten to. There are some things we need to discuss before we fly out in the morning."

The man turned away abruptly, closing the door behind him. Josh stared at the closed blank space, wondering why the older man was so gruff, then he lifted his suitcase onto the bed keeping one eye on the reptile. He pulled out the light weight shirt and checked trousers his mother had given him for his last birthday. Bekah was right, they were pretty awful. She'd refused to let him wear them at home. He grinned remembering what she'd threatened him with if he dared to return with them. Only his mother would buy something like this but it had seemed a shame to just throw them away.

He lay the clothing at the foot of the bed then looked again at the gecko. It hadn't moved, staring at him, as if in defiance. Me or you it seemed to say.

There were towels in the bathroom. He stripped down, first checking behind the door, the ceiling, the walls, for any other unwelcome visitors before removing his glasses and settling in to the lukewarm spray which ran cool over his tired body. His thoughts wandered. To Bekah. How hard it had been to leave her just when the baby had started kicking. What would Bekah think of his new boss? He seemed to have a chip on his shoulder. Guess it was understandable if his wife had walked out on him. Wished he wouldn't call him kid, though.

He towelled himself dry, wrapped the cloth around his waist and made his way into the bedroom. Checking the time, he lay on the bed. It was only ten past five: forty minutes before he was to meet Carlton downstairs. Rolling onto his side, he stretched over and opened his briefcase removing a sheaf of papers: articles on the geology of the Bengal Basin, and laying it beside him remembered that his glasses were still by the sink.

The gecko on the wall was a blur. Maybe he should get up and get his glasses. Keep the thing in his range. He lay his head on the pillow. 'In a minute,' he murmured closing his eyes.

Shumacker's words floated back to him: 'You've been specially picked for this assignment by me, Felstein. This is where you'll be learning your trade. Things they didn't teach you in University, things you'll never learn anywhere else. So pay a lot of attention. Here's a list of equipment you need to take out with you and don't forget your vaccinations and malaria tablets. Oh, and by the way, give Carlton Ramsey these papers to sign and fax them back to me when you get to Dhaka.'

The dinner bell rang. Once then twice. Josh opened his eyes. For a blank, lost moment he had no idea where he was. He fumbled for his glasses which were nowhere to be found, then grabbed at his watch as if that could tell him where he was. Bangladesh. He'd missed his first meeting with Ramsey.

He scrambled to the bathroom, lunged at his glasses, haphazardly threw himself into his clothing, closed and grabbed his briefcase and rushed out of the room across the landing and down the stairs.

Without stopping to neaten his appearance, he ran into the dining room breathlessly apologising. Carlton gazed up from the magazine which lay in his lap, his eyes filled with irritation.

As the young man raced into the dining room, Carlton grimaced at the garish American clothing that he had long discarded for the more subdued and sophisticated European styles. It hadn't taken very long for him to grasp that any kind of blatant display of Americanism, especially in places like Bangladesh where military apparatus mostly came from the Soviet Union or China, was counter-productive. A softly, softly big stick approach was more his style.

He looked askance at the young man who had opened his briefcase and was tugging out wadges of paper and a large black bound notebook. Enthusiasm was tiring in a place like this. At his age it was necessary to pace himself.

Young Americans always had to work and rush through meals, while he had learned to appreciate a slow glass of red wine, the rich textures of the food. Then again, the kid probably only ate at Macdonalds. That is, Carlton reminded himself, if he was allowed to eat that kind of food.

Felstein looked at him with an open pleading expression and he felt a twinge of guilt, remembering what he'd been like as a young man. But the guilt was combined with a slight aversion, which he tried to repress every time he saw the large nose on the boy's semitic face.

Maribel would have half heartedly scolded him for his prejudice and then later, in the confines of intimacy, would have admitted some amount of it in herself as well.

The other's voice broke through the ghost of his thoughts.

"Mr. Ramsey, sir, Mr. Shumacker sent me with some papers for you to sign." Felstein handed them over.

Carlton glanced through the papers. His retirement offer. The boy's face appeared innocent but he could see the connivance underneath. The little bastard was in on it.

"I'll sign these later." Carlton tossed the document aside.

"But Mr. Shumacker…" Felstein said.

"Yes?" Carlton responded defiantly.

"Said he wanted me to fax them back to him."

"Did he?"

A brief moment of panic crossed Felstein's face. Good. Let the twerp know I'm not going to be that easily pushed aside. Felstein leaned over and pulled some other papers from his briefcase. Now what?

"I've been keeping track of the drilling." Felstein changed tack. "We're just above the second gas zone. Is that right?"

Carlton nodded reaching into the breast pocket of his light cotton shirt. He felt for the metal tube containing his cigar, his fingers grasping then angrily tugging the container away from the button which held it secure. His stomach rumbled and he wished Felstein would shut up.

He slowly unscrewed the metal cap, removed the rolled leaf bullet, twisted it in his fingers then lifted it to his mouth and bit down hard. This was from the duty free at Singapore and it wasn't as good as the London ones, but it made him feel better anyway. Maribel would never have allowed him to chew during dinner despite what he was feeling and in a way he recognised that he did it to spite her, even though she'd never know.

Felstein was served his soup first and started eating right away.

'Damned Americans,' Carlton grumbled to himself. 'They've got no idea of etiquette outside their own little sphere.' The kid had better be taught fast before he bungled up in a meeting. Felstein reached over to help himself to the butter. Carlton glared at him. The boy stopped mid-air.

"Uh, sorry Mr. Ramsey. Did you want some of this wine?"

Carlton grunted as Felstein clumsily lifted the bottle pouring the liquid, his inexperience evident as a drop of red dribbled onto the white starched tablecloth.

"If you twist the bottle after you pour you won't end up leaving a mess." Carlton's voice was harsher than he had intended but it had the desired effect plus some.

Felstein's eyes widened. "Gee, I'm sorry!" He poured himself a half glass and twisted the bottle as he had been told. It worked, the offending drop disappeared into the neck. "Well, you can tell how often I drink wine."

Carlton took a sip, hiding his consternation behind the glass. Surely he wouldn't have been so touchy if Maribel had been there. She would have taken care of the boy, excused his conspiracy as innocence. As it was...

"Forget it," Carlton said, sighing inwardly as Josh struggled to cut rather than break his bread roll. "I'm a bit off today. As you can see."

"No problem Mr. Ramsey... Sir."

Carlton's temper was assuaged for the moment. The boy was obviously uncultured, giving his origins away every time he moved or opened his mouth. He tried to change the subject, tried begrudgingly to have some sort of conversation. "I see you got your Master's from North Carolina University. I used to know a fella there by the name of Wilson. Ever meet him?"

Felstein nodded. "Yeah, sure. He's still there. I took a seminar with him on micropalaeontology."

"We were at Yale together." Carlton scowled as he pushed away the soup bowl. He was going to have to remind Maribel to tell the chef to put less salt in the food. "Is he still wearing that ridiculous cap?"

"I've never seen him without it. He's pretty strange. We used to call him the pod man."

Carlton leaned back in the chair as Habib placed a plate filled with rice and sauteed meat of some kind in an unknown sauce in front of him. He assessed his charge in a dispassionate, cold manner. "He was shot in the head on one of his field trips in the desert. About the time they were testing those bombs in Nevada. Before your day, I would imagine. That's why he wears that stupid cap. Hides the scar."

The boy's mouth fell open. "Wow! He never said!"

Carlton picked at the meat on his plate. Goddammit, the sauce was too spicy and the meat tasted like something they'd scraped off the pavement.

Josh was picking at the food as well.

"Too spicy for you too?" Carlton pushed the plate away.

"No. Just wondering what the meat is. Do you think it's pork?"

"This is a Muslim Country kid. They don't usually serve pork here."

"Oh, I hadn't realised that."

"Yeah, it figures." Carlton called Habib over. "Bring me some plain rice, Habib. No sauce. No meat. Just plain white rice. And see if you can find some of that cheese Mrs. Ramsey bought... Sorry about the food kid, when Maribel's gone everything goes to hell."

"Maribel? Is that Mrs. Ramsey? She's not here?"

"No. She's in Houston with our daughter Stacy whose just had her second."

Felstein continued gulping down his food. Carlton searched for something, anything more to talk about but he was just too annoyed. Finally, Habib brought over a plate of rice with some sliced cheese.

"You want some cheese?" Carlton asked.

"No thanks. That was fine for me." Josh's plate was cleared. The kid raised his hand as Habib moved away. "Habib," he asked. "Is there any coffee?"

Christ! Carlton slapped his fork onto the remaining rice. "Hold on with that coffee and let me finish eating. We'll have some in the lounge later. Got it kid?"

"Sure, okay, whatever you say." Felstein gave him a curious look.

Carlton felt another twinge of guilt but he couldn't help feeling antsy. He should try to give the kid the benefit of the doubt. He made another effort.

"What part of New York did you say you're from?"

"Williamsburg. Do you know it?"

"Can't say I do. I'm a Connecticut man myself. Beautiful State. You been there?"

"No. Is that also where your wife is from?"

"Nope. Her parents were from Texas but she was born in Indonesia. Lived all over the place," he said proudly. Felstein didn't respond so he continued. "Maribel's the daughter of an oil man. You see, my whole family have oil in their blood. What about you? What does your father do?"

"Did. He fixed washing machines." The boy mumbled the words. It was obvious it was something he was ashamed of.

"I see." Carlton examined the cigar intently.

"I'm the first in oil," Josh said.

"And the rest of your family? What do they do?"

"I've got two brothers — they're both doctors."

"Oh! Doctors! That's impressive," Carlton laughed. "What made you go into geology? It's an unusual profession for your people, isn't it?"

"What do you mean my people? You mean all Americans? You're American."

"You know what I'm saying."

"No, I'm sorry I don't!" Josh leaned forward.

"Come on, you can't tell me that you guys aren't either doctor's or lawyers. Isn't that true?"

"You guys? Exactly what are you talking about?"

"For Christ's sake, you damned well know what I'm talking about! It's everything, your background, your heritage. It makes you the person you are. Why deny it?"

Felstein was gripping the table, his eyes narrowed behind the thick glasses. "What difference does it make what my background is? I'm an American. That should be good enough!"

Carlton looked the boy straight in the face, unable to conceal the disgust that he had for him — his looks, his manners. Everything that they had tried to keep out of Yale back in the old days — and succeeded.

"No, it ain't enough son! You're in Muslim country now. You're not back home in New York. Maybe you don't like to hear it but you look and act what you are; you wear it like a talisman around your neck."

Felstein went red in the face but when he spoke his voice was steady. "I was sent here by Head Office. Presumably they chose me for my academic and professional qualifications not the religion I was born into. If you didn't think their choice was appropriate you should have said something before now."

"Maybe I did. Maybe I didn't." Carlton spat out a piece of cigar onto the plate now wanting desperately to back down. This was too similar to another argument. An argument that he never wanted to think about again. "Well, let's not get too sensitive about it. Just let me give you some advice. People here may not spot you're a Jew and I suggest you don't tell them. If they ask, which they always will, tell them you're Bahai or something."

Felstein was silent, his dark eyes filmed over. Carlton perceived the cold coming from the boy but he felt too antagonistic to back off. "Let's get this business out of the way," he said gruffly. "Habib, we'll have that coffee in the staff room now."

2

THE NEXT MORNING, RASHID DROVE the two men to the airport; the atmosphere was icy between them. They said nothing as the ground staff shouted at them to identify their baggage and nothing as they boarded the plane and were seated next to the other.

After take-off, Carlton unbuckled his seat belt to reach into his pocket. He pulled out a packet of life savers. "Would you like one?" he proffered the candy.

"No, thanks," Josh said, his face turned toward the aisle, his eyes focused on the opposite window, though he saw nothing but a blur of anger.

"Look, kid," Carlton's voice was conciliatory. "You shouldn't take offense so easily. Anyway, I'm a sour old sod when Maribel's not around. I was just venting my spleen."

Josh swallowed hard. It was good of the man to attempt an apology but it didn't help matters any. He felt bare, as if someone had stripped him naked: so open to the elements, so easily identifiable. He was branded by the stigma of it, his so-called Jewishness, just as he had been in University: the snide remarks, the astonished faces, the broken dates. He'd learned quickly that you never told anyone you were Jewish.

Josh glanced at the man beside him. New England old family looks, close cropped white hair, neat accent and snobby manners. Ancestors probably landed at Plymouth. The old bastard! But he was here to learn the trade and he would do it no matter what Ramsey threw at him.

"Okay, no hard feelings," he mumbled.

Carlton nodded and looking out of the window said, "In that case, you'd better sit here and I'll tell you what you're looking at."

They changed seats careful not to touch.

"The rainy season has started late this year." Carlton's voice was gruff, as if it was he who had been wounded by the remarks he had made the night before. "Those patches of land you see down there will all be covered with water. It's the silt that makes the soil good for farming. Though it's a hell of a way to live."

Josh surveyed the patchwork of small farms. Those little white dots must be buildings. He wondered if the roofs were as flimsy as the ones he had seen in parts of Dhaka.

Ramsey tapped him on the shoulder. The stewardess, a young Bengali woman, offered him a drink from a tray. He took what seemed like a coke. It tasted like syrupy water. He forced the swallow.

Carlton watched.

"Get used to it, kid. These people are dirt poor, coke of any kind, dilute or not, is a luxury."

Josh poured himself into the landscape using it as an anchor for his emotions. He had thought he'd known poverty in New York where his grandparents had lived but this kind of penury made Harlem black kids look like rich bankers.

He concentrated on the scene trying to bury his feelings. He'd been looking forward to working with Carlton Ramsey. Had heard the man had been to just about every exotic location the Company had ever drilled in. If there was one person you could learn the business from it was him. But Carlton's personal views hadn't filtered down along with his professional reputation.

He pushed his glasses further onto his nose as if he were pushing away the feelings he had. He must be a scientist now, noting facts, making observations. No longer a man at the mercy of his emotions.

Cutting the watery plain in half was a meandering river with large broad bends sweeping from left to right, sand bars on one side and a levee on the other. Better than any text book on geomorphology.

The shadow of the plane fell over an old oxbow lake, horseshoe in shape and clear as day from the air.

Carlton's voice cut into the sanctuary of his thoughts.

"Where the Brahmaputra River crosses the border from India to Bangladesh it changes name to the Jamuna River. That's probably the Jamuna we're looking at now. The next major river you'll see is the Kalni. The whole damn system floods every year and nourishes the soil. That's if God is on their side. If he isn't, the water levels rise so high they can wipe out thousands at a time. Poor buggers." Carlton paused, as if trying to digest the enormity of his words then abruptly spoke up again. "You know how long it takes this country to replace two hundred dead?" He didn't wait for an answer. "One day." He shook his head, "It's no wonder they've got so many problems."

Josh gazed at the man beside him. He read prejudice into every word Carlton uttered and braced himself for confrontation.

"Aren't children a kind of security for them?"

Carlton nodded. "Yeah, sure. Well, you can't blame them."

Awkwardness slipped between them once more as the thin brown stewardess collected the cups. Josh returned to the comfort of the window. The ground below was the bleakest of drowned fluvial plains and he wondered again how anyone could live in such conditions.

The plane began its descent, the hills in the distance a welcome relief from the monotonous, wet flatness. Carlton buckled his seat belt then shut his eyes while Josh continued to take in as much of the scene as he could so he could tell Bekah about it.

Bekah.

Sometimes he wondered if he were hiding behind her courage and strength. If it hadn't been for her, he probably would have succumbed to his mother's insistence that he continue with medical school. And, he knew for certain, Bekah would never take the garbage that Carlton was handing out. By now, she would have charmed the socks off of him, despite his bigotry.

Shylet airport was less crowded, less bustling and more informal than Zia International in Dhaka. There was no customs or immigration here, so no payments had to be made to collect the luggage or leave the airport. But the pungent odour was the same.

Josh picked up his bag, winded by the heat.

"Carlton! So, nice to see you again, old man!" Josh whirled round. The speaker was handsome: broad and muscular, his hair a distinguished mixture of black and grey and he was as tall as Josh's six foot.

Carlton was happy to see the man, immediately searching in his pocket. He offered a cigar.

"It's one of my last," Carlton whispered loud enough for Josh to hear.

"And this must be our Mr. Felstein." The man patted Josh's arm and then took his hand, shaking it vigorously and firmly, nearly crushing Josh's in his own. "I am Khalig."

"Nice to meet you. Call me Josh."

"Ah, Josh, yes. A very sincere name. A pleasure to meet you." He then affectionately slapped Carlton on the back. "Myra tells me your good wife has abandoned you. She's sent her best and promises to make you a meal as soon as you tire of the well site fare."

"I'd like that, Khalig. I haven't had decent food since Maribel left. Tell her that I can't wait. Oh, by the way, here are those items you asked for. Let's just hope they do the job."

He handed Khalig the box and without a word the man hurried in front of them, as if the package contained something that he had to quickly dispose of. Carlton slowed to let Josh catch up.

"Khalig's family owns half the tea gardens in Shylet. He was educated in England where he met Myra, his wife. He's our representative here. Claims he's close to Ershad, the President, though I have my doubts."

As they made their way to the jeep, a young boy came running up to Khalig who whispered something in his ear. Khalig handed him the box. The boy grinned eagerly and ran off. When Josh asked his supervisor what was in the parcel, Carlton waved his hand dismissively, "Just some things Myra requested."

Khalig got into the driver's seat and invited Josh to sit up front with him.

"Shall we go for a drive?" Khalig asked. "Let our Mr. Felstein see the countryside before you chain him to the drilling rig?"

Josh looked hopefully at Carlton though he expected, if he showed too much enthusiasm, Carlton would refuse. Their eyes met. The old man was inscrutable.

To his surprise, Carlton nodded and said, "Just give us the usual, Khalig. There isn't enough time to go all the way to Jaintipur."

The impressions were unmistakable: the smell, the ridged tan clay roads, the rows of straw and corrugated roofs on one room dwellings. There was an unexpected feeling of dignity from the people they passed, like the constant flow of a deep river.

Everything was open. There were no locks, no bolts, they lacked the air of defensiveness. The defensiveness of ownership, the fear of loss. And everywhere people stared from impassively calm dark eyes.

Children waved or ran alongside the vehicle. Josh waved back. It was like a crazy run down bazaar: men wearing sarongs and white or blue cotton shirts or long sleeved shirts with long trousers and even though it was terribly hot and humid, only the young wore shorts.

A mass of rickshaws with their bonnets drawn filled the road. But amongst the men squatting by the roadside, or roaming around the marketplace carrying sacks of grain, Josh noticed the absence of women. It had been the same in Dhaka. The whole scene seemed lopsided.

No, he was wrong. There was one woman shielding herself behind the authority of her husband under the hood of a rickshaw. But there were no women on their own.

A bus, brightly painted, pulled alongside. It was full of men who stared with intensity at the jeep and then at Josh, meeting his eyes whenever they could. They never smiled, nor did they look hostile. Just curious and direct. There were hundreds of men and children everywhere. Who did the shopping? Who took the children to school?

They passed bony cattle mixing with the traffic, and there were goats. Goats everywhere: on fence posts, on sway backed chairs, on gates. Like cats, goats sauntered about in the heat and lay wherever the inclination took them.

Gradually, the cluster of villages was left behind. The clay track became even rougher and the vegetation on either side of the road thickened until there were no sights of eyes, no rows of tiny huts.

Long ropes of twining ivy wrapped and catapulted around the impenetrability of bamboo, rattan and palm. This was the first jungle he'd ever seen. It was so thick, so verdant. Everything a jungle ought to be. Khalig swung the jeep off the track and switched the engine off. He indicated to Josh to get out of the vehicle.

The trees were filled with the chatter of monkeys and the buzz of insects and calling birds.

Khalig put his finger to his lips. Out of the corner of his eye, Josh saw a young child. He couldn't have been more than two, with his fat little sturdy legs. He was running, cocksure with an expression of fearlessness.

It was amazing. He had never experienced such freedom of spirit. A young child like that where he came from would never be as confident.

Other children began to appear, in swarms, giggling and tugging, coming from nowhere, clamouring for the bags and the lollipops Carlton was handing out.

"I promised the World Health Organisation I'd give these salts to the kids when I saw them... You give to your mother," Carlton said to each child as he handed out one bag and a lollipop. "They know what they're for," he said as an aside, but Josh had his doubts.

One of the smaller boys grabbed a candy from Carlton's hand and ran off only to return moments later demanding a second which

Carlton gave him. He disappeared again slipping through the maze of giggling children, soon returning for a third.

Curious, Josh followed the boy. There was a narrow path leading through the jungle which had not been apparent from the road. The leaves were sodden with humidity, the warm water dripped onto his head. The air hung rich with the scent of crushed leaves.

As he followed the path, he no longer heard the cries of the children, only the birds scurrying and calling through the thick leaved branches. He came to a clearing. Wooden huts with thick straw roofs lay in a cluster. The clay looked swept and the huts well kept. They were more substantial than the city buildings and lacked the desolate look of corrugated iron.

In the open doorway of one, half a dozen children were holding lollipops. The boys were half dressed, the girls in dresses with shorts underneath. Round bellies protruded outwards. The children clustered around the doorway or lolled against the hut, their hands behind their backs. This is where the women were: clinging to the rafts of their secluded homes.

Before noticing him, one of the women stepped out of the hut and reached for something under the eaves of the roof. She was dressed in a purple sari with a short sleeved powder blue shirt underneath. In her arms a young child stared and behind her more women peered out.

Unexpectedly one of the women smiled so he raised his hand to wave but it only caused the others to withdraw into the darkness of the hut leaving the children to gawk.

"Felstein!" Ramsey's angry voice startled him.

The children by the hut suddenly ran past him their giggling altered to silence as he turned. In front of him, the jungle children and their fathers blocked his path.

"Get back here," Carlton growled over their heads. Josh stepped towards the staring faces.

"Move it Felstein!" Carlton shouted.

Josh shifted into the crowd but it did not yield. "Excuse me," he murmured apologetically knowing they wouldn't understand him but feeling that he should say something. Fingers jabbed him in the gut and then one voice started grumbling, followed by another. Soon the crowd were angrily berating him, though they had stopped prodding.

Josh felt in his shirt pocket, pulled out a little book. It was the only one he could find in the bookshops back home. Survival guide to Bangladesh. He leafed through the language section as Carlton shouted at him again. There was no translation for an apology.

"Asalaam alaikhum," Peace be unto you, he repeated over and over. Would it mean anything to them? The men began to laugh. Bodies pressed against him but slowly they began to let him through. Just before he passed the corner, he glanced back. The faces of the women pushed out of the doorway, like turtles coming out of their shells.

Josh closed the jeep door as Khalig pulled away from the site.

"You were lucky they didn't kill you." Khalig's voice was only half joking. He continued. "The tribesmen don't like strangers looking at their women."

"Are they really that strict?" Josh put his hand out on the dashboard to steady himself from the jarring of the bumpy track.

"They are murderous." Khalig's amused tone contradicted his words.

Carlton tapped him on the shoulder. "Khalig here thinks some of his countrymen are savages."

"Are they?"

"No, they're just unpredictable. Anyway, it's all tribal politics. Isn't that right, Khalig? You can't find a more friendly people as far as I'm concerned."

Josh nodded as if he understood but in truth he didn't and wondered what, if anything, the two men were really saying. That it was forbidden for foreigners was understandable if wives were not meant to be seen, but was it really that dangerous? He wondered whether they were testing him to see how gullible he was.

As they drove, Carlton waved at the children. "They're real cute those kids, aren't they?"

Josh wished that his new boss would be as positive to him as he was to the children, but obviously being Jewish was worse than being Bangladeshi. He wondered again about the man, still couldn't figure him out. But Carlton didn't speak and so he concentrated on the outer world as they bumped along the track.

"What are the salts for?" Josh finally broke the silence.

"They're for cholera. It's a big disease out here, especially for the children. They get diarrhoea and it drains the fluids straight out of their little bodies. The poor buggers die of dehydration. Of course, there's a simple solution: a pinch of salt and a fistful of sugar in water. That's what those packets I'm giving out are. It's like Gatorade back in the States, except here it saves lives."

They slowed to a stop behind a long line of traffic waiting to cross a steel girdered bridge over a small stream. A yellow and blue truck filled with bags of gravel had stopped for no apparent reason blocking the entrance.

Khalig pounded on his horn and when nothing happened got out of the jeep and stormed off to the front of the line. Josh got out too, leaving Carlton feigning a nap. The place was lush and ravaged at the same time. Palm trees and shanty huts co-existed on friable sand banks. No one except Khalig seemed particularly disturbed by the blockage until an argument started at the entrance of the bridge.

A few minutes later Khalig stormed back to the vehicle. He yanked the rear door open and pulled out a food cooler, opened it and offered a drink to Carlton who hadn't moved. Carlton refused the drink so Khalig passed the cool fluid to Josh as he approached the vehicle.

Josh took the can and walked away from the line of traffic. Everywhere he stopped to look, a group of men gathered behind him to stare in the same direction. Nothing else he'd ever experienced was like this. He couldn't get enough of it.

The truck slowly rumbled to a start and precariously pulled across the bridge to the shouts of encouragement from lookers on. Khalig jumped into the driver's seat, waited for Josh to join them then steamed over the bridge. He roared past the truck to angry shouts.

All along the track buses swayed, crammed with people and bags and bundles of long stemmed vegetables. Khalig had no patience with them. He pulled away as soon as he could, leaving behind a cloud of dust swerving off the main road and finally coming to a stop in a clearing surrounded by sandy hills.

Josh followed Carlton to a nearby outcrop of rock.

"What do you think that brown colour comes from, kid?"

Josh reached out taking a sample in his hand. It was sandstone which crumbled between his fingers. He brought it to his nose.

"Is it oil?" he asked incredulous.

"Yep. You've hit it on the head. Oil, oil everywhere but none to find."

Then Carlton led him down a track until they came to a lake which stank of rotten eggs. The intensity of the stench was nauseating. Josh covered his nose and his glasses fogged up. The water was an ominous cream brown and it bubbled as if it were boiling.

"It's terrible!" He pulled his glasses off and tried to clear them.

Carlton's eyes narrowed, he didn't seem to be affected by the disgusting odour.

"You see the bubbles coming out of the water?"

Josh nodded.

"Back in '55, Camco were drilling the area. Hit a big gas sand but just when they were ready to log the hole, the damned thing blew so bad it made its own crater. That's what you're looking at now, a gigantic hole full of gas and beneath it somewhere, a drilling rig." Carlton chuckled. "Damnedest thing."

"How deep is it?" Josh put his glasses back on.

"Who knows? This kind of ground, it's mostly sand. The rig is probably still sinking. Christ knows where the bottom is."

"I can't believe this! Isn't it law that they clean it up?"

Carlton grimaced and searched in his shirt pocket for his cigar. He hesitated before answering and Josh thought he was glowering. At him? What was the older man thinking?

"The environment is the last thing people worry about out here."

"But Camco is a big oil company, aren't they responsible?"

Carlton waved his hand dismissively and turned away. Josh remained where he was for a moment looking at the disaster that lay before him. He wouldn't be surprised if people were hostile if Carlton's attitude was the norm.

They drove away in silence. As the sun fell behind the darkening clouds, the barbed wire enclosure of the drilling site came into view. The landscape seemed to have been pulled out by its roots and shaken into a brown smear of mud.

They pulled alongside two armed guards in uniform who spoke softly and secretively to Khalig then opened the gates. Khalig drove through.

"As I was saying before," Carlton broke into Josh's thoughts. "You don't find much oil in these parts. The government's got an oil well in Shylet and that's it. Ours is the only find since that well. That's why this is so important. All the other drilling efforts have either ended up being dry or have been only small gas accumulations."

Josh didn't respond.

"You all right?" Carlton enquired leaning over.

"Yes sir."

"Good. See that flame?" Carlton pointed to a long length of tube which was flaring an intense and constant fire, shooting into the air about four or five feet high. "We're testing the oil leg right now. There's a layer of gas sitting just above it which we're burning off. When that's finished we'll go ahead and continue drilling down to the final zone. What do you think?"

"I think it's a waste of resources to burn the gas in such a poor country."

"Well you're wrong there," Carlton's voice echoed with satisfaction. "This area's already serving most households and there are also fertiliser plants which run on methane."

"But why flare it?" Josh asked. "Why can't they sell it?"

"There's no external market for it." Carlton opened the jeep door and said, "Hell, I don't even know why we bother."

"I don't get you." Josh followed him out of the jeep.

"They don't appreciate our efforts." Carlton thrust the words over his shoulder as he walked away.

3

THE FLARE OF GAS SHOT OUT, a jet of orange against the backdrop of a sodden sky shadowing the stray trees neglected by the bulldozer's might. Josh and Carlton walked around the well site. Puddles of tan clay and oily water glowed wherever a rut had been made by a tyre or a heavy footprint.

"You ever see a drilling rig before?" Carlton asked.

"No sir."

"This is a heli-rig. It's been flown in from the jungles of Burma where we were drilling a few months ago. It's smaller and lighter than most land rigs."

The drilling site was surrounded by ridges of tea gardens: gentle terraces with low lying shrubs. Beyond the terraces was the outline of distant hills, a rapidly fading dark blue along the horizon to the north into India.

They entered the mess together and Carlton shook hands with the French cook and ordered up some food. The quality was better than Josh had expected, but Carlton grimaced throughout the meal.

Afterwards, Carlton showed him to his quarters. It was one side of a Portakabin with a bed, a nightstand, desk, chair and metal locker. In the middle of the cabin was a toilet and a shower and next door was Carlton's room.

Josh looked about him. The expression on his face obviously revealing what he was doing, for Carlton said, "Shouldn't be any snakes here... But then again you never can tell about these things. Just a few weeks ago, I was in the logging cabin when, what do you know, a great big cobra comes slithering out from under one of the units. Blow me, if it hadn't been there since we drilled that well in Burma."

Josh tightened his fingers around the edge of the table.

"He comes sliding into the middle of the cabin and we're practically breaking our necks to get out. Only thing is, the door's stuck. So I give it a good kick to open it. Anand, you'll meet him later, goes back in and climbs on the unit trying to shoo the thing out with a stick. Except the damned thing slides under another unit. By the way, it's always good to have locals on your side, they're able to handle these kind of problems."

Carlton laughed, but there was nothing funny about the story. He then stretched over the bed and switched on the air conditioner which roared into action then settled down to a rumble.

"Is it still in there?" Josh wished he could stop himself from needing to know.

Carlton scrutinised him, the smile now nowhere to be seen.

"You've got to come to terms with these things, kid. There are more dangers out here than a few harmless snakes and lizards."

Josh nodded but his hand still gripped the table waiting to hear the answer.

None came.

Carlton continued lecturing him, "When I was your age, we used to live in tents on the well site. This is luxury."

Josh didn't respond. It was anything but luxury. Carlton turned to leave.

"What about the snake?"

The older man's eyes were cold, smug. Josh pushed his glasses back even though they weren't sliding down his nose.

"Anand accidentally ran him over shifting the logging unit. We threw it out the door. It's probably still there if you go looking," said Carlton.

Josh kept still — he'd look later.

"You'd better have a wash and get some sleep kid," Carlton said, "We'll have an early start tomorrow morning." Then he went through the bathroom into his own room shutting the door firmly behind him.

As the door closed, Josh searched the room, looking under the bed and table to make sure the place was clear. He sat on the mattress, cold sweat on his face and hands. Where would a cobra be hiding? He shook the covers and ran his hand down the sheets then jumped up, lifted the mattress and peered under that.

He'd only been six the year he and his family had made the voyage to Israel for his brother Abraham's bar mitzvah. They were staying at a cousin's house that first night and the endless hours of travel had made him sleepy and irritable.

"Oy, just look at the boy," his mother had stroked his forehead. She knelt cupping her warm hands over his cheeks, kissing him on the nose. "I'll put him to bed, he's so exhausted." His mother led him into a dark and musty room fussing over him, pulling the shirt over his head and tugging at his trousers.

He climbed under the covers and she pulled them tightly around him.

"I'll be back in a few minutes Joshala, then I'll read you a story."

He could hear the music in the next room. Could discern his father's happy voice calling out the words to a favourite song. He waited and waited for *Eema* to return with the storybook. Where was she? He didn't like this room. It was dark and there were frightening shadows pressing in on him. Now awake with the unfulfilled promise, he tried to force his way out of the covers. In the struggle something ran across his leg.

"Eema!" he screamed.

The thing ran over his chest and onto his face as he fought for his freedom.

"Eema!" He screamed again and threw up, the vomit running back against his mouth.

He was a grown man now. He undressed, shaking off the childhood memory. But when he was down to his underwear, despite himself, he left his underpants on, just in case he had to get out quickly.

There was a bottle of water and a glass on the bedside table. The water had been imported from Scotland, presumably it wasn't safe drinking the local stuff. He gulped down his malaria tablets and checked under the bed once more. The rickety metal frame sagged and groaned with his weight.

He punched at his pillow and shifted about uncomfortably trying to will himself to sleep, but the air conditioner made a racket loud enough to keep an army awake. Condensation dripped onto his face and ran down his cheek onto the pillow. He pushed the back of his head against the wet patch and closed his eyes to no avail. There was no use counting sheep. Think about Bekah. That was easier. If it hadn't been for her encouragement he wouldn't be here now and, despite Carlton's aggravation and the discomforts of the sleeping quarters, being in the field was exciting, there was no doubt about that.

With that thought he began to doze: that light feeling that descends through the body, making it seem as if it's lifting, floating, like a warm sigh brushing against his face, so soothing.

A movement stirred the hairs on his legs seizing him from his sleep. He sat up. Something had slithered over him. He was sure. His skin crawled as he pushed the covers off and stripped the sheets back to the end of the bed. There was nothing there. It was just him.

He lay back again staring at the blankness of the ceiling letting the specks of dust shimmer like floating atoms in the dark. There was no use fighting the insomnia. The day's journey played through his mind: the jungle canopy, the beautiful woman by the hut and the shy staring faces of the children. What would his own child be like? The thought bewildered him. His own child! Only three more months to go.

The morning rain clattered against the tin roof of the Portakabin above his head. It sheeted down from swirling black clouds turning the drilling site into a squelching pool of muddy water. Josh ignored the downpour to walk around the area, get to know his way about and meet some people.

The site was separated from the terraces by a chain link fence with barbed wire at the top, though there was a small gate leading into the tea gardens at one end. He walked over to the guards unit.

The soldiers pulled to attention.

"Just come to introduce myself." They smiled at him but did not relax, nor did they look like they understood him. He extended his hand. "My name is Josh Felstein from the United States. I'm a geologist." He spoke slowly but their expressions didn't change. "Anyone speak English?"

At that moment, Khalig drove up to the gate.

"Good morning Joshua, is something the matter?" Khalig's tone was intimidating.

"No, I was just trying to introduce myself but I don't think they understand me."

Khalig rattled something quickly to the guards and they relaxed slightly and nodded. Josh smiled and extended his hand to the closest man again repeating his name but his offer of a handshake was not taken.

"I have told them who you are, you needn't worry about them anymore."

Josh was about to explain himself when Khalig opened the door, "Hop in."

He did as he was told.

"They are Ershad's men. We pay a fee to have them protect us."

"But why do we need protecting? The local people must realise they can only benefit from having oil on their land?"

Khalig laughed and reached over patting Josh on the shoulder.

"You have a lot to learn my friend. People here believe the government gives all the oil away to imperialist oil companies like your Standex or Camco."

"But that's not true! Surely there's some percentage deal?"

"Yes, of course there is. It's just unclear who gets what percentage." Khalig winked at Josh who again tried to read between the lines. If there was anything to be read at all.

They pulled up outside the Portakabin which contained the kitchen and dining area and Josh got out but did not enter the cabin. Khalig drove away and a few minutes later Josh saw him talking with Carlton gesticulating wildly. The two men were clearly arguing.

As Khalig headed towards the drilling rig Carlton stormed up.

"Khalig wants us to stay inside the compound for the next few days. They've imposed a curfew on foreigners but that's no big deal. And kid, don't go walking by the gates again. Understood?"

Josh nodded submissively but he felt stung by the implied criticism. Why was it so important that he not talk to the guards?

They went into the mess; Carlton ordered some eggs on toast and Josh did the same. Though they sat facing each other, neither offered any form of conversation.

Carlton was the first to rise. "When you're finished, I'll show you how the place runs." He pushed his chair under the table. "We should be hitting that final section soon, then we're going to log and case the well. If the lower sections contains hydrocarbons we'll go ahead and test that too. See how much oil or gas we have. No use leaving the job half done."

"What happens if there isn't enough oil?" Josh asked finishing his eggs.

"If the tests are no good we may close up operations here. It wouldn't be a moment too soon if you ask me. Too damned much money with not enough returns." Carlton grabbed his cup and gulped down the rest of his coffee. Josh followed suit.

"Right then!" Carlton opened the door. "Let's see what they're doing on that rig."

Josh ran out after the older man. The prospect of getting his hands dirty, of learning the oil business, not from text books but from hands-on experience, overshadowed any other difficulties he might be having.

Carlton began his tour at the mud pits.

"Pay attention," the old man's voice resonated with condescension. "The mud circulates from these pits through the well bore then back again. They act as the grease for the drill bit and they keep the rocks from caving into the hole."

They walked by the slimy, stinking mud pits — pumps sucking and choking — past grease spattered diesel engines and piping assemblies until they came to the base of the stairs leading up to the drilling floor.

The smell of diesel, the sound of the pumps and the grinding drill bit, lifted Josh above all his other worries. This was exhilarating. His reason for working in the industry. It was just as he had imagined: men in orange coveralls shouting above the screaming metal, oily mud splashing onto his boots, the warm rain battering onto the roof of the driller's cabin.

Yes, this was magnificent, awesome even! Nothing Carlton could say could touch him when he was standing on the drilling platform.

"This is our Chief Driller Bob K!" Carlton yelled above the clamour. "He makes sure everything is running smoothly on the drill floor. You see him first when I'm not around if you think anything is going wrong."

Josh held out his hand and was shaken by the huge driller, whose front teeth were missing and whose nose had been flattened.

"How ya doin'?"

"I'm fine. Thanks."

"Hey, yawl another damned Yankee! Goddam!"

"'Fraid I am." Josh relaxed with the friendliness.

"Well, damn Yank or not, new mugs're always welcome round this shit hole. Yawl come on down to the mess after ten tonight. We got a little game of poker goin' if you wanna lose your shirt." Bob K winked at him, "I can give you some tips on where you can get some action, if you know what I mean." The driller grinned and slapped him on the back then pulled out a tin of chewing tobacco from his coverall pocket and offered some.

"No, not for me."

"It's good stuff. You should try it." The driller took a pinch and stuffed it into his already tobacco-swollen cheek.

Josh grinned, declining the offer once again. "How long have you been out here?" He asked the driller.

Carlton suddenly grabbed his arm, growling into his ear,"Do your socialising on your own time, boy. I haven't got all day."

Josh shrugged at the driller who winked understandingly.

They walked around the drill floor. Pipe was going down the hole, wires running to the top of the mast. The sound of screeching metal against metal rang through the hills. Carlton tapped Josh on the shoulder and reluctantly he followed the older man's quick steps down the stairs and around the piping assemblies to the logging cabin where Carlton introduced him to Anand.

"Anand's going off shift now and you're taking over," Carlton announced as they entered the cabin.

Despite himself, Josh glanced around, as discreetly as possible, to see if the room was clear of snakes.

"Enough of that!" Carlton's voice was all business. He pointed to the complicated instrumentation on the wall and rattled off a quick list of instructions. "I want you to keep your eyes on the gas readings, the mud weights, check the circulation and make sure you know what that drill bit is doing."

The plethora of moving dials looked like the inside of an aeroplane's cockpit. Josh stared blankly.

"If the readings go above average," Carlton continued, "you get out there quick and find Anand. He'll get the drillers to tie the hatches down until I get back. You stop it at just the right moment or the whole rig goes up like a bomb. Got it?" Then Carlton charged out saying that he was going into town despite Khalig's insistence that they stay inside.

Josh stared at the wall of unfamiliar instruments, the blood rushing into his face. He was in trouble now. Surely Carlton should have given him some time to get acquainted with the way things worked before he had left him. He stood in the middle of the cabin and watched the needles moving in rapid jerks against the background of charts. He had no idea what he was supposed to do and how he was going to stop anyone from letting the rig blow.

4

CARLTON CHUCKLED TO HIMSELF. The kid seemed real anxious when he had left him. The drillers would stop the drilling long before Josh could do anything about it. As soon as the well took a kick they'd put a halt to their activities. Better to make the boy feel he was accomplishing something rather than leaving him roaming around aimlessly, even if the job was meaningless. He waved down Khalig at the gate.

"I want to send my wife a telegram. Take me to the Hilltown Hotel in Shylet."

Khalig wouldn't dare argue any further. That was good because curfew or not, there was something Carlton wanted to say to Maribel and it couldn't wait. Besides he'd ignored curfews before and hadn't met with any trouble. Khalig signalled to the guards who opened the gate. He whispered something to the soldier closest to him who nodded and saluted.

Carlton returned soon after lunch. The gas readings had not altered so the drilling had continued. They were thirty metres below prognosed target but he wasn't worried. What he was concerned with was the rumour that he'd heard from the desk clerk in the Hilltown: a mob of Bangladeshi were marching up from Dhaka to protest about the well.

He considered mentioning it to Felstein then decided not to. The boy seemed to have an anxious enough disposition without him fanning the flames further.

The day passed without incident, and dinner for a change tasted half decent. Khalig's wife, Myra, had sent a sponge cake and some English Cheddar cheese which he reluctantly shared out with the rest of his crew. The kid seemed to be getting on with people. In fact, they seemed to respond to him remarkably well. Considering.

Carlton made a final inspection around the drilling site then ordered

Josh to take the first watch with the loggers.

"Make sure you keep an eye on those gas levels," Carlton reminded the boy, then he went to his cabin, washed off the grime of the day, finished some paperwork and climbed into bed.

He stared blankly at the ceiling. The air conditioner was on low and he listened to the sound of its motor humming gently letting the questions that Felstein had asked him at the bubbling gas lake surface in his thoughts.

He hadn't wanted to tell the kid the truth. Not this early in his career when he was still so fresh and idealistic. Big oil companies needed watchdogs like everyone else and here in Bangladesh there were no such animals, not to control the likes of Camco or Standex who were doing as they pleased. It just wasn't cost effective.

Then he thought of the argument he'd had with Khalig. Felstein had predictably upset the guards by trying to get familiar with them. What a nuisance he was turning out to be. Khalig wanted all civilians to keep away from the army people. Orders from the President himself. Well, the exclusion wasn't going to apply to him. He was running the show and he'd do what he wanted no matter what.

That's why he'd gone to the Hilltown. To send Maribel a telegram wishing her a happy anniversary and asking her to come back to Dhaka. He didn't like the idea of her being in Houston without him, especially now that Shumacker had been transferred there. Don't be a fool, he chided himself, it ended bloody years ago. He moved irritably onto his side. He wouldn't be able to sleep if he kept thinking about that son of a –

Josh leaned happily against the counter of the logging unit looking at the chromatograph which indicated how much gas was down the hole. Anand was teaching him how to read the instruments and he was picking it up fast.

The place was swarming with insects and so damp and humid you could grow mushrooms in your boots. It was great. There was no way he could ever have gained such valuable experience if he'd been stuck in an office back in Houston.

He was indebted to Shumacker for choosing him, so unexpectedly, from amongst the many more experienced and probably more deserving geologists. But considering Ramsey's attitude to him, Josh questioned again why it was that he had been chosen. Maybe it didn't matter. Maybe it was just luck.

He filled his lungs. Despite the waves of diesel fumes, the air, once he got used to the fetor, was sweet and heavy with moisture. The odour, Anand said, was a combination not of earth and sewage, but the smell of jute manufacturing mixed with the burning of cow dung, rice straw and husks used as cooking fuel.

Anand's father was a government official so Anand had been able to go to Dhaka University. After the first year, during protests against the President, the Government had closed the college and so Anand was sent to England for two years to finish his studies.

"The students in my country," Anand explained, "have been used for political purposes too long. It is ruining the education of normal Bangladeshis. We have no choice but to get involved in politics. And then we have no time and no chance to return to our studies. It is a dangerous situation."

Anand had been working for Carlton for over a year.

"What do you think of our boss?" Joshua asked convinced he already knew the answer. Anand probably was just as burnt as he by the older man.

"Mr. Ramsey? He is a very good man."

"I'm talking about Carlton Ramsey!" Anand must be covering his back!

"Yes, Mr. Ramsey," Anand continued sincerely. "He has been very good to me as he is to many others."

Anand opened his desk drawer and pulled out a rock hammer and various drilling manuals. "You see, these are only some of the things he gives me from his own collection. This hammer and these books. You cannot get such things here."

Josh nodded but it wasn't enough to change his mind. A rock hammer and a few books didn't add up to much.

"He helped me to find this job and has been training me since. Soon I will be able to work as a well site geologist, perhaps even in your country."

The sting of the older man's snub was even more harsh.

Carlton relieved him at six and despite the tiredness Josh kept himself awake long enough to watch the morning pour into the valley and over the tea hills. He walked around the drill site again. The sky had cleared and the sun was a blur behind a distant mass of lacy trees.

The light came like the tide, splashing over the terraces, reaching into the nooks and crannies, the folds of the hills revealing forms that had not been obvious in the dark. Dozens of men and women, like

41

frozen statues lined the contours leading down into the bowl of the well site. Where had they come from?

It was unnerving. What were they staring at? Looking over his shoulder, as if the eyes of the statues were boring into him, he returned to the logging unit.

"Excuse me, Mr. Ramsey, have you seen all those people on the terraces?"

Carlton stepped out of the cabin. "There are always locals watching us drill. It's a days entertainment." With that Carlton returned to the logging unit.

Completely dissatisfied with the answer, Josh stalked back to his room to get some sleep.

Josh felt every muscle sink into the springs of the metal bed through the thin mattress. But it was good. The air conditioner was running full pelt and he had positioned the pillow so the drips of water would miss it.

As he closed his eyes he could see the remnant of sunrise behind his eyelids. These moments filled him with a deep satisfaction, when he was able to wash away everything he was, all the conflict, the confusion, leaving in its wake only fulfilment: his chosen career, his relationship with Bekah. These were the times when, if there were indeed a God, he felt close to him, willing to let him enter his heart.

The drift into sleep suffused him with calm, deeper into relaxation: dreams of children playing in the jungle. A movement down the pathway, mothers smiling from bamboo thatched huts. Then the scene changed suddenly. The huts on fire, explosions rocking the ground as he ran towards them to save the women.

He sat up. Another explosion shook the cabin followed by the wail of sirens. He jumped out of bed, pulled on his trousers, shirt, shoes, grabbed his glasses and raced outside.

People were scattering in every direction. There were screams from the rig as another explosion shook the ground. Josh ran to the logging unit. It was empty. He bolted over to the area around the rig where the guards were pointing and chattering at the shaking mast and workers were sprinting away from the billowing rig. Sirens echoed against the hills, the smell of gas acrid and burning.

Josh squinted into the sunlit glare. The terraces were still lined with locals staring and pointing, umbrellas shading them from the heat.

He heard Carlton shouting and followed the sound of his voice. The old man had taken control: he looked unbelievably cool.

"Mr. Ramsey, did we take a kick? Is that the gas you were worried about? Are we going to lose the well?"

"Hold on to your hat and we'll see," Carlton answered. "We've got a fire down there and if something above it ignites we'll lose that baby."

"But what can you do about it? I mean, is it going to blow up?"

"We're trying to shut her in. Then we'll pump some mud in and see if we can get her stabilised. If we can't kill the fire, you'd better get out as fast as you can." Carlton laughed and then yelled out another order.

Josh watched his manager's performance, hanging on his every command, trying to memorise the entire scene, to pick up as much information as he could. He admired the way Carlton handled himself, the way he knew just what to do.

"Come on, kid," Carlton said, "I'll show you something." He hurried after Carlton to the mud pits.

"We've just managed to close the well in. That's put the fire out, which is good. Next thing we'll do is pump these heavier muds down the hole, they'll push back the fluids and keep the sands from falling in. Just hope it does the trick."

The mud pumps kicked on, circulating sizzling water stinking like rotten eggs: the smell of sulphur.

"It's a great gas kick!" Carlton was clearly delighted. "There might be something to this area after all."

Flying ash greased Josh's glasses. He took them off and rubbed them clean, returned them to his nose, then followed Carlton back to the rig as the pumps sucked and squeezed. The drillers began a cautious return. Anand waved from the logging cabin. Carlton was right, the fire had gone out. He followed his manager to the logging unit and listened intently while Carlton and Anand discussed strategy, then Carlton told him to try and get some more rest — there was going to be a lot of work to do from now on. Josh nodded and headed off to the cabin pausing briefly to look again at the hills surrounding the site. Surely, the numbers of spectators had trebled just in the past hour.

He found Carlton on the way to the mess and asked him once more about it.

"Look kid," Carlton pushed the mess door open, stepping inside, "I'll be frank with you. This isn't normal but you have to pretend it is. It looks like we're going to have some trouble either tonight or tomorrow. You just stick to your duties and keep out of harm's way."

43

"But –"

Carlton put his cup on the table. "Whatever you do young man, remember you're not at home now. These people have different customs than you're used to. You never know when you might say or do something offensive." Carlton squinted at him hard.

"That's not very fair." Josh stood his ground.

"Fair or not!" Carlton continued, "You keep to your duties. If I see you out of bounds I'll have you sent back to Houston. You understand?"

Admiration mixed with anger. They fought for dominance. Josh clenched his fist in the pocket of his trousers.

"You understand, boy?"

"Yes," Josh answered.

"Good. Now we're going to log those bloody formations then run casing and test before anything else can go wrong down that hole! You get some sleep and report to me at 13:00 hours."

Josh returned to his room, lay down on his bed replaying the scene on the rig. He should take notes. But no, he'd remember that fire for the rest of his life. He glanced at his watch. It was already eleven thirty. No way was he going to be able to get more sleep. He got up and brushed his teeth and got himself ready for work dreading having to deal with Ramsey again. No matter how hard he tried to be reasonable, the old man got under his skin and the more Carlton dug at him the more he wanted to kick back.

He was sure that if he asked Anand why there were so many people collecting around the site he'd get a straight answer and find out there was nothing to worry about. He had an unshakeable belief that the Company would take care of them. The barbed wire and armed guards certainly helped.

The mirror reflected back a tired face. He should probably have listened to Ramsey and tried to get some more sleep but there was too much going on outside.

Anand had left the logging cabin, so Josh wandered aimlessly around the drilling site, finding himself, finally, near the gate, looking once more at the scores of people lining the hills. A guard came over smiling and nodding his head. Josh offered him one of the cigarettes that he'd bought earlier from the driller for just such an occasion.

The soldier glanced nervously around. He signaled for Josh to follow him and they walked behind a sentry post where they couldn't be seen.

The guard smiled encouragingly. He took a cigarette and said, "Asalaam," and then he laughed, "Asalaam alaikhum."

Josh smiled back and repeated the phrase. Peace be with you. He was making some headway.

"What is happening here?" he said motioning with his arms to the surrounding hills.

The guard appeared confused.

"Those people," Josh pointed to the figures in the hills. The guard rapidly answered but Josh couldn't understand a word. He tried again.

"Many people," he gestured with his hands but again the answer came too quickly. He offered another cigarette which was taken but there was clearly no scope for conversation. The guard began backing away and Josh said, "Khuda hafiz. Goodbye."

The guard smiled again repeating his words and Josh was glad that he had established some friendly contact.

He walked back to the logging cabin to see whether Anand had returned. He was running the winch down the hole, lowering the electric tools so they could send back resistivity and conductivity readings of the rock formations and their fluids. And he was too busy to talk other than to say that the fire had caused little damage. They had hit a small pocket of gas while drilling. It had flared up and was just as quickly gone. Even though it had looked a lot worse, it had not ignited anything shallower which really was a miracle and a credit to Carlton's management of the crisis. If the older man had misread the situation, the rig would have gone up like a missile.

The logging tools clicked into place as the information from the instruments down the hole was relayed back to the screen in the logging unit. Josh sat in front of the monitor, watching the responses: the types of rock that were there and what fluids were in them.

He lost track of time and his surroundings. This job was no chore. He could do it night and day. This was everything he'd ever hoped for. No, it was more than he'd ever hoped for except for one thing. 'Nothing good comes free,' he heard Bekah remind him. 'Tough it out!'

He got up and traced his finger along the contours of the seismic map on the wall. The area where they were drilling was an enormous underground high. There were lines of faults zigzagging through the overthrown sediments. Geology was something special, it captured the imagination. Whole continents moving and banging into each other, crumpling rock climbing into mountains, rich oil that had created huge industries and changed civilisation, beautiful crystals which had created and destroyed great kingdoms of the past and would soon be the technology of the future.

He sighed deeply. This was where he truly belonged.

As the sun was setting, Carlton stepped into the logging unit. He looked worried. "Must be at least two hundred of them come up from Dhaka. Kid, stay in the logging cabin, your quarters or the mess. I don't want to see you walking around."

"Sure, but –"

Carlton ignored him and said something to Anand who nodded and then hurried out of the cabin.

"I'm going to talk to the drillers," Carlton mumbled. "I'll see you back here in twenty minutes." He opened the door of the cabin and Josh looked out. Ramsey was right there were hundreds now at the gate, ominously hushed and lit by spotlights hooked up along the guard posts.

"Just need to get something out of my cabin." Josh jumped out.

"Okay, but make it quick," Carlton replied stalking off to the rig. As Carlton came into view of the gate, the sounds of jeering broke the strange silence. The guard post and the cabins were pelted with stones. Then a shot rang out and in its aftermath a dreadful silence dropped, like a cloak thrown on a fire, smothered for the moment.

Josh paused for a few seconds before he left his quarters. He hadn't eaten yet and his stomach grumbled hungrily. He'd just drop by the mess, make himself some sandwiches and return to the logging unit. As he neared the mess, he could see the Chief Driller and Carlton storming towards the guards.

The crowd ignited again.

Josh stepped behind a small shed keeping out of view.

Carlton was talking to the guards. They seemed to understand him. Carlton even laughed! The Chief Driller was jeering at the crowd. Carlton said something to him and the driller raised his middle finger to the mob and shook his fist at them. Carlton pulled the upraised arm down and tried unsuccessfully to tug the driller away who lunged towards the crowd like a dog ready for a fight.

The guards paced back and forth in front of the hut. As the driller walked away, the sounds from the mob crescendoed, the gates rattling in time to the chants.

Buses were arriving every minute. Bangladeshis hanging from every available space, dropping off at the gates, creating an army of civilians, carrying megaphones, hurtling their voices into the air. Emotions flamed as the speeches came bellowing over loudspeakers.

The guards were becoming more agitated. They aimed their weapons at the rioters. Then the sputter of a sub machine gun smashed the screaming crowd backwards, heightening the wailing and chanting.

Carlton was walking towards the cabin with the driller in tow. Josh sensed the older man's eyes land on him. He bent down and hurried to the mess, opened the door then quickly closed it behind him. He grabbed a cup and poured himself some tea. A few minutes later Carlton opened the door. He was alone.

"I'm fed up with you boy. The next time you disobey my orders you may well find yourself dead."

"What do you mean by that?" Josh countered.

"The sight of you drives them crazy. You understand?"

Josh clenched his fists but restrained himself. "I haven't had anything to eat yet today. I just came over for a sandwich. Is that all right?"

"Yes." Carlton poured himself a cup of coffee.

Josh started cutting the bread into slices filling it with peanut butter and jelly. "I have a right to know why this is happening," he said calmly.

"You've got no rights while there's an emergency on. Just do as you're told."

"Come on, you don't have to behave this way."

"I don't huh?" Carlton prodded him in the back, "You want to know what's going on. I'll tell you. That mob thinks Ershad is giving away all their oil."

Josh twisted out of the way of the old man's aggression, "But that's crazy. Everyone knows we have to sign percentage deals."

"Jesus kid, no wonder I hate telling you anything. You have no idea what you're talking about."

"I'm listening."

"It's all politics. Places like this. Got nothing to do with the oil or contracts or revenue. Everything to do with who wants power. Right now, the opposition want Ershad out."

"But what has that got to do with us?"

"For Christ's sake! You get enough people agitated, you stage a coup. Don't you understand yet?"

"But isn't there anything we can do to make them understand?"

"Like what? Tell them that they're being manipulated? You think they'll believe us? Jesus!"

"What about Khalig? He can talk to them. Surely it's just a matter –"

"Sure, we'll just mosey on out and tell 'em there's nothing to worry about. And they'll all just pack up and go home."

"I just think there should be some way to let them know the truth."

"The truth about what? You don't understand one thing about this place. Until you do keep your mouth shut!"

"Look, I don't have to take this from you!"

"You know Felstein, I've dealt with your type before. It just goes to show how alike you all are."

Josh suddenly lunged at the older man smashing him against the wall. Carlton quickly shoved his palm under Josh's jaw pushing him away.

"Come on, boy." Carlton danced away from the wall. "Prove you're a man."

Josh came back at him swinging. Carlton deflected the first then second punch. "Come on kid, you can do better than that."

Josh swung again. Carlton punched straight through his efforts, connecting his fist on jaw, sending him flying to the other side of the room. Josh sat up rubbing his chin. The old man was as strong as a bull. As he struggled back to his feet, the roof and walls were pelted with stones. A piercing scream filled the room.

Carlton dashed out of the door, Josh close behind. The Chief Driller Bob K, was surrounded. Taller and larger than his attackers, Bob was plucking them off one or two at a time, tossing them away like scraps of meat to a dog. Reinforcements poured in armed with sticks. They came in from behind, bearing down on the driller. Tips of club ends lifted into the air before smashing down. The driller disappeared only to come up again and be brought to his knees by another blow.

Carlton began running towards the guards. For the briefest of moments Josh wondered why no one else was doing anything to help, then he bolted out of the cabin and jumped into the mob, punching his way through.

He caught a glimpse of the driller. The man was unconscious, and they were dragging him away, streaking blood across the oily ground.

Josh started shouting for help. He pushed his way toward the driller. Someone hit him from behind and he fell to the ground. He struggled to get up and was hit again. He had a sense of bare feet running by

48

him, stepping on his hands, someone kicked him in the forehead. He knew he had to get up but none of his limbs responded. His cheek was cool against the sticky clay as darkness slipped over him.

He heard voices. American voices. He opened his eyes, looking up, his vision a blur. He groped around for his glasses. They had been cracked in the middle and as he sat up he hung them loosely upon his nose.

Carlton was standing menacingly over him. "What the hell do you think you're doing?"

"I was trying to help."

"The guards could have busted the fight up. How were they supposed to shoot at anyone if you're in the middle of things? They've got Bob K now. You can hold yourself responsible if anything happens to him."

Carlton stormed away leaving Josh lying in the mud. He sat up and saw Anand and the others walking away. Not even trying to help him. A sense of foreboding ran through him, as if he were a very small boy who had done something terribly stupid.

Was it really his fault they had taken the driller? He put his hand to the back of his head and felt a large bump, sore to the touch. He struggled to his feet dizzy and shaken but determined to face the old man again and finish what they'd started.

He stumbled into the mess ready for another fight. Carlton was on the radio to Khalig. He paused when Josh stepped in and pointed to the first aid kit on the table. Next to that was a hot cup of tea and a roll of tape. Carlton reached over and grabbed the tape then pulled Josh's glasses from his nose. He began mending the frame in between talking to Khalig.

It knocked the impetus out of Josh's anger.

Carlton hung the receiver back on its hook. He didn't speak as he handed the mended glasses back and moved to the table. He looked down at the tea cup. It hadn't been touched.

"Drink up, boy. It'll help your head."

Josh lifted the cup to his lips. The tea was strong and hot and full of brandy.

"Sit down. Let me look at that bruise."

"Thanks, but no thanks."

"Look kid, I've got enough to worry about without tending to your hurt pride. Sit down and let me look at it."

Josh obeyed. What choice did he have?

Roughly, Carlton put a wet cloth against the back of Josh's head. The antiseptic burned. Then Carlton handed him a few pills.

"Take 'em."

"What are they?"

"Chrissake, they're painkillers."

Josh put them in his mouth and tried to swallow but a lump of anger stuck in his throat. They began to dissolve, bitter on his tongue. He grabbed the tea, swilling it into his mouth but the pills refused to go down — just like everything else the old bastard was handing out.

The chanting rose and fell, the air filled with apprehension. Guards paced the perimeter fence as it clanked and rattled abuse. There was an echo of hammering some distance off.

The mob began praying. There was a fervour to it that reminded Josh of his father praying in synagogue: that rocking, yearning, beseeching. A prayer for relief, for something new, something better. He was anxious, couldn't sit still. The sound of the hammering filled him with dread. What were they doing? He kept glancing out of the window then sitting down only to jump up a few minutes later.

The afternoon light began to shift against the hills. Gradually, the sounds of hammering stopped and were suddenly replaced by the rumble of engines in the near distance. There was shouting and the echo of gunshots. The crowd stirred as if it were one body. Aggrieved voices called out.

The cabins were pelted again with stones. Then the importuning of the megaphones drowned out the distant engines. There were more shouts. More protests as the roar of engines approached the now opening gates. Two army tanks rumbled in, armed soldiers crowding out of the top. Khalig's jeep swung in after. He drove up to where Carlton had appeared.

The driller was sitting in the passenger seat. Josh ran over and opened the door of the jeep and dragged the injured man out.

"Sons-a bitches," the driller grabbed on to Josh's shoulders stumbling forward. "Sons-a fuckin' bitches," he cursed as he fell to his knees forcing Josh down with him.

Carlton was talking to Khalig. Josh heard them laughing. What would they find funny in a situation like this? A few minutes later Carlton made his way to the other side of the jeep. He took the driller's right arm and hoisted it over his shoulder. Josh took the other and together they dragged the man to the mess and sat him in a chair.

Carlton rummaged through the first aid kit.

"Felstein, I've got whisky in my bedroom. Go get it."

In Carlton's room, Josh rummaged in the older man's bag for the bottle. He became aware of a picture in a pewter frame. It was of a woman in her fifties: neat, blue white hair, but the expression was one of holding back, perhaps even resentment. This must be Maribel then.

The driller drank greedily, finishing the contents.

"Fuckin' assholes tried to hang me! Built a fuckin' scaffold right in front of my fuckin' eyes."

"What happened?" Josh pulled his chair closer.

Carlton elbowed him aside, "Kid, how'm I supposed to bandage him with you in the way?"

"You got any more whisky I can have?" the driller tugged on Carlton's sleeve.

"You've had enough." Carlton pulled his arm away.

The driller grabbed the bottle again, tipping it upside down, shaking the last drops into his mouth, then he let the flask fall. "Sons-a bitches," he slurred. "Arrived just in the nick of fuckin' time. Like the goddamned cavalry." He laughed and winked at Josh. "They don't like us knockin' up their precious cunts –"

Then he dropped his chin to his chest and started snoring.

Carlton said, "We'll carry him to his bed. I've seen him in worse shape than this."

Together they dragged him to his cabin. Carlton took the man's boots off and tucked him in. As they stepped outside, a stone was thrown onto a nearby roof. It bounced off and landed at Carlton's feet. He kicked it and ignored the jeering from the gates. Now that the tanks were in place there was a lot less to worry about.

By midnight it was nearly quiet again. The whirring and clicking of the insects, the humming of the engines and the sucking of the pumps returned the site to normal.

5

JOSH ROLLED OVER IN HIS BED against the cabin wall under the clattering air conditioner, condensation dripping onto his right shoulder, the white sheet tangled between his legs. A single mosquito buzzed in his ear and he waved his hand to shoo it away. He scratched at his neck, mumbling in his sleep then rolled over onto his right side.

His forehead, as he turned, hit against something hard and metallic which woke him with a start.

He sat up.

The metal lifted and prodded, pushing his head against the wall.

"You get dressed," a Bangladeshi voice whispered harshly in his face.

Josh reached over to the bedside table for his glasses and the metal rod crashed onto his hand. He shouted out and was hit again.

"You'd better do as they say, kid." Carlton's voice came from the back of the room.

"You move!" the Bangladeshi thrust at him again.

Josh slowly swung his legs over the edge of the bed; the weapon shaft probed at his chest, making him sweat.

"You get clothes... Move!"

Josh reached for his glasses again. He heard the trigger click; the weapon pressed into his neck.

"No touch!"

"My glasses, I need my glasses to see."

"You no see."

Carlton's sarcastic voice cut through the shadows. "He can't get dressed without his glasses."

A figure jumped out breathing heavily. "Okay, pick up," it said washing Josh with the smell of sour yoghurt and curry.

Josh couldn't control the shaking of his hand as he placed the mended glasses onto his nose. It clarified the images in the room.

There were soldiers and Carlton was standing impassively behind them. His throat was dry, he could barely stand, made himself put his legs in the trousers, forced his fingers to button the shirt while the soldiers jabbed at him babbling wildly, to hurry, to move.

They were smaller than he. Perhaps he could catch them unawares: grab the weapons, overcome them. Another figure jumped forward from the dark recesses of the cabin and grabbed his hands, binding them with a rope or a rag.

They prodded him out of the cabin. He stumbled on the metallic step, still barefoot, then landed on a sharp piece of stone. Where were the guards? Why weren't they aware of what was happening? Was Ramsey behind this? But why? Had he made such an enemy of the man?

He struggled to move his feet. Ancient scenes of pogroms and Nazis rumbled through his psyche. Should he really go passively, isn't that what people just like him had done? His aunts and uncles? They shoved at him, propelling him along. Carlton's words returned. He'd find himself dead if he didn't obey. But he hadn't taken the old man's threats seriously. Why should he have?

No. He refused to believe it. He was being paranoid, ridiculous. It had to be a mistake. They had to be taking Carlton too and maybe others. He heard the protesters jeering at the front gate and forced himself to keep going, to think of other possibilities.

If there had been a coup, then Carlton and he would be enemies of the State. But these men were soldiers, or dressed like them. His thoughts rebelled. No, it can't be. He looked wildly around for Carlton but he was gone.

"Where are you taking me?"

"No questions!" The point of the weapon shoved into his back, sending shards of pain through his spine. "Move!"

He was pushed to the perimeter fence behind the mud pits, into the filthy stream separating the tea gardens from the drilling site. He fell onto his knees in the muck and filth. The fumes of the sewage, penetrated into his fabric, unravelling him. He was losing his nerve. He fought against vomiting, fought against the dreadful nightmare, the poisonous snakes looming in his mind, fought against the urge to run whatever the consequence.

The soldier yanked him up, pushed him through a hole in the fence. He staggered to the other side. Something slithered by, rustling under the wet leaves. The scream inside his head resounded but refused to leave his throat. They pushed him into a clearing where a broken down, rusty van waited.

There was another soldier there, looking at the vehicle, kicking its tyres and checking the doors. He recognised the man! It was the guard he had given those cigarettes to. The one he'd exchanged greetings with. They were saved! My God, it was awful but everything was going to be all right. His knees gave way. He started to say something but the gun stopped him. He lifted his arms to attract attention. The man looked up. Looked straight at him. His eyes like nickel blanks.

Sullen words were exchanged between soldiers, the familiar man turned his back and walked away as if he hadn't seen anything at all. Josh wanted to lunge at him, shake some sense into him. Instead he crumpled to the ground in despair.

The door of the van screeched on its rusty hinges as they pulled it open letting the musky night air wash against Carlton's skin. He lifted his head to see what was going on. The kid's face was filled with fright and then the damnedest thing, he could have sworn that Josh gave a sudden smile just before they gagged and shoved him in. Idiot! Did he think this was some kind of adventure?

The doors were shut and locked, leaving them in total darkness with the smell of urine and animal shit. The engine idled but they did not pull away. They stayed there for an interminable time. He heard gunshots in the distance and then megaphones blaring. It was a clever cover, if the riots had anything to do with their abduction.

He straightened his back against the rough wall of the van and tried to sleep. But his eyes refused to stay closed and the cloth around his mouth was cutting into his flesh. After about an hour or maybe two, the truck began to roll away bumping over the rough ground, jolting him against the jagged metal within the cab.

He focussed on the kid. What a way to start a career, but this business had always been dangerous and the boy had to accept that. It was comical, in a way, that this may be the true ending of his own career instead of the early retirement. Another euphemism: early retirement for death. His father had been the same way, work had been his life and he'd died soon after he had retired. Bad heart. Just like him.

He rocked along with the motion of the truck, not fighting it. He'd been in a million vehicles on a million dirt tracks all over the world and had learned that you just let your body roll with the punches.

The boy was bouncing around and banging against the sides of the truck with every jolt. He wished he could tell him to relax.

They drove for hours. Carlton had no idea what direction they were heading in. The road was monotonously bad and despite his riding the waves, his backside was bruised and getting sorer by the minute. It was to the boy's credit that he hadn't made a sound. He wondered if he were asleep. That would be quite a feat. He discounted that option. He was probably wide awake and feeling twice as sore.

The truck finally rolled to a stop. The engine cut off. As the air filtered in, through the cracks and leaks in the metal work, it was fresher and cooler than it had been in Shylet. That could mean only one thing. They must be in the hills. They had been travelling for about two or three hours. That would make sense. The road had been passable. They hadn't crossed any streams so they had been on the dirt track up to Jaintipur.

The truck started again and this time they went off the main route and pushed their way through jungle, the branches hitting against the sides of the metal, thumping like angry gods.

They stopped again. The doors jerked open to the morning light. They pulled the rope from the boy's feet first and then yanked him off the truck. He fell and they kicked him unnecessarily. Blood massed at the back of his head as he was dragged upwards.

Now, it was his turn. The rope wouldn't yield and it was cutting into his flesh. Then his legs were free and he struggled to keep balance as they pulled him off the van. He had been right. They were probably near Jaintipur right on the border of India. The sweep of hills with their distant waterfalls was somewhere he knew well.

They marched through a narrow track: palms hanging overhead or brushing against their sleeves, the branches snapping in his eyes.

The boy stumbled blindly in front and each time he fell they kicked him. Carlton only knew the most rudimentary phrases in Bengali but their exclamations needed no translation. No wonder the kid was falling. He wasn't wearing his glasses. After all that bother in the cabin.

They walked along the crest of a hill. A large cobble-filled river was flowing rapidly, only visible when the trees opened up enough to see beyond the pathway. Then they came to another trail and swung right going deeper into the hills.

He was not as fit as he used to be, but out of breath and yearning for one of his cigars. His legs were hurting too and he wondered how long they expected to march him like this before he collapsed. The kid still had his head bowed but he kept walking. That surprised Carlton. He had thought the boy would have given out long before now.

They finally came to a small clearing. Two wooden huts stood side by side. They'd been purpose built, like dog kennels, one with a straw roof and the other wooden. Only the straw roofed hut had a door. The wooden one had a small hatch which bolted from the outside. The Bangladeshis were crafty carpenters when they wanted to be.

Carlton scanned the area over the low lying roofs of the huts. Something white reflected back at him. It sparkled like snow. That was impossible. It was probably the white sandstone of the rock face and other than that the vista was of jungle everywhere. No one would find them here.

They pulled the bolts across and opened the hatch, just big enough to fit his bulk, untied his hands and shoved him in. It was the kid's turn. They didn't untie his hands which made it near impossible to get in through the hatchway. The guard shouted something, lifted his rifle and smashed Josh on the head causing him to land with a heavy thud inside the hut.

Carlton undid the cloth around his mouth and then began to work on the ropes around the other's inert wrists. The hatch was slammed and bolted from the outside. They were in total darkness with the smell of new wood and tar and the absence of any sound. He felt the ropes around the boy's hands loosen and then fall. "You all right boy?" he asked but didn't get an answer. He moved back towards the wall and lightly banged his fist against the wood to test it. It didn't move. He leaned against the wall, struck by the sudden realisation: this abduction had been planned long before the riots, perhaps even before they had hit oil. The implication was unnerving.

"Kid, you okay?" he moved over to the boy. "Talk to me for Christ's sake." He reached out to touch the other's leg. Something rapidly slithered through his fingers and away. He jumped falling backwards, hitting his head on the wood. Damn lizards! He sat upright rubbing the back of his head reminding himself that at least there wouldn't be many spiders in the hut.

Josh hadn't moved. Was he unconscious? Carlton returned to the boy and tried to drag him to the wall, sit him up if he could. This whole mess was insanity. Sure, he'd been through this before: the political problems in Indonesia in '65 when the government withdrew from the United Nations. He had been followed home one evening and attacked

56

outside the house. Nothing had come of it. He'd overpowered the lunatic and had him arrested and besides, back then they all had personal security guards. Except his had been sleeping in the car.

What an assignment this was turning out to be. He sat in silence opposite his charge. Couldn't even tell if that last blow had killed him or not. He reached over and touched the boy's foot. It was cold. As he squeezed the toes, the smooth skin suddenly reminded him of his own son, Joe. Beloved son who might as well be dead.

"Come on kid, talk to me will you? Does your head hurt? You had a nasty gash there while we were walking." He could sense the other moving slightly. "Now look, these things happen all the time. It's part of the game. Something always goes awry when you work overseas. You just have to go with it and everthing'll turn out fine."

But he knew his words held no conviction.

He pushed himself against the wall and closed his eyes. When he opened them again he found he could just see the kid's outline in a corner of the hut. It was unnaturally still. He crept over, reached out and touched the boy on the shoulder then moved his hand briefly to his forehead. It was cold as ice.

Damn! He wished he could see better. He tried looking into the boy's eyes but they were closed. Was he breathing? He found then lifted the hand. It too was cold and clammy. He searched for the pulse. It was fine, a bit slow but still as strong as could be. He took his shirt off and something dropped out of his pocket. He groped around for it. A cigar! His last dying wish: a bloody cigar.

He folded the shirt up tightly and put it under the boy's head and then moved back to his wall where he fondled the aluminium cigar case, savouring the moment when the aroma would reveal itself as he unscrewed the cap. But he decided against it.

He left it sealed then slipped the case into his trouser pocket. The pleasure could wait, for when he really needed it. Right now he had to figure a way out.

Against a backdrop of silence, he tried to discern the noises around the camp, but he could hear nothing, only the kid's breathing — now gulping sighs, sounds from a child's mouth. There was nothing else to listen to, no other movement, no rattling of metal or the wind through the trees. Everything was still and quiet as if the small camp had emptied of their captors and they had been left to rot. It spurred him to action.

He got to his feet but couldn't stand completely, the eaves of the roof too low to allow it. The first thing was to check out the place where last light had ventured in before the hatch had been slammed shut. With his fist he pounded on the wood. And when that did nothing he took his shoe off and started whacking the panels with his heel quickly replacing it on his foot as he heard a squabble of voices and the bolts being slid across. The light startled him. "Toilet!" he shouted. "Toilet!"

There were two guards. Both heavily armed. They were not the ones who had brought them here and there was no sign of the others.

"Toilet!" he shouted again and pointed to his crotch. He searched for the Bengali word, "Paikhana!"

One of the guards seemed pleased, his moustached lip curling in a half smile. He understood. Damned paikhana, toilet. Carlton was beckoned out. He was taken to a tree and the guard pointed then said, "Paikhana."

As he urinated, he surveyed the area and the quickest way out. The town was probably back where they had crossed onto the jungle track. If they could make it to Jaintipur they'd be able to find help. He looked around for water, food, anything that would keep them alive but there was nothing. He just hoped they had something stored in the adjacent hut.

The rain began to drop and the guards grew impatient. He zipped his trousers up and they led him back where he climbed through the hatch, catching a glimpse of the boy huddled in the corner before they shut them up again.

It was aggravating. Perhaps the kid was a coward. Too frightened by his own shadow to move out of the dark. He could have done some valuable reconnaissance in his unguarded time. Together they could have decided a course of action.

A jerk of pain lunged through his chest. With the utmost control he slid against the wall into a sitting position, scratching his bare back on the way down. He waited for the pain to clear. When at last it did, he reached his hand into his trouser pocket and touched his cigar.

The boy stirred.

"Well, how are you feeling?" he asked.

"Not too good. I think I passed out."

Carlton felt a flush of guilt. "You must have been hit pretty bad."

He could just sense the kid lifting his hand to his head,

"I'm gonna be sick." Josh shuffled towards the front of the hut.

"Hold on! Hold on! I'll see what I can do." Carlton smashed at the wood with his shoe. The hatch opened and he stepped aside. The boy fell chest first, vomiting on the way out. The guards tried to pull then push him away as Josh stumbled off, retching.

Watching, Carlton again remembered his own son. Holding him as a child, letting him be sick and not giving a damn whether he was covered in it or not. The vulnerability, that was it. It drove him mad. Despite that, he tried to climb out of the cabin to help but was stopped.

He waited, watching the rain mix with the boy's blood and run down his neck. What was the damnable word for water? He should know it. If only he could remember. Water and whisky, to wash the wounds — and he didn't only need the whisky for the kid.

Josh stumbled back to the hut prodded by the smaller of the watchdogs. They were a puny lot, but with the strength of submachine guns behind them Carlton felt he could do nothing but wait for the right opportunity. If it ever came.

"Water," he called out, but the guards appeared confused. "Water!" he shouted louder, knowing full well that hollering at them was the worst thing he could do. What difference did it make anyway? Their eyes were blank with stupidity. He yelled and cursed, losing his cool. They panicked at the sound and pushed the kid in, tumbling him through the opening causing him to fall on Carlton. The hatch was slammed shut and bolted. Carlton pushed the boy off then smashed his fist against the door.

"Sons of ignorant bitches!"

"Mr. Ramsey?" The boy's voice sounded younger than it should have been.

"Yes, what is it?"

"Was that your shirt?"

"Yes," and he rubbed his hand over his bare chest.

"I think I've ruined it."

"Doesn't matter."

"I'm sorry…"

"Forget it, just try and take it easy, will you?" Carlton took the three crouched steps to his place in the cell and sat down. "Hey kid, check your pockets, will you?"

Josh did as he was told. "I've got my phrase book. Some coins and my Swiss army knife."

"That's good. That's real good. Now all we need is some light. Hand me that knife of yours."

The boy stretched forward. In the dark their hands touched before they could transfer the knife. Carlton started poking at the wood with the end of the blade trying to find weaknesses in the structure of the joining boards. He worked his way along his side of the hut.

"You feel good enough to try on your side?" Carlton rested on the floor, his arm ached.

"Sure." Josh took the knife and checked the wall for breaches. But he found nothing.

"There's got to be a way out," Carlton said. But his charge didn't respond though he gave him plenty of time to answer. It was obvious. It was going to be up to him to get them out of this situation. Either the boy was too hurt or he just didn't have the guts.

"Give me that knife back and I'll check the roof." Carlton felt the cool plastic of the army kit on the palm of his hand and fumbled to open the blade again. He jabbed at the roof, first on his side of the building and then, making the kid move over, on the other side "Bastards," he cursed, jabbing fruitlessly.

The bolts suddenly slid open. Quickly, he dropped to the floor, depositing the knife in his shoe. The guard screeched something and threw in two bamboo mats then disappeared for a moment returning with two Styrofoam boxes. Carlton went to the hatch as it was closing. He threw his shoulder against it, flinging it open.

"Kid, open your damned book," he called into the hut, "Find the word for candle or light." He struggled with the door keeping it open.

The boy moved closer, flipping through the book. "Try to stall him."

"You have candle?" Carlton asked. The guard sneered and pushed. Josh came closer to the hatch flipping through the book fast,

"Din is day," he said. "Try that."

"Good thinking... Din." Carlton shouted and pointed to the sky full of dark and bleeding clouds. And then he pointed inside the hut, "Din, din!"

"Din!" the guard repeated. "Ji, ha!" The hatch shut but a few minutes later it reopened and a candle was thrown in.

Carlton fell to his knees in the dark scraping his fingers in the mud, mumbling under his breath every damned curse he could think of.

The kid was on the ground beside him, searching too. He said, "I've got it!"

"What the hell good is it if we don't have any way to light it?" Carlton countered. He heard the boy sigh. What the hell good was he?

"I've got a flint attached to my knife," Josh said.

"A flint eh? You think that'll work?" Carlton handed the knife over.

"We need kindling," Carlton heard the other's voice.

Kindling? Where'd the kid think they were going to get kindling from? Damned Paikhana, that's how. He got to his feet and smacked the hatch with his shoe and when no one opened it, he smacked it again and again. Won't let the bastards have a moment of peace. Finally it worked. "Paikhana!" he shouted at the opening but the door was once again slammed. "Sons of –"

"We can use the paper out of this book," the kid interrupted him. Then he struck something against the knife, once then twice. Carlton saw a spark light and die. Then another spark and another. Slowly a thin glow of flame began to expand into a continual source of light from the burning candle. Despite himself Carlton was impressed.

"Glory be to God, wherever he may be," Carlton said taking the candle and examining the Styrofoam cartons that had been thrown in. "I assume this is grub," he said. "You'd better eat while you can." Carlton handed Josh one of the boxes. "Food might come scarce." He examined the carton. ARM was printed on the bottom. He laughed. "Now you can see why the poor don't benefit by Western charities. All their donations go to the army."

The boy held onto his drooping glasses and squinted at the printed letters,

"What do they stand for?"

"American Resource Mission. They're big in Dhaka. They keep the army in money."

Carlton chuckled again and opened the box. Sitting on a mound of rice were two small yellow yoghurt balls.

"Christ, we'll have to use our fingers," Carlton said distastefully.

"My knife has a spoon on it. You can use it, I'm okay without."

"It's your knife boy."

"Go ahead, I'm okay."

Carlton inspected the food. He hated yoghurt.

The kid put the milk ball cautiously in his mouth then said, almost cheerfully, "It's sweet." He took another one, popped it in his mouth and swallowed.

With the thought of the slimy acidic taste, Carlton grimaced. Then, abruptly, the boy lifted the tray to his mouth and started shovelling the rice in. Carlton shook his head as he watched Josh gulp his food down. The recuperative powers of the young were always amazing and with those silly broken glasses the poor boy looked like a starving orphan.

Carlton undid the spoon from the rest of the gadgets and dipped it into the rice, slowly eating the white starch. It tasted musky.

"You want this yoghurt?" Carlton asked.

"You should eat them. They're not so bad."

"Can't stand the stuff." Carlton pushed the tray away. "Go on take them." The candle light sputtered.

Josh fixed his gaze on the food.

"Go on, then."

The kid hesitated. What was the matter with him? Jesus. Get on with it!

Finally the boy took the carton.

They sat in the flickering light, companions who had lost any possibility of intimacy, strangers with nothing to say. Josh was the first to break.

"Do you think they're soldiers?"

Carlton nodded. "Looks like it."

"Do you think the president's been deposed? Is that why they're holding us?"

"It's hard to say."

"Do you think they've taken the others?"

"I doubt it."

"But why do you think they've taken us? They must know we're not involved in the politics or anything. Or even, if Ershad has been deposed why would they benefit by taking us?"

"For Christ's sake kid, how the hell am I supposed to know?"

"Maybe they just want Ershad to hold elections and then they'll let us go. Or maybe the people just want a better deal with Standex! We could be in the wrong. They could really have a reason for being upset."

"There's no reason for anyone to be upset," Carlton responded acerbically.

"But surely you've got to have some idea why we're being held!"

"Jesus, kid! When are you going to get the message. How the hell should I know?"

The boy stopped. That was good. Carlton pressed his head against the wall. He wished he were alone, or if not alone then far away from Felstein whom he hadn't wanted to have anything to do with in the first place. He shut his eyes and clasped his hands together, closing himself as best as he could against any further intrusion.

6

DESPITE CARLTON'S GRUFFNESS, Josh still wanted to know what he thought their real situation was. The older man knew more than he was saying and his secrecy was like a gate that swung open only for those that Carlton deemed acceptable. The isolation of it enhanced the fear.

Compared to this, nothing bad had ever really happened to him. The occasional mugging in New York, the hostile stares as he and Bekah walked arm in arm in North Carolina. Why had he thought before that he had to be on his guard?

No one had ever bashed him about the head nor stuck a gun in his face or fired at him. He longed for the safety of home. He would never again devalue it as he had done before. Josh reached out and touched his foot. On the march over he had cut the skin between the toes and now the cut had spread, swollen and raw into the middle of the arch. Why did they hate him so? 'The sight of you drives them crazy.' Carlton's words pressed in on him. Why? Why did they treat Carlton with respect and him like dirt?

His head began to pound as he pressed the questions over and over, using them as assaults against his self-respect. His eyes focused on the shirt. The cloth was streaked with blood. Stained with an act of kindness that made no sense at all.

He lifted his head to look again at the other man, the face partly in shadow which altered every time the flame of the candle shifted. Carlton seemed at peace, with his eyes closed. Relaxed. Impenetrable.

At that moment the darkness of the blue of Carlton's eyes showed itself. Carlton bent forward, grabbed the candle and struggled to his feet, his shoulders stooped, knees slightly bent.

Josh's eyes were drawn to the ground. Why hadn't he noticed before? Carlton was wearing shoes. The bareness of his own cut feet was just another example of the difference in treatment. Was this really some kind of crazy scheme to get rid of him? Kidnap them together and set the older man free, leaving him to... But what would Ramsey possibly gain by it? He could have sent him home at a moment's notice. Surely there was nothing to gain!

Carlton whispered, "Listen, I'm going to use the candle to find some discontinuity in the wood. Tell me if you see the flame flicker." He slowly moved the candle along the boards.

Josh didn't move. Why play into the older man's hands, making a fool of himself any further?

"Are you helping or not boy?" Carlton growled.

Josh moved to the wall Carlton was concentrating on, but he wasn't watching the candle. He wanted to ask Ramsey what he was up to. Perhaps if he showed that he'd figured it all out, Carlton would confess. Then he'd have the truth. No matter how bad, he would know what would happen to him.

"For Christ's sake kid, anyone would think you liked it in here. Are you gonna play the side or not?"

"Can you explain something to me?"

"Whaddya want to know?"

Josh took a deep breath and let it out slowly through his mouth. If he was right, as remote as it might be, he would be fighting for his life, for his very sanity. If Carlton were plotting to kill him...

"You said the sight of me drove them crazy. That I'd be dead if I didn't obey."

"I don't know what you're talking about." Carlton held the light up to the wood, not turning to face him. What was he hiding?

Josh continued. "You said that in the mess during the riot. I want to know why."

"You shouldn't take things so personally. I meant any white person. Not you in particular. Look at what happened to our driller."

"Yeah, but..."

"But what? Speak your mind dammit!"

But did he really want to know? Josh hesitated, weighing the consequences of his questions.

Carlton spun around. "For Chrissakes kid, spit it out."

"Why do the guards treat us so differently?"

"Is that all that's bugging you?"

"That and –"

"It's an age thing they have out here. They're so used to treating their elders with respect it doesn't come natural to abuse me. Don't worry they'll get around to it. Make you feel better?"

Josh had no answer for his superior. Carlton was clever, as if he had known the questions would come sooner or later, as if he'd rehearsed the answer. He'd have to let it go for now. Carlton continued running the candle around the wall. A dramatic dance of shadows, Josh thought, between two men on two different planets.

"There!" The candle's flicker made Josh jump.

"Where?"

"Just there. Here give me the candle I'll show you."

Against the framework, the flame quickly bent and straightened again. Carlton opened the knife and started patiently chipping away at the wood.

As the candle melted away, dripping splatters of wax on the muddy ground, a sliver of light began to appear on the opposite wall of the tiny hut. A ray of hope thought Josh. How he wished he could tell Bekah the news: that they had managed to bring some illumination to an otherwise –

The bolts scraped against their metal holdings.

Carlton dropped to the ground as Josh slumped against the wall. The hatch swung wide swamping them with the cloudy day, drowning out the scrap of light they had so carefully nurtured.

Carlton was laughing, or growling, Josh couldn't tell which. There were several people outside. He could hear what sounded like logs or equipment being dragged by. Someone was laughing and then a harsher voice stopped the merriment abruptly. The void of light left by the open door darkened as an officer flanked by two soldiers peered inside like visitors at a zoo. The officer said something to the men beside him and they laughed and pointed at Josh. What were they laughing at?

"You!" The officer shouted at Carlton. "Up!"

Carlton slowly got to his feet subtly pushing the knife towards Josh's leg as he did so. Josh dropped his thigh onto it.

"Why are you holding us?" Carlton asked.

"No questions!"

Carlton sat down again and crossed his arms. "Then I guess we don't need to cooperate with you fellas. You're really disappointing me. I sure had you people figured out to be a lot more –"

"Silence!" the officer hissed taking out a small hand pistol and aiming it at Carlton's head. "Stand!"

Carlton replied calmly, "First tell me why we're here, then I'll cooperate." Josh gawked at the coolness, the insolence. What was he hoping to achieve? Surely they should try and get on friendly terms with their captors? Wouldn't that make their life easier?

The officer garbled something incomprehensible to the soldier next to him who answered sharply as he was shoved into the hut.

"They think we're animals," Carlton said as the soldier grabbed at his hair twisting his head sideways. The superior shouted again and handed the gun to his man when Carlton refused to rise."Shoot!" he screamed.

Carlton smiled sourly as the gun pushed his head sideways. "Kill me already fellas? I won't be worth much to you dead."

The soldier paused then looked to the officer at the door to decide for him.

"The other one," the officer said and then suddenly laughed. "Kill him. He is worth nothing."

As the eye of the weapon focused on his chest, Josh felt his breath stop: the constriction in his throat, choking him. His hearing seemed to amplify the sound of Carlton's breathing, the movement of the soft clay under the guard's feet and the sound of the trigger as it slowly squeezed backwards.

Carlton suddenly jumped, hitting the soldier's hand. The bullet went thudding into the ground near Josh's leg and before he could respond Carlton was dragged to the opening and pushed out. The hatch was slammed and bolted shut closing the darkness back in over Josh's eyes. He hadn't moved. Had been suspended in a space where movement and breath were magnets to danger.

The darkened silence brought him back to awareness: his body lay soaked in fear. Where were they taking Carlton? What were they going to do? Was it now that they let Carlton go to safety leaving him here as fodder to their incessant sadism? But then why go through the act of saving him? Why not let the guard shoot him when he got the chance? Piece by piece he was cracking apart, laboriously he used a web of control to keep together. He would not fall prey to this nightmare.

Gradually he managed to ease his breathing, bring down the rapid beat of his heart, letting memories, images, like the flicking of pages in a scrapbook, pass through his mind. He clutched at shreds of conversations, replaying them each time his thoughts returned to what had just transpired.

Thoughts of his childhood floated by: playing baseball with his brothers in the park just behind the house; coming in as the sun was disappearing into waves and shades of clouds and blue, yielding to the first three stars that heralded the eve of Sabbath. Just before dinner his father would call he and his brothers to the living room for a discussion about the value of human life, understanding what motivated people, the importance of finding good in others and letting it reveal itself so God could see it too. Then his uncle Chayim, the numbers tattooed on his arm always hidden by his shirtsleeve, would interrupt as if on cue, "Try finding good in Auschwitz and those Nazis." He would shake his head. "Your father," he would say and then give a sweet smile and shake his head again. "He's led such a sheltered life."

Josh would watch his mother light the Sabbath candles, put her hands around the glow reflecting against the skin of her euphoric face, and the song of the blessing would fill him with peace and joy. Then she would go into the kitchen and after a few moments return with a roast chicken sizzling on a serving plate waiting to be carved.

He groaned with the thought. His mouth watered and as he tried to swallow he realised that he was so thirsty it seemed that every sense was on fire and had to be extinguished. He pushed the need away and moved back to his own corner of the hut where Carlton's shirt lay in a damp bloody mess. He still could not comprehend why the man had given him his only shirt to soak in blood, the kindnesses too contradictory.

He sat in a daze. Time moved without his acknowledgment. His eye strayed to the small shaft of light on the opposite wall and rested.

His mother's voice echoed: 'I told you something like this would happen. Why didn't you listen to me? Oy God! Why can't you ever listen?'

"Go away," he groaned, but he knew that he would never escape her worry and recriminations. Her constant chattering inside his head. They had become too much a part of his own internal structure.

The sound of the rain on the roof ignited again the burning dryness in his throat. Without warning he had to urinate. The urgency of it filled his groin with an explosive pressure. He grabbed his crotch and rushed at the door, pounding the wood with his fist. Nothing happened.

A cold panic filled him as he pounded again. Had they really left him? Had they really taken Carlton away? He beat at the door until the rawness of his skin forced him to stop. There was someone there.

He could sense them. He heard the hesitant scraping of the bolts. The hatch opened. He climbed out controlling himself as best he could in his desperation then ran to the nearest tree, grappled for his zipper and relieved himself against the coarse bark, only too aware, behind his back, that the guards were laughing at him. Did they take such pleasure in treating another human being like this?

As he finished he moved to face them. He wouldn't let them grind him down. "Where's Ramsey?" he demanded but they ignored his question and signalled for him to return to the hut. "Mr. Ramsey!" he repeated. "Where is he?"

They motioned again for him to return, this time the rancid smiles gone from their faces, but the night air was so much cooler than inside the steaming hut. He tried to stall them.

They approached waving their weapons menacingly. He raised his hand and grabbed the phrase book from his pocket. The guards paused, amused once again. As he searched through the book he could hear in the distance the ripple of water from a stream or a creek, the sound of it tormenting.

"Drink!" he called out searching for the word in the book. "Pani!" he cried as he found it.

The guards laughed again.

"Pani! Water!" he repeated. He wasn't getting through. "Pani! Drink!" He lifted his hand to his mouth as if he were holding a cup.

Their sadistic faces changed expression again.

The smaller of the two spoke. Josh could barely hear the words but he swore that one of them was 'pani'. He had gotten through. The other one ran to the adjacent hut and brought a cup, grinning as he held it out for Josh to take.

"Asalaam alaikhum" Josh said extending his hand but as he reached the cup, the guard tipped it over letting the water splash onto the ground.

He froze, fixing his gaze on the guard's face and was butted in the gut with the weapon. Words of his uncle Chayim resounded past the pain as he straightened: 'Cry on the inside. But always show the bastards your smile.'

Josh did so, then lifted his chin and doggedly returned to the hut and the humid dark. They would eventually give him something to drink. He fell into a restless sleep. He was on a long march amongst hundreds of people through a bone dry desert. They were humming a dirge. It seemed like a funeral but there was no coffin. At the head of the march he could see the Star of David held high, gold and glistening against the sinking light.

He was exhausted, his feet reluctant to move another step, as if he had already been walking endless miles and could go on no longer without rest. He fell to his knees. Someone rushed up to him. He lifted his arm. They would help him. But there was no helping hand. His mother was standing in front of him. She was filled with wild energy. Her dark curls waving like snakes and her eyes probing and penetrating.

"Eema!" he moaned but she wagged her finger and said,

"Look on the bright side, Joshala. There's always somebody who feels worse than you." Then she disappeared and he opened his eyes.

There were scratching sounds outside the hut and he wondered if it was animals looking for food. The air had become denser. His arm hurt from leaning on it and his mouth was bitter and dry. The darkness seemed endless and Carlton's continued absence lay heavily on him.

He reached out for comfort. For the one person who had made him feel as if he belonged. "Home is in the heart," he whispered. If only he could see Bekah. Hear her wisdom. He lifted his hand in the darkness to touch her face, the wisp of the scent of imagined rosewood heightened the sense of her presence. She would know what to do. Would get him something to drink. Would understand how alone and vulnerable he felt.

Time moved so slowly. The scurrying stopped, or the hammering of rain on the roof drowned it out. It didn't matter. It made him feel as if he were suspended in some sort of motionless void.

He fell asleep again into a merciful blankness where this time memories and confusions let him be. Then he woke again to a lonely nothingness. He tried to stretch his legs out, his arms to the side to get rid of the ache. How long would they keep him in isolation here before they did something decisive?

The bolts were suddenly pulled across, the hatch opened, a breath of rain-cooled air pushed its way in. Josh filled his lungs trying to consume as much as he could. Like a magician, Carlton appeared wearing a fresh shirt looking cool and clean. He was holding a lit candle as he climbed in. The man wore fortune like a cloak and he carried it with him where ever he went.

"Sons of bitches!" Carlton growled as they slammed them in. "How are you feeling?"

"Fine." Josh measured caution with relief.

"You need anything?" The light flickered against the wood casting giant shadows against the slatted walls. Would it make any difference if he said?

Carlton scrutinised him. "Well?"

"I could use some water."

"Haven't they given you anything to drink?"

"No."

The man cursed under his breath as he returned to the door taking off his shoe with one hand while holding the candle in the other. He whacked the wood a few times and the door opened.

"Pani," he said softly. "For my young friend."

The hatch did not close this time. Carlton waited expectantly by the opening. Why did he feel so confident that they'd respond to his request? A cup was handed in and Carlton passed it over.

"Don't drink it all at once, it might have to last a while."

Josh took the cup and slowly sipped the water. It was cool and refreshing and he reluctantly pulled the rim away from his lips and set the cup down beside him as a sacred treasure. The door remained open and he could see the outline of the guard outside.

"Are they waiting for the cup?" Josh asked.

"I don't know what they're waiting for." Carlton stuck the candle in the dirt so it would stand by itself. He moved to his corner and said, "Maybe they're listening."

"They don't understand us, do they?"

"Not the underlings. The officers do." Carlton shifted his back against the rough wall.

There were voices outside, then the door was slammed and bolted. The air hung heavily — a curtain creating barriers to speech. Josh tried to make eye contact but Carlton avoided him. When would the man let him know anything? The absence of confidence made him desperate. Desperate to be confided in. To be included in the circle of one that Carlton called his own. He could wait no longer, the knots in his stomach tying tighter.

"What happened?" he said.

Carlton took a deep breath as if he were willing himself to communicate. "They took me into Jaintipur and made me send a fax to Dhaka. That's why it took so long. They cleaned me up first so it wouldn't look too suspicious. There's a stream just over the hill."

Josh nodded. He had heard it. He waited for Carlton to tell him what was on the fax and why they were being held but the older man didn't seem too willing to continue.

The waiting was interminable.

"Why are they holding us?" he finally asked wanting to grip the man by the shoulders and shake him.

"They want two million dollars from the Company."

Josh leaned forward. "Just money? What for?"

"Looks like its been staged by a break away army unit... To depose Ershad."

Carlton leaned over and picked up the Swiss army knife playing with the blade as if he had lost interest in the conversation.

"Do you think they'll pay?" How Josh wanted to snatch the knife from him, make him act with some humanity.

Carlton hesitated an endless moment before answering, the pause a scale of balances, weighing up the effect of the response. "Let's just hope so," he said.

"But you're important to the Company!" Josh protested. "They'll pay for you, won't they?"

Carlton lifted his eyes. The shadows of the trembling light made his face look as if he were a thousand years old. He reached over and snubbed the candle out and said hoarsely, "We'd better get some kip." Then Josh heard him rustle against the floor.

In the night the old man cried out in his sleep.

"Ramsey?" Josh whispered but there was no return. Carlton grunted and then snored lightly but the gentle sound didn't lighten the worry that something was wrong. The ground was too hard to sleep on but he was young. He could take it despite his head and foot injuries. Probably easier for him than someone of Carlton's age. He groped around for the blood drenched cloth, crept over to where Carlton's form lay and gently put the shirt under his head. Then he returned to his own corner to stare into the darkness.

Something was in there. Out of the corner of his eye he could just see the slightest sheen of movement. He groped around for his glasses and found them in the corner. Another movement, a scurrying from one side of the hut to the other and then nothing. He rubbed his hand lightly, cautiously against the wall and settled against it. His breathing shallow. The thing slithered by his foot making him jump and cry out.

"What the?" Carlton's voice was groggy.

"There's something in here."

"Geckos probably. Consider 'em your friends. They'll keep the spiders out."

"They don't bite?"

"No." Carlton picked up the bloodied shirt. "What the hell is this doing here?"

"I put it there."

The old man made no sound until he started choking. "Do you have any of that water left?"

Josh carefully found the cup and handed it over. Carlton sipped slowly, not finishing it. He handed it back.

"Thanks kid." Josh heard the rustle of cloth. "I was dreaming about Maribel and that little granddaughter that I haven't met yet. Damn, she was cute in my dream. Just like her grandmother."

Josh was quiet, surprised at Carlton's words and his voice. He sounded almost tearful, but maybe that was because he had just woken up. Josh tried to think of something to ask his companion but questions about family and loved ones seemed superficial and somehow irrelevant. What he really wanted to do was fill the gap that Carlton had left before he'd fallen asleep. What were Carlton's thoughts about the Company? Would they pay that kind of money and who would deal with getting them out? Would it be someone from Head office or would Khalig be responsible?

"I'm real sorry kid." Carlton's voice was still teary as if the sleep had caught his rougher self off guard and his gentle persona had taken over.

"For what?"

"For this whole fiasco."

"It isn't your fault, like you said, these things happen."

"I blame myself. I should have told Shumacker it was too dangerous."

"You mean you knew this could happen!"

"No, no, of course not. We would have stationed armed guards at our huts if I had... Though," he chuckled, "the damned bastards probably would have kidnapped us themselves."

"Hard to know who's on your side," Josh heard himself say.

"Do I have to keep apologising to you all night?"

"No."

"Well then, that settles it."

"What does it settle?"

"Nothing. Forget it."

Josh knocked his back against the wall. He was tired of playing games. He wanted to hit out, smash through the mindlessness, but the older man was saying something now. What was it?

"While we've got nothing better to do and nowhere to go and can't sleep why don't you tell me about yourself?"

Josh grimaced. What trap was Ramsey trying to lead him into this time? "It isn't interesting."

"Of course it's interesting. It's the most fascinating thing in the world right now. Where'd you say you were born?"

Josh shook his head. Crazy to let him do this again.

"Come on kid, you can answer my questions."

"New York. I've already told you that." Josh said no more. He was sure that Carlton's ratty side would have woken up by now and he didn't feel up to the abuse.

"1964, right?"

"Yes. Why do you know that?"

"My son was born in '64. Joseph Carlton named after his mother's father and me."

Josh pushed his anger back feeling himself approaching safer ground. "You see him much?" he asked but the response he received sounded oddly angry and regretful.

"Christmas, maybe. That's if we bother to go back to the States."

"What does he do?" Josh continued more determined to keep Carlton talking about himself. He had used the same tactic on his grandparents when they had asked him about Bekah — wanted to know about her religious background, was she willing to convert? What about the children? Didn't he realise that Hitler was finally getting his way when Jews married out of their faith? They hadn't been as easy to distract as Carlton was.

But Carlton had still not answered his question.

"Sir?"

"He's a… He… does something in photography."

"Oh." Josh had gained no idea what his son did and wondered if it now seemed wise to pursue it. It was odd. In the dark, when the only clear thing was the voice, somehow subtleties, shades of intonation, were clearer. In his early college days, he had helped to counsel inner city children. They would take them on field trips. Spelunking. In the caves they would find a place to sit, turn off the lights on their hard hats and talk about what mattered to them most at that moment. Some of the kids had found it frightening, as if the obscurity of light brought too much truth out in the voice.

Carlton said no more.

"Are you okay?" An unwilling concern made him reach out and he rebelled against it.

"Yes. Thanks, kid."

Kid! The very word was becoming a symbol for everything unacceptable. He heard Carlton groan, hand rubbing against bare skin.

"Are you sure?" he asked.

"Sure, I'm great. What do you think?"

"I don't know. I guess you'll just have to break down and tell me."

"Sure kid, whatever you say."

"Do you think you could do me a favour."

"What is it?"

"My name's Joshua or Josh or even Felstein."

"I know that."

"Please don't call me kid."

"It's just a name. You take everything so personal."

"Maybe I do."

"If you feel that way about it. Sure... Josh... Well, I guess we'd better get some sleep. Goodnight," and then Carlton paused and repeated his name once more.

"Goodnight, Mr. Ramsey." Josh lay on the floor and wasn't sure whether he actually heard or only wanted to hear the older man say, "The name's Carlton."

7

REBEKAH LEE FELSTEIN WAS JUST COMING out of a long dream when the ringing of the phone by the side of the bed woke her. "Hello?" Her voice was soft as she drifted in and out of sleep still trying to clutch on to the remnants of the images and dreams fast disappearing.

"Mrs. Felstein?" The man's voice was deeply Southern and as uncertain.

"Yes?"

"This is Callahan Shumacker from Standex Petroleum. Your husband may have mentioned me. I sponsored him at that introductory weekend in the Houston office a few months ago."

"Oh yes, Mr. Shumacker, he's mentioned how kind you've been to him." She sat up. Why was he calling her?

"I'll be in Houston for another few hours. I'm wondering if I could drop by sometime this morning and have a chat with you." His tone told her something was wrong. She pushed the covers off.

"What's happened? Is Josh all right?"

"I think we'd better meet in person," Shumacker responded.

"Tell me now. Please!"

"I don't think that would be wise," Shumacker said, "Why don't I come over? As it happens, I'm only about a half hour or so from you. You're still in Sugarland, aren't you?"

"Yes, I am but –"

"I'll see you then." He dropped the phone on its receiver before she could say anything more.

Bekah moved into the bathroom as quickly as her body would allow, the baby inside making her much less than her normal agile self. Perhaps it had sensed at that moment that something had gone amiss because it started squirming about. She put her hand to her stomach to try and soothe.

She grabbed her toothbrush and scrubbed furiously at her teeth. "Calm yourself, Bekah," she said to the mirror. "He hasn't said anything has happened." But she could feel it. There was something wrong.

She tried to sense Josh. Sometimes when he was in the bedroom and she was in the bath, she'd play a game. Could she see, in her mind's eye, what he was doing? Sometimes she could. But this time nothing came. Nothing, just a blank darkness of foreboding. He was so out of touch.

She sat on the edge of the bath, dread creeping into her sinews. Something was definitely wrong.

She rose slowly and left the room, began to dress, then made herself a cup of herb tea and waited in the living-room for Shumacker to arrive.

The doorbell rang soon afterwards.

"Mrs. Felstein? The man was smiling. Perhaps it wasn't that serious. She let herself relax.

He stared at her stomach and then at her face and she wondered which perturbed him more.

"When's the baby due?" he asked as she stepped aside and let him enter.

"Three months." She remained cheerful, friendly even, though the man was obviously uncomfortable. "Would you like some coffee?"

"Yes, thanks." But he wouldn't sit when she showed him to an easy chair.

"I'll only be a minute." She went into the kitchen. There was definitely something wrong. But she needed to be cautious about what she said. People were touchy enough about her and Josh, every move she made could influence his career. Her hand shook as she handed him the cup on her return.

"Please sit down," he said refusing to sit himself. If she complied it would force her to look up at him at a disadvantage, but she needed to sit. Her legs ached.

"I don't want you to be alarmed Mrs. Felstein." He was pacing the floor then stopped and looked down at her, trying unsuccessfully to make his face look kind.

Get on with it, she thought.

"The Company has everything under control," he continued, "But I must inform you that your husband has been taken by the Bangladeshi. I'm sorry. These things sometimes happen."

"Taken! Do you mean kidnapped?"

Shumacker nodded.

"When did it happen?" Her hand tightened on the side of the sofa. How could she not be alarmed?

"A few nights ago. We received a message from the kidnappers yesterday and we're trying to evaluate what course of action to take. I assure you that we'll do everything in our power to get Joshua and Carlton Ramsey to safety." The words were spoken in an awful monotone as if he were playing a tape recording apologising for a delay. Apologising for any inconvenience caused!

"Who is Carlton Ramsey?" she was stalling for time, trying to get a grip on herself.

"He's our manager of operations. He was training your husband."

"Oh Lord!" The baby kicked again. "What do the kidnappers want?"

"That's not your concern." His tone was supercilious and in the situation it aroused a deep distrust. "What we want you to do," he continued, "is stay calm, keep in touch with us, let us know where you are if you plan on going out of town and we'll do our best to keep you informed about your husband."

"I'm going out there!" she said suddenly.

"No ma'am, that wouldn't be a good idea, especially in your condition."

"I am going. My condition can take care of itself." His face clouded over, filling with an expression she recognised on other men of his type whom she had defied.

He continued, "I have to warn you that you'll be putting yourself in unacceptable danger and you'll be a hindrance rather than a help. The best thing you can do is stay here." He crossed his arms and towered over her.

She felt uncertain, attempting to evaluate whether he was right or not. He was tense. Of course, she was making life difficult for him. But she had to. And then for a moment she faltered. Would it be better to think about it first then decide? No. Not when Josh was involved. She made her decision. It wasn't up to him or the Company what she did. She stood up awkwardly and faced him inclining her head upwards.

"I must go. Surely you can understand that." She spoke the last deferentially and watched as his eyes glinted with the hint of victory.

His tone softened. "Ma'am, I can't tell you what a mistake you're making."

"Mistake or not," her voice remained low and soft, "I'm going to be as close to my husband as humanly possible and no one is going to stop me!"

"Now Mrs. Felstein, you listen to me. The Company cannot and will not take any responsibility for your health or welfare once you've left this country. Do you understand?"

"And what about my husband? Are you responsible for his health and welfare?"

"Of course we are."

"Then you can take care of mine." Bekah heard her voice rising, tinged with hysteria. Shumacker must have heard it too. He stared coldly at her, giving her a look which clearly said that he was dealing with only half a human. Well he could think what he wanted, she was going and that was final.

"I'll let you know what flight I'll be on. I expect the Company will find me suitable accommodation."

His face became a mask of sudden pleasantness but his tone did not reflect his expression.

"I'm sure your husband would appreciate knowing that you were safe at home rather than trudging through the third world meddling in affairs you know nothing about."

"I know what my husband would appreciate, Mr. Shumacker, and it isn't sitting on my ass being passive while his life is in danger!"

The man smiled, the expression didn't move up to the steely hardness in his eyes.

"If you're imprudent enough to go, it will be at your own expense. Of course, you can stay at the headquarters in Dhaka. In that event, I suggest you worry about the health of your baby from now on. Malaria is only one of the diseases that you will be exposing your child to."

"Thank you for your concern. I'll discuss it with my doctor. Now please tell me what the kidnappers want."

Shumacker was caught unawares by her persistence. Had he expected some nice sweet little wifey who went along with everything her husband's superiors said? Is that what he was used to?

"How much?" Bekah demanded again. Shumacker stiffened and said,

"That's confidential." He seemed satisfied by his obtuseness and its effect.

The fingers of her right hand closed in a fist, her nails digging into her palm, steadying her, keeping her from exploding. She had to play this one cool. She wasn't going to let the bastard see he was getting to her. She'd had plenty of practice playing that game.

She took a deep breath and willed herself to soften. She let her crossed arms drop by her sides, lifted her chin stepping closer to him.

"Surely the Company wants me to know what we're up against," she said, gently, softly, wooing him.

He glared at her suspiciously but she sent wave after wave of kindness to him. His fingers fiddled with the button on his suit jacket, unconsciously unbuttoning it, letting the jacket fall open revealing a starched white shirt and a severe dark tie. He rubbed his nose, hesitating, weighing up the odds.

She smiled at him, felt her lips pull back reluctantly to show her teeth.

"How much are they asking?" she repeated.

He fidgeted with his tie, loosening the knot.

Finally he said, "Two million dollars."

"What?" Suddenly her hope, her commitment, the strength which she had used to manipulate and gain control over the corporate creep, collapsed.

"Yes, it's a lot of money." Shumacker snapped back into his previous smug paternalism, the spell broken. "We're going to negotiate for some kind of settlement. I'm sure we'll come to a suitable compromise."

"What does that mean?" she beseeched, though in her gut she knew: they weren't going to pay! It was as if the man had hit her in the stomach.

"Now don't get excited Mrs. Felstein. Like I said," he returned to the frightening monotone, "Standex will do everything in its power to free your husband and his supervisor."

He went to the front door then paused in silhouette as he opened it, "I would reconsider going. You don't know how foolish you're being." With that, he left.

Bekah rushed into the bathroom slamming the door behind her, gagging into the toilet. Desperation flooded over her as she slumped to the floor. She pulled her arms about her and rocked back and forth, her shoulder brushing against the bowl making a shushing sound. Then slowly she gathered the threads of her panic about her and tightly knit them into a quilt of determination. And as she rocked, she decided exactly what she would do.

The first thing was to call Josh's brother Abraham. He could break the news to the rest of the family. She'd call the Bangladeshi Embassy and find out about a visa. Her passport should still be valid from her trip through Europe a few years before.

Next she'd call the airline and then her mother. She struggled off the floor. She and her baby would respect her more if she fought for her husband's life. She knew she was right. Shumacker's words replayed: 'The Company will do everything in its power.' A load of shit.

"Momma, it's me, Bekah."

"What's the matter, child? You sound terrible."

Bekah could not restrain the tears, especially at the sound of her mother's sympathetic voice.

"Now what's going on, Bekah? You tell your mother and don't you hold anything back." Her voice was like warm honey.

"Josh! He's been kidnapped in Bangladesh!"

"Oh my Lord! How could that have happened?"

"I don't know. Some Company idiot came over to tell me, but he didn't actually say anything other than to try and intimidate me into not going to Bangladesh."

"And what are you going to do?" The sound of anxiety was not hindered by the distance.

"I'm going." And she thought, 'Don't try and stop me.'

"Is that wise?" Bekah was grateful for the calmness in her mother's voice. Even if it was forced.

"No," Bekah said less defensively. "But I'm doing it anyway." 'Momma please don't oppose me now,' she entreated to herself.

"May I come with you?"

"Oh Momma, I wish you could but there's no use in both of us going out."

Her mother sighed. "Isn't there anything I can do?"

Her mother had come through again. As she always had. Her wise woman. Her mentor. Always knew the right thing to say.

"I don't know what you can do. I wish I did."

"When are you going?" Her mother sounded sad but determined not to pressure. She was the bravest person Bekah had ever met. She had been the only one of her kin to take Josh in and make him one of her own.

"I've got to get my visa first but it shouldn't take long. I'm going to call the Embassy and then I'll book the flight."

It was only then that her mother revealed her anxiety but she did not put it into words, rather it was the stillness that hung between them.

"Momma, please don't worry about me. I'll be fine. I promise."

"Yes, of course you will be." The strain of pretending was breaking the equanimity.

"I'll call you this evening with all the numbers and details. Okay?"

"All right Bekah, I'll be here."

"Bye Momma."

"Talk to you soon, sweet child. And Bekah, take care of yourself."

Abe Felstein hadn't agreed with what his sister-in-law had wanted and told her so. He had warned her of the dangers of flying at her term of pregnancy but she had persuaded him to do as she bid. He wrote her a note saying that he was her physician, which he wasn't, and that she was only five months along, clearing her for the flight that she would take come hell or high water. All obstacles dissolved away in her determination.

Josh's family were such a trip, Bekah thought. Carrying the burden of their version of right and wrong on their shoulders. It was right to love and respect your parents, as she did, but wrong to go against any of their wishes. Right to open yourself to God and follow all his Commandments, his rituals, but wrong to turn your back on it and find out for yourself what your beliefs were truly made of. Right to follow a moral code, but only one that fell within the boundaries of doctrine. All the answers were there, they said, you just had to look for them.

Funny enough, her mother had studied the Old Testament and knew it better than any Jewish person she had ever met, including Josh's brothers. Her mother had named her after the wife of Isaac, Abraham's only son who had been led to slaughter though he was intended to be the first child of God's chosen nation. It was a symbolic name to represent her mother's everlasting optimism. Not Rebeccah, the Jewish spelling, but Rebekah from the Catholic, Douay translation.

His family hadn't wanted her to marry Josh. That was obvious from the first time they had met her. The brothers and grandparents had stood with their mother against the whole thing. And she had even been willing to convert if it would help smooth the path. It appealed to her sense of destiny: the struggle their ancestors had both endured had been nearly identical.

Josh had forbidden her to even consider conversion.

It was as if their marriage was an opportunity for him to step out of his world and join another. But he couldn't turn his back on it, no matter how hard he tried.

And despite the friction, she had insisted that they maintain contact with his family. It was she who bought all the presents, sent the cards, phoned on the holidays, arranged the visits. It was she who finally made the call to his mother to tell her what had happened to her errant son.

"Mrs. Felstein?" Her mother-in-law had made it clear that Mother or Mama was not acceptable from this particular daughter-in-law. "I have something I must tell you."

She had hesitated knowing the impact the words would have on his mother and when she finally spoke the shocked silence on the other end confirmed the prediction.

"I consider you personally responsible," his mother wailed, finally. "If it weren't for you he wouldn't have gone into that stupid goyisha profession…"

Bekah could feel herself stiffen with resentment. Why couldn't his mother, just once, see beyond her own boundaries and give her the comfort that she needed.

Mrs. Felstein continued, "If he had become a doctor, he wouldn't have had to travel to these god-forsaken places. But no, you! You! Shicksa! Pushed him into this business!"

"Mrs. Felstein. Please."

"My boy!" her mother-in-law had wept, "My boy, how am I going to live if anything happens to him?"

The plane tilted as Bekah glanced out of the window. Despite her penchant for travel, she was never easy during take-off. This time the movement of the plane did not make her nervous. It was bringing her closer to her destiny. Her fate. This moment was a turning point and she wondered how well she'd be able to weather it.

The stewardess came over, offering drinks and food. Too pensive to eat, she asked for another cushion. Her back had begun to ache and she shifted uncomfortably around in her seat. As she was handed another pillow, the stewardess offered to move her up to business class, which was virtually empty. She would be more comfortable there.

"Thank you," she said warmly. "This is so kind of you. I'm very grateful."

The stewardess helped her with her things then left her to her thoughts, which predictably fell back to her husband and the baby that

82

would be theirs. Joshua. How she was always so protective of him. He was so vulnerable. So other. And he was right to be. He wasn't like other men were, always trying to prove their masculinity. He was worried about more important issues: humanity, caring, striving to be the best he could be. And his vulnerability was his best quality and his worst, they resided in the same space.

In her idiotic days she had dated only big men, with muscles and egos to match and they'd taught her one by one what she didn't want in her life, not for herself, not for any children she might have. Though, if she hadn't known all the bastards she would probably not be as appreciative of Josh as she was. Kind. Reliable. Sincere. Honest. She had no doubt why she loved him. He was everything she wasn't. He was sensitive; she was like a bull in a china shop. He tried to find the tactful way to put things; she just came out and said what was on her mind.

Funny how the contradictions of life confused him. The great paradoxes which she thrived on, he couldn't handle, thought of them as pure hypocrisy. Perhaps he was right after all. What benefit did they get keeping in touch with his mother. Yes, perhaps he was right after all.

Josh had wanted to turn his back on his mother after she had refused to attend the wedding. But she had convinced him to forgive and forget. What good would it do anyone if he held a grudge? He had gone along with it, choosing compassion against anger every time. Compassion. It caused the world, when she could truly feel it, to open around her like a flower. But even she had to admit it was not easy to be able to absorb his mother's continual displeasure every time they went to New York to visit his family.

No, it hadn't been meant to be easy. It was his love that made it worth all the hassle. Which would have been there no matter what, she reminded herself.

Her younger sister wasn't much better. Using Josh as a sounding board to her own prejudices. She was behind Farrakhan these days. Martin Luther King jr. was more Bekah's style. Were either of them right? Did anyone truly understand the situation? Truly understand how to make people equal in a struggle where each was sure that they had been cheated out of their birthright? She sighed. The only way to go about it was to approach each person individually. To love or to heal or even just to understand.

That was the way her mother was. After all the hardships, the experiences that would make anyone else bitter to the core, her mother had come out of it believing that every person was worth listening to. There were so many more people to love than to hate. Oh Momma! Her vision filled with tears. Why hadn't she said yes when her mother had offered to come with her!

She closed her eyes. There was going to be a layover in London and then one in Bombay. It was going to take forever to get to Bangladesh. And then what would she do? She hadn't any idea. Thoughts of Josh washed around the storm of worries. How her heart ached to know he was safe.

The plane emptied in Bombay. With only a scatter of passengers left it seemed odd. Such a huge craft with so few people. As she travelled closer to Josh she tried again and again to sense him, only to find the same darkness, the same void.

She stepped into the thick hot air, grasping the hand railing. The stewardess offered a hand which she refused: no heat and no fetor was going to get to her now.

The terminal building was chaotic. Despite her pregnancy, people shoved at her from all sides.

"Mrs. Joshua?" A kindly looking man approached her.

"Yes?"

"I am Rashid. Mr. Shumacker has told me to meet you."

"Well thank you Rashid. I was wondering how I was going to get to the Company house."

Rashid took her cases and escorted her rapidly through immigration and then through customs and the bevy of armed guards. As they walked out of the airport building, Rashid scowled at the beggars and urged her along as she paused to look. They gawped but didn't bother her for money. Not the way the children had done in Africa.

"Come Mrs. Joshua, you must hurry," Rashid urged. "Not good for baby to stand too long."

She grinned at the man. Who was he kidding? She followed him to his jeep and he carefully placed her in the back and slowly bumped out of the airport.

"Rashid? Do you know where my husband is?"

Rashid turned his head, perilously, to face the back, a despairing look on his face. She got the message and said nothing more, only half taking in the helter skelter of the city streets. Rashid pulled off the main road into a side street, where the buildings were more sturdy.

They pulled alongside one with the Company name on a sign at the top.

"This is our office. You stay here until we find Mr. Joshua."

She laughed. Did they think it was going to be that easy to keep her prisoner? She appeared compliant, not showing Rashid her true intentions. She'd get settled in first. Scout out the area and see what her options were. As soon as she had accomplished that, she'd hit the American Embassy.

A young man came rushing over, picking her bags up. Rashid introduced him.

Habib seemed confused.

"You, Mrs. Joshua?"

"Hello, Habib," Bekah greeted him warmly.

He repeated the question. "You Mrs. Joshua?"

"Yes I am. Have you met my husband?"

"Yes. He live in Texas, but not cowboy. You no cowboy. You red Indian?"

"No, I am African American, one of the good guys."

Habib scratched his temple, concentrating on his confusion then he looked up with his liquid friendly eyes and smiled as if he suddenly understood something terribly important.

"You come to get bad guys?"

"Yes," she said and followed him as he hoisted her suitcases up the stairs.

"Bad guys very bad. They take Mr. Joshua and Mr. Carlton far away!"

"Do you know where they are?" she asked the boy without much hope.

"Oh yes, Mrs. Joshua, they somewhere in the north. That for sure."

Bekah made a note to ask him more later, but just now she was desperate for the toilet.

"This your room, Mrs. Joshua. You need something, you ask Habib. Okay?" Before she could say more, the boy ran from the room and left her to herself.

She found the bathroom and when she was finished she sat on the bed, at last weary from the journey, the obstacles in front of her beginning to dawn.

Before she had met Josh, she had travelled alone through Europe and Africa. What a trip that had been. But she'd never stepped foot in Asia. She didn't doubt she'd survive, but with the baby kicking inside her, she faltered. It wasn't only her own life at risk. Her impulsiveness had taken her down some pretty muddy dirt tracks. To a medicine ceremony in Zimbabwe, a snake dance in Zaire. She had met people who looked so like her in Botswana, people who had come up to her in that little village in the Kalahari and had touched her face as if she were a long lost sister.

Everything depended on keeping her courage. Like Lady Macbeth. That was it. 'But screw your courage to the sticking-place, and we'll not fail.' If only this hadn't happened so late in her pregnancy.

She slowly unpacked the cases taking everything out, arranging things neatly in the drawers. She'd be here for a while. That she felt in her bones. As she knelt, awkwardly, pushing the case under the bed her eye caught a slight movement on the wall. A lizard. Josh was terrified of them. What did they call his terror? Herpetophobia.

She lay on the bed. Poor Josh. He'd be going insane if there were lizards around. An immense wave of exhaustion ran through her. She closed her eyes trying to give herself space to gather her wits.

Somewhere in her sleep, Bekah heard a woman's voice calling angrily. The words merged like fluids in a dream state.

"Excuse me!" the voice demanded, tugging at her consciousness. "Who are you? And what are you doing here?"

Bekah struggled to sit up. In the vagueness of awakening she saw first a disturbance of purple around the petite shape of an older woman. "I'm sorry." She rubbed her eyes to clear them. "Who are you?" She knew exactly who the woman was.

"Young lady, I don't know how you managed to get in here. This isn't a tourist hotel. You're obviously in the wrong place though God knows how you managed it. I'll get Rashid to show you out."

8

BEKAH EASED HERSELF OUT OF THE BED.

"My goodness!" the other woman gasped, her eyes fixed on Bekah's midriff.

Bekah extended her hand, moving forwards, but the other woman backed away looking frightened.

"I'm Rebekah Felstein. You must be Mrs. Ramsey."

"Oh my!" Mrs. Ramsey coloured deeply. "But! You don't look like a Rebecca Felstein!"

"You're not the first person to tell me that."

"I'm so sorry. I must have seemed awfully rude. I had no idea that you were col... uh, bla... uh, going to be here. No one told me."

"I didn't give anyone much notice. There wasn't time was there?"

Mrs. Ramsey seemed to Bekah as though she might suddenly fall to the ground or the opposite, fly off in a frenzy.

"But! When are you due?"

"It's not for another three months. I'm fine... I think."

"You're mad to have come here. Don't you realise the danger you've put yourself and your baby in?"

Bekah smiled as if the act of smiling would disperse the hysteria, bring them to the same level. "I don't think I'm putting anyone in danger. And there isn't anything else I can do. I'm sure you can relate to that."

Mrs. Ramsey shook her head as if she were shaking away a fly buzzing around her head. "You are sadly mistaken young lady. I cannot relate to that at all."

"Then tell me. Why are you here?" Bekah was so calm it clearly made matters worse.

"My place is by my husband's side."

"And so is mine."

"But you're –"

"I'm?"

"You have no idea what you're doing, you're too young and you're –"

"And I'm?"

"You're pregnant, of course."

"Mrs. Ramsey." Bekah kept herself under control understanding too well the intentions beneath the words. "My husband's life is in danger. I'm not going to sit by and let something happen to him without trying to help."

"No, it's impossible."

"Nothing's impossible where there is a will to change."

"My goodness what world have you come from?" Maribel shook her head in disbelief.

"If it's so impossible, why do you stay?"

"I have to. Of course, I have to!" Maribel put her hand to her forehead then slumped against the door frame as if she were dizzy.

"There's no difference between us, then." Bekah rubbed the small of her back which ached with the strain of the argument.

"You know nothing of this place," Maribel continued mercilessly, "I know these people, I know how difficult things are. There is no way you would be able to understand!"

'Garbage,' Bekah mumbled to herself. She tired of the meeting. It was getting them nowhere. "Why don't we find somewhere to sit and have a cold drink. We can talk then."

"Talk? You and me? Oh dear!" Maribel gasped. "Of course. What am I saying? We have a staff room that's comfortable, and the servant…" Maribel glanced uncomfortably at Bekah, "Habib, can get us something to drink."

Habib was solicitous as he helped them to their seats, obviously nervous in front of the older woman. Bekah put her hand on the boy's arm.

"What's wrong Habib?"

"No, no, nothing Missis. Just very worried for you and Mr. Joshua and Mr. Carlton. Not good. Very worried."

With her warmest voice Bekah said, "Thank you Habib that's very kind of you."

Maribel sat stiffly in the chair. "Habib, what do you have to drink that's cold?"

"We have cola or iced tea or lime juice? You like tea?" Habib asked.

"I'll have the lime juice. What will you have, uh, Mrs Felstein?" she sighed disparagingly. "May I call you Becky?"

88

"I'll have the same Habib," she faced her opposite. "And feel free, though people usually call me Bekah." Then she waited for the older woman to reveal her first name but she didn't. Bekah left it for the moment. It could wait.

Mrs. Ramsey patted her collar, pressing the ends. She flicked imaginary dust from her dress as the boy left the room. "I must look a mess," she said and when Bekah didn't respond she patted her hair, leaving wild strands sticking out from a wilted version of what must have been a carefully kept coiffure. She leaned over and said, "A word of advice. You can't trust anyone here. They are all deceitful."

Bekah watched Habib as he entered. He wasn't deceitful, anyone could see that. To her he seemed completely genuine. Should she take the older woman's words into consideration? She desperately needed to decide who she could rely on and that would take a few days. Right now she needed Mrs. Ramsey on her side.

"Mrs. Ramsey?"

Maribel put her glass down, staring at her as if she were some unruly child.

"Were our husbands taken from this house?"

"No, of course they weren't. They were at the well site."

"Is that up north?" Maribel nodded but volunteered nothing else. Bekah waited again.

"Were you here? Did you know what was happening?"

Maribel suddenly stood, accidentally knocking the glass over, liquid spilling onto the table. Habib ran over, righted the glass and started wiping the mess.

"No, I wasn't here. Why must you ask me such things?"

Bekah rubbed her forehead with her hand, pushing back the thick dark hair with her palm, then she looked up at the source of anger and saw tears.

"Mrs. Ramsey?" she said softly.

"You couldn't possibly understand!" Maribel sobbed turning away and grasping at a handkerchief from a pocket in her dress.

Bekah stood and reached out touching the woman on the arm but the touch was responded to as if it were an insect landing on soft skin.

"Why don't you try and tell me." The burning sensation of rejection didn't daunt her. If she could get the information she needed from this... this bitchy irrational person, she would be able to do the rest of her leg work by herself.

Habib stole into the room and set another two glasses of lime juice on the table in front of them. Bekah smiled at him and his return was genuine, without any sign of deceit. She was sorry that he had to put up with this kind of behaviour from his employer all the time.

Maribel sat, lifted the glass to her lips and gulped thirstily at the fluid. When she finished she put the glass down gently. Without looking up she whispered hoarsely, "I was visiting my daughter in Houston. She's just had her second child. Someone had to go to her."

"Yes?" Bekah leaned forward encouragingly.

"My husband. Carlton. He had promised that he'd go with me to Houston to see them." She snorted angrily, "As usual, the Company came first despite the fact they were booting him out." Maribel sat back and covered her eyes, her mouth revealing the barely suppressed grief. "If he had kept his promise. To me. To my daughter. Just this once, he'd be all right now."

Bekah rose quickly, moved to the woman and put her arm around her shoulder and squeezed. She felt Maribel stiffen. "I'm so sorry," Bekah murmured comfortingly, continuing to hold her.

Maribel was soon passive, as if the storm of anger had drained the last ounce of energy from her. Her voice was softer, calmer, as she began to speak,

"If I had been here, maybe he would have been able to contact me. Maybe... I don't know. I wish I knew. I feel it's all my fault."

"Of course it's not your fault." Bekah dropped her arm from Maribel's shoulder then after a moment of calmness returned to her own chair.

"You couldn't possibly understand," Maribel muttered.

"Try me." Maribel met her eyes. Through the distress, she looked surprised.

"You're just a child. How could you begin to comprehend?"

Bekah couldn't tell the woman how she could 'begin' to comprehend. It was just something that had been with her all her life. This uncanny sense of what other people were feeling and how to help them cope with it. Her mother had called it an old Saturnian wisdom.

"I can understand, I promise you."

Maribel hesitated for a moment then she continued, "Before the kidnap. I refused to come back here. Even though he asked me to. Can't you see if I had been here, somehow I might have known, or..."

"If they were taken from the well site, what difference would it have made if you were here?"

"It's just a feeling I have. It's too hard to explain. It's as if, somehow, he did this to get even with me."

"What!" Mrs. Ramsey's guilt was inexplicable.

"You see. It was a waste of time trying to explain this to you. You don't understand." Maribel stood, walked to the window and pulled aside the curtain. Instead of delving further Bekah decided to change tack.

"Do you have any idea where they've been taken?"

The answer was muffled against the glass. "The fax was sent from Jaintipur."

"Do you think they're there?"

Maribel shrugged, withdrawn again. Bekah pressed the palms of her hands against her eyes. She was tired. So tired and so worried. And now this –

Suddenly there was a hand on her shoulder, nails digging into her clothing, pinching her skin.

"The Company will never pay you know. You do realise that?" Maribel cried out. "Not for an old man and not for some Jewish nobody no one cares about!"

Bekah gasped with disbelief. The woman was insane. My Lord. She got to her feet pushing the hand away. She wanted to scream but Maribel suddenly collapsed on the floor.

"Habib!" Bekah was on her knees beside the woman, dragging her into her lap. How frail she was. In her fury, she seemed so much bigger. Within seconds she opened her eyes, let Bekah help her onto a chair.

"Perhaps you should rest." Bekah stayed beside the shaking woman.

"I can't rest," Maribel clutched at Bekah's arm. "Don't you see?"

Bekah got to her feet. The older woman was right. Rest was impossible. She had to make a plan of action. Surely this woman would know who to go and see. But was now the best time to ask?

Maribel straightened her dress.

If not now, then when? Later might be too late.

"Do you think they could be in Jaintipur?" Bekah asked softly.

"I couldn't possibly tell you."

"You know?"

"No, no, I don't mean that. Of course I don't know. The army is looking for them. I don't know where."

"They've involved the army?"

Maribel laughed weakly, "Ershad's men. But you can't trust them –"

"Sorry, who's Ershad?"

"The President for God's sake!"

"Why, why can't we trust them?"

"They've probably been promised a cut of the ransom to keep their mouths shut. Don't you know anything about this place?"

Bekah found it hard to breathe. She could believe in elements of corruption anywhere, but this was conspiracy on a grand scale! The baby kicked. She put her hand on her stomach to comfort it. "Do you know why our husbands have been kidnapped?" she persisted, "Why do they want that kind of money?"

"It's something to do with getting rid of Ershad. It always is. There are so many factions here all fighting one another for power."

"Can't we get the American Embassy to help us? Can't we protest to Ershad? I'm sure there's something we can do."

Maribel took a resigned breath and exhaled it pressing her back against the cushions then shaking her head wearily, she said, "The Embassy, the army, the police, they've already been contacted. It's really up to the Company to rescue them. There's nothing we can do. Nothing!"

"That's absurd." Bekah pulled herself up tall. "No one is totally helpless. There is always something you can do."

Maribel raised her head. With the light shining on her soft, aged skin, Bekah could see faint lines of dried tears through a beige incandescent foundation and pink blusher. Despite her age, the older woman momentarily seemed like a young child, her eyes hopeful and searching, and then just as suddenly age and cynicism replaced the hope.

"Not here! You can't do anything in this place," Maribel said.

"Well, I can!"

Maribel shook her head. "You can't even go out by yourself."

"Why?" Bekah's hand had reached the side of her bulging belly and then found its way to her hip, resting there in defiance. "Of course I can go out."

"Not without Rashid you can't."

Bekah cocked her head. This woman definitely had an attitude. A little doll woman, she thought. Little doll rules don't apply to me. "I go where I please, when I please."

Maribel grimaced. "You'll learn."

Bekah wanted to let loose, tell her to stop pitying herself and do something positive. She wasn't the only one suffering! But her own mother had trained her too well. To respect her elders. Before she could say anything else, Habib reappeared with Rashid.

"You want to go to consulate?" Habib directed his question at Bekah. He looked worried.

"Rashid!" Maribel sounded controlled, almost commanding. "Tell Mrs. Felstein whether it is safe for her to go walking by herself in Dhaka city or anywhere else for that matter."

Rashid pursed his lips and shook his head slightly. "No, Mrs. Joshua it is very unsafe for you to go out on your own."

"I'm sure that's not true!"

"My people have different customs from yours. In Bangladesh we have what is called purdah. It means seclusion of women. Women must stay within their own home areas."

"You are a Muslim, yes?" Bekah enquired and received an affirmative reply from Rashid. "But you can tell I'm a westerner, can't you?"

"Yes," he replied again, "but it is still unwise for you to be seen in the streets, especially alone."

"I respect your culture Rashid and I've studied the customs of Islam, so I recognise that it's preferable to cover up, but I'm not going to be kept prisoner here. I want to visit the consulate and I want to visit officials and I may even want to go up north to see the well site."

"I tell you, it is not possible." Rashid sounded worried. "Mr. Shumacker has forbidden you to leave the building."

"Shumacker!" Bekah pointed to the older woman accusingly. "Is he here?"

Maribel looked shocked, "No, of course not. What has he got to do with this?"

'We'll see what I can or can't do.' Bekah murmured as she swept past Rashid. Slowly she climbed the stairs to her quarters. If she could only maintain the angry and driven energy. But the baby weighed heavily upon her and she was beginning to flag after the long, long trip and the strange and unwilling atmosphere. As for the kidnap, she had yet to let herself really think about that.

With Bekah gone from the room, Maribel Ramsey felt uncomfortable alone with the two Bangladeshis staring at her as if they expected her to know what to do. She stood slowly and thanked Habib for the drink then followed Bekah up the stairs returning to the room that she had shared with Carlton.

Initially, she was glad of the peace. But as the minutes passed, thoughts that she would rather not deal with returned to haunt. This terrible thing had turned her entire life upside down. Oh, but if only she hadn't had that darned argument with Carlton before she had left. And if only she had told him that she did love and forgive him, couldn't bear to see his health deteriorate in front of her eyes because of his own stubbornness. If only he had accepted the early retirement rather than staying in this squalid place.

The wardrobe door had swung open. One of Carlton's favourite shirts hung loosely on the hanger and she lifted it out of the closet to straighten it.

"Carlton how can you do this to me?" She stroked the material lovingly as if she were stroking him, then abruptly hung the shirt back. Her eye caught her reflection in the mirror on the door. She looked shocking! She rubbed her hand through her normally immaculate hair, messing it even more. For the first time in her life, she couldn't be bothered to fix herself up.

No, she'd never been this frazzled before. Not when he had been offshore in '64 and she had nearly lost little Joseph Jr., or when they had been in Karachi in '79 and the company building had been stormed, or in Nigeria when the oil price had collapsed and they were rushed out of the country.

She had always believed the Company would take care of them and they had. But now, things... attitudes had changed. The Company seemed indifferent, uncaring, and Callahan Shumacker was giving orders from Houston. Just the mention of his name filled her with dismay remembering what lay between them forever unresolved. After little Joe was born she had entered such a terrible darkness. Now she knew they called it post natal depression. Back then it was just sheer neglect by one's husband that all wives were supposed to put up with. And Callahan had been there like a white knight, ready to sweep her away from her grief. But now? Would he do the same?

She grabbed the cuff of the long sleeved khaki shirt. 'Not like this. Carlton please, don't go from me this way.'

The window rattled. It was raining. Though there had been a drought earlier in the year, now the rain was endless and buried the country in water. It seemed appropriate: the sky crying. 'Cry for me,' she thought.

Wasn't there anything that she could do? But she felt defeated. Too many years of following Carlton from pillar to post had put an end to the side of her that fought for what she wanted. It was the fate of all the women she knew. She did as she was told and waited. Endlessly waited. That's what she had become so good at.

Her thoughts flew to the pregnant black girl. So silly. Couldn't begin to understand the ways of the world.

Foolish thing. What was her name? Bekah. Throwing her weight around. She'd only make more trouble than there already was.

She whirled around to the wardrobe again. 'Carlton! Why couldn't you have gone quietly to your retirement?' But she knew the answer. He was all work and no play. Even when they were on holiday he'd find someone to talk business with. Hadn't made her life terribly easy, but she had always promised herself their retirement. Now look what you've gone and done!

How she yearned to be in their new house in Connecticut, sitting on the porch and sipping lemonade in the sun with the grandchildren running around. After all the years they'd been together these were the ones she was most looking forward to. These were going to be her years. And they were so precious. And he had to ruin it. She scrutinised herself again in the mirror: her grey-green eyes were mournful and the skin underneath smudged with mascara.

She was like a piece of driftwood on the edge of the water: lifted in high tide and dropped in low or swept away in tumult. Her whole being was shaken and she could do nothing! Nothing!

She dropped onto the bed and closed her eyes willing herself to escape from this torment of uncertainty.

Then suddenly she sat bolt upright. Khalig! Of course! If they could contact Khalig, he might have some information. She ran from the room, stopping to knock on Bekah's door.

"Rebekah?" she called. There was no answer and she knocked again, this time softer. If the girl were sleeping she shouldn't be disturbed. She began to turn away, then tried the handle and opened the door.

Bekah was lying on the bed, rolled over on her side, one hand on her swollen belly. Her soft oval face was smooth, released from the awful tension that plagued them both. She was very pretty once you got past the darkness of her skin. But Maribel couldn't. Not really. It was just too unexpected.

In sleep, the hardened determination had faded, leaving the girl childlike and yet with child — an odd contrast, but one she had seen before in her own daughter.

She wondered what it would be like to be a black woman and then let the question escape unanswered. She had no idea. All her life had been spent with Indonesians, Asians, Africans or Arabs. But in all those years she had never made friends with any of them, they were either servants or workers. Her place had always been with the other American wives with an occasional British or European thrown in.

She sighed then glanced at the sleeping girl again and turned to leave the room.

"Are you looking for me?" Bekah's voice was soft and sad, and Maribel was drawn to her, despite misgivings.

She answered haltingly, "I've thought of someone who may know what happened."

Bekah sat up. "Who? Where?"

"There is a man in Shylet who worked for Carlton." She hesitated waiting for Bekah's response. The girl had moved to the edge of the bed expectantly.

"Perhaps if we could contact him, even if he had the least bit –" she broke off. "Oh, I don't know. It was just a thought." She went to the door. Khalig probably knew nothing.

"Wait!" Bekah's plea brought her to an unwilling halt. Now she regretted coming in here. The girl would be useless in all this.

"Any lead would be helpful," Bekah implored. "Who is he?"

Maribel put her hand on the door. As she opened it she sighed ruefully. "His name is — Oh forget it. It was silly of me. Forget I said anything."

She stepped out of the room and stood on the landing, looking down into the marble floored hallway beneath.

"We can work together." Bekah's voice was soft behind her.

"We can make no difference to this situation," Maribel said as she proceeded down the stairs far, far away from the foolish young woman above her.

She ordered Habib to bring her some tea and a small snack but she left the food untouched. She hated feeling this way. The limbo and the long silences between communications. The absence of knowing where Carlton was. Always, always gone. Yet all the times before she had known that he would return.

She hadn't heard Bekah come down the stairs. The girl wasn't wearing shoes as she padded gently into the room despite the burden of child she carried.

"Who is this man you mentioned?" the girl asked, her voice soft.

Maribel sighed and put her cup down. "It isn't of any value, I'm sure."

"Let me be the judge of that."

Maribel suddenly laughed. But it wasn't a happy laugh. It sounded even to her own ear as if it were a harsh bird disgorging itself. "His name is Khalig," she said unexpectedly to switch attention from the horribleness of the noise.

"And? Do you have his number? Can we contact him?"

Maribel nodded.

"That's great," Bekah said. "It's the next step forward. Wonderful!"

'The foolish girl, trying to praise,' Maribel scolded to herself. It was like receiving blessings from a prostitute. It held no virtue whatsoever.

Bekah rushed out of the room, returning quickly with a pen and a paper. "Okay, I'm ready to write it down…"

"I don't have it," Maribel said. "Rashid should. When he was in Dhaka and the well was drilling, Carlton used to speak with Khalig every day and he had Rashid do the dialling."

Bekah nodded. "Okay, let's get Rashid and then we'll call him."

"Don't count on it," Maribel answered. "You'll be lucky if the telephones are working."

Bekah looked so expectant Maribel thought she must do something to appease her. After all, one phone call and they would drop this idiotic attempt to raise a world that lay drowning at her feet.

Bekah followed her into the hallway.

"Habib! Rashid!" Maribel called noticing the clicking of her heels on the marble floor next to the silence of the girl's bare feet. "Habib!" she called again. Where was that boy?

"Yes, Begum," he suddenly appeared behind a door. Wretched lout. He'd been listening all along.

"Go find Rashid and get me Khalig's number and do it now!" Habib disappeared again behind the door.

"What is Begum?" Bekah asked as they waited in the hall.

"It means Mrs. It's a term of respect, though I know the young rascal has no such feelings for me."

"Why do you say that? He seems sweet."

Maribel shook her head, "It's something about him. I don't know. It's just… this whole situation!"

Bekah put a hand on Maribel's arm. The older woman could feel the warmth and the strength emanating through the dark skinned fingers and she felt herself relenting. Involuntarily words started pouring from her.

"My husband. He has a heart condition. His blood clots. I doubt he even knows how serious it is. And he doesn't listen to the doctor. Oh! You know how men are!"

Oddly, unloading onto the girl made her feel better. Something about her was so soothing. "He was supposed to have retired, last year. Of course, he refused. He just kept demanding, 'One last assignment', One last rotten…"

"Oh Lord Jesus," Bekah murmured.

Maribel sighed deeply. There, she had said it. Now the girl knew what the real situation was. Wouldn't judge her too harshly if she was rude or upset.

"Thank you for telling me, Mrs. Ramsey."

"Call me Maribel, please."

"Maribel, yes, of course."

Habib suddenly raced into the hallway, "Missis! We have another fax from kidnappers. Mr. Rashid is taking it to Mr. Shumacker in hotel. He leaves right now. You catch him."

"Shumacker! What do you mean? What hotel?" Maribel grabbed at the boy.

"Sonargon, Begum. Mr. Shumacker staying there."

"That man! He's here and he hasn't even called!"

"Must hurry!" Habib said running out of the room.

Maribel rushed after him, through the front door, catching Rashid as he climbed into the jeep.

"Rashid, I insist that you give me that fax!"

"I am sorry Mrs. Carlton, I am following orders. Mr. Shumacker says I must take them directly to him. No one is allowed to see. Please let me go."

"Rashid! I'm begging you, please tell me what it says. For God's sake. He's my husband!"

Rashid hesitated then sadly shook his head and drove the vehicle away from the building.

"That's how they treat women in this country!" Maribel screamed. "You see what I mean? Women? They're nothing here!"

"Maribel?" Bekah's smooth voice reached into her fury. "Maybe Habib saw it. He'll tell us… Habib?"

He appeared again from behind the door.

"Did you see the fax?" Bekah asked.

"Yes, Begum. But I no allowed to say nothing."

"Habib." Bekah's tone could soften stone. "You care about our husbands, don't you?"

"Yes, Missis. I like Mr. Carlton and Mr. Josh very much."

"Then you can help them by helping us. We need to know what was on that fax."

"Mr. Rashid fire me if I tell you. He say to me."

"Mr. Rashid will never know. We won't tell him, will we Maribel?"

Maribel shook her head, "Of course not, Habib. Of course we will never say a word."

The boy was sceptical but Bekah was working on him. The girl was evidently skilled at making people feel at ease.

"Fax says... bad guys to get money soon or..." The boy was stumbling over his words looking frightened. "Or, big trouble."

"Habib," Maribel softened her tone. If it worked for Bekah, perhaps now she had to lay aside her anger and manipulate the boy into doing what she needed him to do. "Has Rashid left Khalig's number?"

"No, Begum," Habib answered and then he smiled half heartedly, "but Habib knows where to find."

"That's wonderful." Bekah moved to Habib's side and squeezed his arm.

"Will you dial it for me?" Maribel asked, momentarily wishing that she was better able to motivate the boy. But obviously Bekah was more effective at it than she had ever been.

Habib led the way to the phone, hastily riffled through some papers and started dialling. He scowled, hung up then tried several times more.

"No good, Missis. Phone no work today. Maybe try later."

"You see what I mean? This is the most awful place on the planet!"

"Habib," Bekah asked. "Why does the phone not work?"

"Monsoon season, Hemanto, now in September. Everything very wet. Calling very difficult!"

"Can we send a fax?"

"Yes, maybe fax work, maybe not. We try."

In the fax room, Habib handed Maribel some paper and a black marker. She scribbled a message onto it and placed it in the tray. Habib dialled the number. After a number of tries, they watched as the paper slid through.

"Okay, that good," Habib nodded his head as he spoke. "Everything okay."

"Now to find that son of a so and so, Shumacker," Maribel cried. Stopping only to pause at a mirror, coldly looking at her reflection, she roughly dabbed her eyes with her handkerchief and patted her hair into place. She looked at Bekah, her chin tilting upward, emphasising lips set in anger. "You were right, I think it's time we took some action, don't you?"

Bekah flew up the stairs, slipped on her shoes, grabbed her bag and rushed after the older woman. They hurried down the clay road, the dirt kicking up around their ankles. By the time Maribel paused by the corner to wait, Bekah's loose trousers and long sleeved shirt were saturated with sweat.

"Riksha!" Maribel called at a rickshaw driver waving her raised arm downward. He stopped alongside them.

"You're kidding," Bekah whispered.

"I most certainly am not," Maribel replied as she climbed onto the cab seat. Bekah struggled in after her and the driver yanked the hood up over their heads.

"Sonargon Hotel!" Maribel said, "Khoto, how much?"

"Ek-sou" the driver announced.

"That's ridiculous. I offer no more than 'choy' six."

"Ath!"

"All right, ji, ha!" At last they pulled away from the curb. Bekah was very impressed. "What was that about?"

"I always learn a certain amount of the local tongue. You have to do something when you're stuck in these countries year in and year out. Anyway, it's a hobby of mine. I can speak about five languages fluently and scraps of another ten."

"What did you say to him?"

"He had the audacity to ask for four dollars. I bargained him down to about thirty cents."

"But why? Why didn't you just give him what he wanted? We need to hurry!"

Maribel met Bekah's eyes. "My dear," she said, "he would have announced to everyone on the street that we had accepted that fare. It would have made us a laughing-stock and he would have gone as slow as he could pointing out to his friends what he'd been able to get."

The Sonargon Hotel was surrounded by a tall chain link fence, separating it from the surrounding mayhem of the city streets. The building was large and luxurious, surrounded by tall palm trees, flowering shrubs and plants the likes of which Bekah had never seen before. The porter helped them out of the rickshaw. The door was opened by a bowing doorman.

Maribel marched straight up to the reception which was alongside one wall of a large room with sofas and tables and hurrying busboys. "Kindly contact Mr. Callahan Shumacker for me. I believe he's staying with you." She tapped her fingers on the marble counter as she waited.

The receptionist dialled the number speaking to the person on the other end. He put the phone down and said, "The gentleman will be with you shortly. If you would like you can wait in our lobby. The waiter will bring you drinks."

They walked to a thickly cushioned sofa and Bekah eased herself down. "This is gross," she whispered to Maribel.

"You shouldn't be surprised," Maribel whispered back. "There's always luxury next to squalor in places like this."

They ordered lemonade. Then another. Maribel asked that the concierge call Shumacker again. An hour passed. They ordered a plate of sandwiches and let another hour pass. Maribel went back to reception.

"I'd like to speak with Mr. Shumacker, please," she said. The receptionist dialled the number and handed her the phone.

"Callahan, it's Maribel." Bekah could just make out the words until they were drowned out by the entrance of a noisy group of military men coming from the elevators.

Maribel returned but did not sit. "He'll be right down." Her voice was tense.

A few minutes later Shumacker arrived, greeting them half-heartedly. He sat on an adjacent soft chair and put his hands on his knees bending forward. "Look ladies, I'm sorry to keep you waiting but you have to understand I've got a lot on my plate. Now why don't you go back to the house and stay put. I'll call you when there's something to report."

Bekah found her voice. "You have something to report. You received a fax this morning."

"Everything has to be kept strictly confidential," he responded coldly.

"Look Mr. Shumacker," Bekah tried again. "Don't you think we deserve to know what's going on?"

"Not when it endangers the safety of your husbands, no I don't."

"And how does it endanger them?" Bekah was growing impatient.

Shumacker stood up. "I'm sorry ladies, there's nothing more I can say." He held his hand out to Maribel who did not take it. He scowled. "Go back to the Company house and stay there. If I see that either of you have left it, I'll have the government deport both of you. Is that clear?"

Maribel's eyes widened. "You wouldn't dare."

"I would and I will. This is for your own safety. Now go. I refuse to take responsibility for you as well."

Bekah got to her feet. "You have no right to behave this way! If you threaten us again, I'll make sure this whole story is publicised from here to New York."

Shumacker's face reddened, he glanced over at the military men who had ordered themselves drinks and were watching the scene with interest, then he glanced at his watch and said, "We'll discuss this upstairs."

The military men waved as they passed and Shumacker nodded his head at them. Bekah paused for the briefest of moments trying to imprint their faces in her memory. Just in case. Once in his room, Shumacker's tone softened. "Now look ladies." He was obviously trying to be reasonable and Bekah was satisfied that she had hit just the right nerve. "I want to emphasise to you the urgency of secrecy in this matter."

"We understand that Mr. Shumacker," Bekah replied. "All we want to know is the progress that is being made to help our husbands."

"We're negotiating with the kidnappers."

"Have you found out who they are?"

"No."

"And?" Bekah waited.

"There's nothing else to tell. We're holding off until we get a response to our offer."

Maribel stepped forward. "What have you offered them Callahan?"

Shumacker's expression softened and he lowered his voice as he answered Maribel's question. "I'm sorry Belle, I'm not in a position to tell you."

"Callahan," she reached out and touched his arm, her hand lingering on his sleeve, "please don't be like this."

He pulled his arm away, his face darkening. "You're not the one who should be telling me how to behave."

Maribel gasped, stepping backward into Bekah who steadied the older woman, trying to reach into the truth of what was between them.

"Please don't be cruel," Maribel pleaded.

"Cruel? You call me cruel? What about you? What about what you and your stinking husband –" he stopped.

"But that was years ago… years ago! How can you –"

Shumacker shouted something back at her. Something about his own wife that Bekah could not understand. Maribel cowered under him as Bekah pushed her way in front of the older woman, protecting her. Her voice louder,

"You have no right to treat us this way!"

"I have every right. I'm in charge and what I say goes."

"You may be in charge Mr. Shumacker. " Bekah lowered her voice, "But you are also accountable to us."

Shumacker laughed, a bitter sadistic sound. He went to the small bar and poured himself a drink, gulping it down. He slammed the glass on the bar. "Let me tell you something Mrs. Felstein. I have allowed you to come here –"

"You did no such thing."

"Don't kid yourself. If I thought you were going to get in my way I would have personally made sure they didn't let you through immigration. Don't underestimate my powers or your own weakness."

Bekah did not respond, his words stunning her into silence. Maribel was still behind her gasping and wiping her eyes with a handkerchief.

Shumacker stabbed his finger in the air sending waves of antagonism her way. "You are going to go back to the Company house and you are going to stay there. When the time is right I'll come and update you with any news that is relevant to you. Until then I want you off my back."

"That isn't acceptable." Bekah stood her ground. "We know that a fax has arrived and we want to know what's on it. You say that you're negotiating but we don't know what you've offered. We have a right to know these things and if you don't communicate with us I will take action against you."

Shumacker grabbed out for her shirt but at the moment of contact Maribel stepped in pushing his hand away. "Callahan," Maribel whispered harshly. "Remember yourself for God's sake. Remember what we once were."

He reacted as if the woman had slapped him, his shoulders curled slightly, injured, trying to regain his strength. The silence in the room was terrible. What was Maribel referring to?

Shumacker started speaking, his voice almost too low to hear. "It's been left to me to sort this problem out. You know how the Company is. They don't want to know."

Maribel reached out, laying her hand on his arm again. "I'm sorry Callahan… I."

He shook his head. "It's too late for that," he said bitterly. "Don't think I feel the same way I did back in the sixties," Callahan continued angrily. "A lot has changed. Between you, me and Carlton. Now it's me making the decisions. It's me who decides who gets what life."

Bekah stepped forward. "Mr. Shumacker." She tried to cut through his anger, into the humanity of the man, if there was any there to be found. "This isn't a personal issue. This is a kidnapping. Two people are in trouble and they need your help. Forget your anger."

"What cotton fields did your husband find you in girl?" Shumacker spat out.

Bekah took the insult, gritted her teeth. "I don't care what you think of me. I care about what you're doing in those negotiations."

Shumacker shook his head as if trying to reason with her was completely impossible. He said, "You won't like the truth. And there's no need for you to know it."

"Let me be the judge of that," Bekah demanded.

"All right," Shumacker growled. "I've tried to shield you from the worst. You obviously don't appreciate it. So why should I bother? This is what's going on. Don't blame me if you don't like the truth."

Bekah braced herself.

"Your husbands are dead men if the Company doesn't meet with the kidnapper's demands within the week and we can't do anything about it until we've consulted with all the relevant authorities."

"But that means –" Maribel choked back a sob.

"It might mean that, yes."

Bekah reached out to Maribel. What did it mean consulting with the relevant authorities? Surely they would have done that by now? "But the money," she cried out. "Of course the Company will pay it if that's what it takes. Won't they?"

Shumacker shook his head in disgust. "Belle, why don't you explain to Mrs. Felstein that money is not the issue right now."

"But the threats!" Bekah shouted.

"Nothing can be done Mrs. Felstein until we've discussed this with the President. All right? Are you satisfied? I'm not keeping anything back. Now go back to the Company house and stay there!" Shumacker strode to the door and opened it. "Now go."

"But what about the ransom? Surely the Company will raise it?" Bekah didn't move.

Shumacker shook his head again. "Go!"

As desperate as Bekah was to have something happen, or to

implement action on her own behalf, Shumacker's words had frightened her into a temporary lull of confused submission. But if she was weak now she would somehow recover in the privacy of her room, gathering her strength along the way.

As she walked into the hall, Bekah felt Shumacker's hand on her back as he shoved her forward into the waiting, caring arms of Rashid who made sure they didn't stray on their journey back to the Company house.

Maribel had closed off again, could not be reached, leaving Bekah to the isolation of her own humiliation and confusion. She sat in the jolting vehicle through the crowded city streets feeling uncomfortably helpless and violated. And when they swerved around the corner and the Company house came into view, Bekah sighed with relief wanting to crawl into a dark corner and lick her wounds.

As soon as the front door was open, Maribel fled up the stairs to her bedroom. Bekah made her way into the staff lounge collapsing on the sofa, despair threatening to engulf her.

9

THE RAIN POUNDED AGAINST THE ROOF of the hut and ran in rivulets down the incline of the mud floor. A tiny slice of light hit Carlton's face as he pressed the back of his head uncomfortably against the coarse wooden wall and swatted at a mosquito which had landed on his arm.

The bolts slid across. Carlton lifted his hands to his eyes to avoid the shock of light. But he had been looking forward to this moment for hours and he wasn't going to waste it lying down. His legs didn't agree with him, they were as stiff as old leather.

"Well, if it isn't my friend Tweedledee," he said to the guard. He had named them, in the hours of solitude when he couldn't communicate with the boy. There were two sets of guards: Tweedledee and Tweedledum, who seemed to have some trace of decency left in their bones, and then there was Genghis and The Wrath of Khan. Tweedledee jerked his weapon upward and garbled something to him.

"I guess it's time for our wash," he said hopefully though Josh was still sleeping. The lucky bastard. He gently nudged the bottom of Josh's foot but he didn't wake.

'Damn!' The amiability of his captor would rapidly disappear if they didn't get going and he couldn't face being closed back up in the foul darkness.

He bent down to shake the boy's leg and the guard cursed at him in a language he was becoming all too familiar with.

The boy stank: sweat, excrement and infection. In the light Carlton could see the underside of Josh's foot, swollen and filled with a yellow-green pus. He shook his leg again. "Josh?" The boy stirred and opened up eyes drugged with sleep.

"Get up, we're being taken outside."

Josh fumbled with his trousers which had edged down. He staggered up, Carlton helped him. The boy was limping badly as he made his way out of the hatch, but he didn't complain.

The rain was soothing, immediately soaking them. It was such a relief. Carlton lifted his face to the sky. The guard jabbed him. "Okay we're coming." He knew the routine and began the short walk to the river. He, but not Josh had been allowed to bathe every day. Josh had been neglected, or worse, persecuted, and he stunk of the abuse. Carlton had the previous day stuffed the boy's shirt around his midriff under his trousers to bring it back fully soaked so Josh could at least wipe himself but it was a dismal replacement for the real thing. And the real thing was almost useless without soap.

But today as he slipped into the river, he was handed a bar of glorious, glorious soap — though Christ knows what it was made from, it smelled like goat dung. He stretched his arms to his side then ducked his head oblivious for a moment of his surroundings. Free from the four dark walls. The sky was baked in hot black clouds and the leaves were sweating and throbbing as the beating rain fell into the jungle.

He wanted to point this out to Josh. Had he noticed that the vegetation appeared to be moving in the wind like a giant monster. But where was the blasted kid?

For crying out loud! Josh was standing on the bank staring into the water. What was with him? Any idiot would have thrown himself in long ago. Didn't he realise that keeping clean was the most important thing he could do for himself? What the hell are you waiting for? He wanted to shout but he was afraid he'd alarm the guards.

He waded back to the bank. "Josh, get in this water now."

Josh hesitated.

"For Christ's sake what's the matter with you boy?" Carlton growled keeping his voice down.

Josh didn't move.

"I'm telling you boy. Get in here. What are you trying to prove?"

Josh shook his head then he hobbled forward, the cuts on his foot obviously causing him pain.

"Give me your hand. Come on." Carlton stepped onto the bank offering his hand but the kid wouldn't take it. "What're you so scared of?"

"Are there snakes in there?" Josh whispered.

"No snakes here," Carlton lied, though he would have sworn he'd just seen one swim by a minute ago. "Hurry up." He grabbed Josh's hand and tugged him in landing him on his belly in the water with a thump.

Carlton moved deeper into the cooling water. The kid didn't let him have a moment of peace. Things were bad enough. Jesus why did he have to get stuck with such a yellow belly. He pushed the soap through his hair then scrubbed his face, working his way downward. Leeches in the jungle were worse than the bloody snakes. He ought to say something. No. He laughed to himself. Better not. When he reached his chest, Carlton glanced at his charge dipping himself in and out of the water. He paddled his way over and handed Josh the soap.

"You use it now and be quick," he said. "Make sure to scrub yourself and your clothing. Christ knows when we'll get another chance."

Josh took the soap and started earnestly scrubbing himself.

"Feels good, doesn't it?" Carlton said.

Josh nodded and dunked his head under the water as Carlton watched the guards. They seemed bored or indifferent, he couldn't tell which but he knew how fast things could change. He scanned the opposite bank for the umpteenth time. He hadn't a chance, it was too steep and he was too easy a target. And if he threw himself downstream? How far could he go before they caught him? He started to move away from the kid. Let's test his theory. Maybe they'd be watching Josh. Carlton could tell he amused them with his stupid fears and phobias.

Carlton was only a few feet away from the opposite bank. They still hadn't noticed him. If he left the kid behind, he could go and get help. He was pretty sure he could pinpoint their location by the outcrops of sandstone surrounding them. He heard a shout then gunfire. Jesus they were shooting at Josh. Branches started crashing down over the kid's head. He heard Josh shout — they'd hit him! Then the kid sank under the rushing water.

He swam as quickly as he could to the spot, diving under. Couldn't see anything. He surfaced again and gasped for breath. The soap bubbled up to the surface and he grabbed it. The kid was gone. Christ they'd shot him.

The bloody guards were laughing. He ducked his head under the water again. Was the current so strong Josh'd been carried away that fast? He could hear the blood in his ears pounding as he held his breath, but he couldn't stay down there. He surfaced again.

One more time. One more time he'd go under and then the hell with the stupid kid. Goddammit! He ducked down again. Something tugged at his trouser leg. Jesus! There he was! Looking up at him! His face swollen with holding his breath. Josh gave him the thumbs up and kind of grinned. Crazy kid!

Carlton surfaced letting out a gasp of air. Then the kid came up too. "For Christ sake what the hell do you think you're doing! I thought you were dead."

"That branch hit me on the head," Josh said, "I thought if I didn't stay down I was a goner."

"I don't know how you can hold your breath so long," Carlton said gasping.

"Used to be on the swim team in high school."

Carlton nodded. That was good. He liked to hear about a boy doing sport, but he said nothing. There was washing to be done before the guards blew the whistle on them.

He lifted his leg to clean his feet, heard that pounding again in his ears. The trees started sloping in towards him, cutting out the light. He fell over, water rushing into his nose.

"Mr. Ramsey?" Josh's hand was squeezing his shoulder dragging him up.

"Take it easy kid," he replied angrily.

"Are you okay?"

"I'm fine, let me be."

"Are you sure?" Josh was still gripping him.

"Of course I am." He pushed the boy's hand off, but he knew that lying was becoming an uncomfortable bedmate.

The guards shouted. "Time to go back," Carlton said dismally. He was like a trained dog, knew all the signals. Soon they'd have him jumping hoops, just to see how fast he could do it.

Josh hoisted himself out of the water and reached out to help Carlton who refused the hand. Despite the pain in his chest, Carlton felt refreshed — his skin had begun to itch and the water had helped to alleviate the irritation.

"Hey Josh, life's improving," Carlton said as they were led further into the jungle away from the huts. "They're either going to kill us or let us use the loo."

The soldiers stopped at a clearing where they indicated a small shovel and then pointed to Josh.

"You go first. Dig a hole. There's probably some boards there," Carlton said.

Josh limped away into the foliage then Carlton heard the clinking of shovel against dirt and pebbles. He faced his captors. "You're being really nice to us today fellas. What luxury." He gave them a big smile. "You guys really know how to make us Yankees feel at home." The guards scowled. Carlton smiled again and put out his hand saying, "Nice, very nice accommodation." The guards backed away.

Let's see what these bastards are made of, Carlton grinned. He stepped towards them and they backed away again. Were they afraid of him? He made a face at them like a Maori warrior, his tongue sticking far out, his eyes bulging. They squabbled at him but didn't move any further back. Pity. If he found the right face maybe he could frighten them away permanently.

He heard a groan behind him, the kid must be getting sick of the local cuisine if his guts were getting at him. Bengali revenge. He'd had it himself several times in the past few months. Carlton stood with his legs apart so the guards wouldn't advance forward. It would give him a few minutes to look the area over.

The track they had been marched in on led away from Jaintipur further into the jungle. He'd been taken cross country, when he'd been dragged to Jaintipur, across two rivers until they'd come to a four wheel drive and he'd been blindfolded at that point so he didn't know which way they'd gone from there. Maybe the next time they had a wash he and Josh could make a break for it? Christ he'd better be careful. He could get them both killed.

Josh appeared handing him the shovel. "I've already dug you a hole," he said and pointed to the spot.

As Carlton walked to the shit hole he checked the vegetation, plucking a leaf here and there. One of the shrubs caught his attention. It looked familiar. He'd had a bad cut on his arm when he was in Java. Couldn't make it to a doctor and had to go to the local healer who showed him how to make a poultice. Wasn't that the same plant? His arm had healed so quickly with those leaves, he'd forgotten he'd hurt himself. It was worth a try. He quickly tore as many of the leaves from the bush as he could and stuffed them into his pocket.

He pulled at his trousers, unsticking them from his legs and squatted. The effort made his chest block up again but he forced himself to keep still. He'd been constipated for two days now, but today relief engulfed him as his bowels finally let go of the sticky waste and dribbling water.

When he'd finished he kicked the pile of dirt that Josh had left beside the hole covering his excretions. Should he run now? Try and get away? No. The jungle was too dense here. He returned to the others. The guard handed him a small tin of water.

"Josh, you wash your hands yet?"

"No sir," the boy replied.

"Use half of this... Wait a second," he stuck his hand in his shirt pocket where he'd dumped the soap.

Josh used the water sparingly and handed the rest back. Carlton looked at the tin.

'Just the sort of thing we could use.' Carlton mumbled and casually began to walk back to the hut with it in his hand. Suddenly he was shoved.

"Hey! What the –" Tweedledum snatched the tin out of his hand and as he tried to grab it back, Tweedledee jumped him from behind, knocking the wind out of his lungs as he hit the ground.

Josh was by his side. Jesus he couldn't even be humiliated in peace. "I'm too old for this crap," he said and let Josh help him up. The boy's hand was wet. He could smell the fear rolling off him.

"Don't let the bastards get you down," he whispered. "They'll eat you up and shit you out if you do."

As they were prodded forward, Carlton tried to push down a rising panic which seemed to fill his chest. He couldn't face going back into the hut. Perhaps if he was by himself, not having to deal with the kid, it would be easier.

"Let me introduce our guards to you, young man." He forced himself to speak, pointing at the smaller of the two. "This friendly youngster with the moustache, his name is Tweedledee. And the older one is his brother, Tweedledum, if you've not already guessed. Now let me tell you something about Tweedledee. He is a good boy. Respects his parents as he's been taught to do. Can't you tell that? Look at the sweet expression he wears on his face. Isn't he cute?"

Carlton's words flowed from a river of sarcasm. A river on the brink of bursting its banks. "And Tweedledum. Now he's a real man. He likes the smell of fear on others. You remember that the next time they knock you down."

Josh nodded.

They came upon the huts. The hatch had been left open. Carlton climbed in. Before he could give Josh a hand, the door was slammed and locked leaving him alone in the dark. It's what he had asked for. How did they know? But the boy was his responsibility despite his feelings about him. Another pain plunged through his chest. It was so damned hot in this hell hole. Sweat ran down his forehead, beading up above his lips. He wiped his face.

If they hurt the kid, he'd... He'd what? He paced back and forth. What to do? He took his shoe and banged on the hatch then realised that the noise he made would cover up the sound of gunshot so he stopped.

He moved back into the dankness. Must keep calm. Think about the business at hand. Idle hands, idle mind. He dug his fingers into his pocket, the smooth skin of the leaf reassuring. He took the leaves out and brought them to the tiny hole in the wall.

There wasn't enough light to do anything with so he stuffed them back into the pocket. He went to his side of the hut and sat down. He had to think of a way out, if not for his sake then for the boy's. Where the hell was he anyway?

As the day slowly passed, thoughts jumbled in his head, melding and merging; images that wouldn't leave. Maribel. He was still steamed up over her refusal to come back. His children. How would they react when they found out he was missing? And the damned Company, what were they going to do? Was he fool enough to believe that they would use their precious money on him?

The hell with them. He had lived his life the way he had seen fit. No one had forced him to do anything. He'd had a great life, a great career. What the hell was he moaning about?

He sat on his mat, straightening the edges out and appreciating the little shard of light which he could play with if he moved his hand in and out of its path. And then he remembered the knife. It was inside his shoe. He scrambled over to the corner and shook it loose, opening out the blade. Perhaps they could escape after all. Why hadn't he thought of it before? Separate the bastards and knife 'em.

He touched the tip of the blade. It wasn't that sharp. He was crazy. If it failed he and Josh were dead. They may be dead anyway. But who was going to save them if he didn't? He wondered what Khalig was doing now? Would he be searching every corner of the country for them? Probably not. He liked Khalig. They had created opportunity for business together, had made possibilities within an impossible situation, had even become friends. But Khalig was always interested in buttering his bread on both sides. And Carlton had helped him, had ordered small pieces of equipment that could be used in Khalig's other businesses. But he understood the man too well. Unfortunately.

He went to the opposite wall and started digging away at the wood with the knife, scraping and splintering until the hole was large enough to see through. He thought he heard shouting and put his ear to the hole but it had gone quiet. Maybe a bird or a monkey. The hut opposite seemed empty. They'd taken Josh away. To Jaintipur, now that he had been cleaned up? He hoped the boy wasn't fool enough to do anything stupid. And then he hoped that he was. He hated this waiting for something to happen. Hated being restricted, being kept in the dark.

He peered out of the hole again. As the wind changed direction it blew water into his eye. It felt good and he put the other eye against the opening for a wash. Then he saw them, about fifty yards away. The boy was moving badly as if they'd kicked him in the groin. One of the guards kicked him in the backside propelling him forward. Carlton closed his eyes, he couldn't bear to watch it.

The hatch opened again and Josh climbed in with as much dignity as his bruises would allow.

"Why'd they beat you, Josh?"

"Fun, I guess." Josh's voice was muffled. "They wanted me to dig another hole for tomorrow."

"Is that it?"

"Yes."

Why was the boy lying? They'd obviously wanted more than that.

"Did you do something to upset them?"

Josh didn't answer.

"I asked you a question." Carlton flicked the knife open.

"I don't go around upsetting people."

"I'm not saying that boy. Don't be so touchy." Carlton didn't pursue it. He would wait until Josh was ready to speak. Josh settled himself in the corner like a wounded dog. Something else had happened. Carlton wanted to shake the boy, get him to talk, but the picture that flashed in his mind of who he wanted to shake wasn't Josh. He held his fist against his chest, the feeling of indigestion driving him mad. The picture in his mind was of his son and he pushed it out as hard and fast as he could.

"I hit one of them in the face," Josh whispered.

"What else Josh? You looked like you got kicked pretty fierce."

Carlton heard what he thought was a sob. "Felstein, get to grips boy."

"They had me strip down." Josh's voice was tense but controlled.

"What happened son?"

Josh didn't answer.

"Come on kid, what really happened?" Nothing again. What the hell did they do to him? He spoke real low. "You're lucky you're not dead."

"Yeah."

Carlton felt bad for the boy. Felt real bad but couldn't show it. "How's your foot?"

"I'll live." Carlton pulled the leaves out of his pocket. "I've found a possible remedy in the jungle which may, or may not, help your foot. You game?"

Carlton waited for a response. Was the boy ungrateful for his efforts? Had he not heard him? "Hey, I'm talking to you!"

Josh spoke from the darkness. A withdrawn voice, one struggling to exist in the space between them. "Thanks."

"Don't think anything of it," Carlton responded, sure now that he had to lighten the situation up. The kid was obviously the type of person who lingered on his problems. That kind of person didn't survive these kinds of situations. "I've got to mash these things against something. I'll tell you what. Give me that phrase book of yours."

Josh handed it over while Carlton moved closer to the hole.

"You've worked the hole open?" Josh asked.

"Yessiree! I certainly have." Carlton pressed the end of the knife into the leaves. "I've been thinking," he said.

"What about?"

"What do you say we have a go at the guards."

Josh's voice was still weak, "You mean with the knife?"

"It's better than nothing."

"How will we get close enough to them?"

At least the kid was thinking about his suggestion.

"I don't know but it's worth a try, isn't it?"

"I don't think it'll work."

Carlton stabbed at the leaves,

"Now let's not be pessimistic son." Even if his plan was stupid, surely it was better for them to consider a way to get out than passively accept their predicament.

He stopped trying to mash the leaves. "It's no good," he said, "I'll just have to crush them in my hands and put them on neat. Christ knows if it'll work. Hand me that old shirt."

Josh reached over and grabbed the bloodied cloth.

"Rip the sleeve off," Carlton commanded.

Josh did as he was told and handed it over.

"Now sit back and stretch your legs out. Twist around for Christ's sake so I can get the light on it. That's good."

He pressed the leaves onto the boy's foot and then bound them against the sores with the shirt sleeve.

Josh winced and asked, "Do you know what you're doing?"

"Not really but I've done a lot stranger things in my day."

He pushed himself back to his corner and sighed. "You know I've been all over the globe looking for oil. It's been my entire life. I've seen some crazy things in my time. Did you know that the sunset in Western Africa is different from any other sunset in the world?" Carlton lost himself in the memory. He stared into the dark space and went beyond it: to the colours of his life, his travels. "It's a fabulous career," he said. "There's nothing else quite like it."

Josh said something distracting Carlton from his reverie.

"What'd you say, son?"

"I asked if you're still glad about your life. Considering."

"Considering what?" Of course he was glad. What was the kid going on about?

"Where we are."

"I don't get you?"

"I mean the way it might end."

Carlton shook his head, "You're pessimistic about everything boy! You know people like you never make it in the oil industry."

He shifted irritably against the wall. What did he have to go and say that for, especially when the kid was so down? It wasn't even true. Hell! Young people these days, you tried to show 'em the right way to be and they threw it back in your face.

"Come on, Josh." Carlton was desperate to clear the air. "Why don't you tell me about your own life?"

"I'd rather not." Josh was sullen.

"Well then let's talk about football or rugby. Shit, kid I don't give a damn what we talk about."

Josh paused. "Tell me about your time in Indonesia, then."

"You really want to know?" There'd be nothing better than to talk about the old days.

"Sure, I'd love to."

Carlton searched around for his shoes and found the aluminium case holding his cigar. This was a good time to have a chew. Maybe he should offer the kid a few leaves. It might help the bruises around his mouth. He uncapped the container and the aroma filled his sinuses, lifting him out of the prison for a moment.

"Josh, would you like some of this cigar to chew on?"

"No thanks."

Carlton slowly put the leaf to his mouth, postponing the moment when the end would touch his lips. He could practically taste the damned thing and then he gently clasped it in his mouth, let the scent of sweet acidity fill his nose. He settled himself in, sticking his toes into the rivulets of water running through the centre of the cabin. If they could cup that, it might be drinkable. He should have used some of it to make that poultice.

He heard the boy's stomach grumble. His own gut felt hollow but he ignored it. He let his thoughts stray back to his first assignment overseas.

"I had just received my Master's from Yale, when I joined Standex. They were still just a small independent at that time." He chuckled, "Those days you could make your fortune as a geologist. Did you know, if you found oil you actually got a percentage of the profits? Can you imagine that?

"I was lucky. They were just breaking in to the Indonesian offshore and needed a geologist to help out and I happened to be in the right place at the right time. Within two months of joining the company I was in Jakarta. The damnedest place. I'd never seen such exotic scenery, and the people! Hell, I'd been to New England and Okalahoma City and that was about it. It was a whole new world to me and I loved it. It was there I met my wife. The boss's daughter. Beautiful woman, so petite, well mannered. Knew more about oil exploration than most geologists."

Josh interrupted him. "When did you get married?"

Carlton sucked on the end of the cigar. "Took us four years to get around to it. Had to prove to her old man that I was fit to do the job. But it wasn't too long before we had the kids."

"You have a daughter and a son, right?"

"What?"

"You've got two children? Is that right?"

Carlton didn't answer.

"Ramsey?"

"Yeah, just the two." He fell quiet then. Maribel was probably still with Stacey and the new baby, having a good time, not thinking about him. Not realising the danger he was in. And his son…

"Where'd you meet your wife?" he suddenly asked Josh, choking back the upsurge of anger.

"Me?"

Was the boy asleep or what? Carlton peered into the darkness.

"Well?"

"At North Carolina U."

"She's a career woman, is she?"

Josh didn't answer.

"Well, is she?"

"She was studying for her Master's when we met."

"That's real interesting." He didn't really give a damn what Josh's wife was doing, not when his own had deserted him.

The bolts scraped across, letting the hatchway swing open. Carlton blinked uncomfortably at the sudden light. The guard shouted something and motioned for him to get up. He cupped his cigar in his left hand and discreetly slid it into his pocket as he tried to stand. His legs were stiff again and there was pain running down his left arm.

"What the hell do you want?" he snapped at them.

The guard had a black eye and it gave Carlton a certain amount of satisfaction. Maybe Josh had more in him than he'd given him credit for. Tweedledee handed him two cartons, two cans of pop and a candle. Things must be improving if they were getting cans.

They shut the hatch. He didn't move, the candle and the boxes of food still in his hands. He heard Josh calling him but the voice seemed to come from a distance away. "Get a grip," he said, as the boxes slid out of his hands.

"Ramsey?"

A hand touched his shoulder and he angrily shrugged it off. "There's your food."

Josh bent down and picked the things up then he started shuffling around for something. "Where's the knife?"

"It's in my shoe."

Carlton heard the flint strike against the metal of the knife, the slow glow of flame catching onto some twigs and paper and then the candle.

"I've got to get out!" Carlton hissed through gritted teeth.

Josh didn't say anything, which didn't make it any better.

Carlton went back to his corner, took the candle and stuck it in the muddy clay then slid to the ground. He opened the tray. Same crap. Rice and yoghurt. He stared at it and then put it aside. He wasn't hungry. He searched in his pocket for the cigar and returned it to his mouth. The boy was eating as slowly as he could, though he looked as if he could wolf the food, tray and all.

He stood up to hand his share over to the boy but a pain stabbed through his head. The ground began to shake. He staggered onto his knees, clinging to the food tray so it wouldn't spill, accidentally knocking the candle over, extinguishing it. He managed to rest the tray on the floor. The cigar dropped from his mouth and for a second he went blank.

The next thing he knew Josh was kneeling by his side.

"What the hell are you doing here?"

"Are you okay?"

He tried to sit up but couldn't. "Of course I'm all right. Don't touch me."

Josh didn't go away. He felt his pulse being checked and heard himself say, "What the hell do you think you're doing?" The boy was ignoring him. He tried to snatch his hand away but it wouldn't move. "Jesus," he mumbled again and tried to sit up. Nothing was working.

"Just lay still Mr. Ramsey."

What does the kid know? He tried to tell the boy he knew nothing about anything, but his words were dissolving themselves before he could get anything out. Josh stood up and went over to his corner but returned almost immediately. He stuck something under Carlton's head then rolled him onto his side.

"Do you have a history of blood clots, heart trouble or strokes?" Josh's face was very close to his. He could smell the yoghurt on his breath and wanted to push him away, but his arms wouldn't move and then he couldn't remember what the boy had asked him.

10

JOSH HAD BEEN HELPING HIS FATHER on a service call in Williamsburg when his dad had collapsed on the floor of the Laundromat. Immediately his fallen form was surrounded by probing, pressing spectators all wanting to help, to give advice. Josh had dropped to his knees and laid his father's head on a towel that someone had thrown into his hand.

He put his head to his father's chest to listen for the heart and found nothing. Then he put his ear to his father's nose to sense the breath, which did not come.

As he struggled to return life to the vacant body, a rabbi from the local synagogue knelt beside him, encouraging his efforts. By his side, a melody sprang from the rabbi's lips, a prayer for continued life, for the mercy of our Blessed God, for the faith and trust in He who is all good, all knowing.

As the ambulancemen rushed in and lifted the body, Josh stayed with them, climbing into the vehicle and gratefully accepting the rabbi's offer to come along. He took his father's hand and joined voices with the religious man as the ambulance careered through the city streets, rocking him back and forth. He felt confident, grateful that now in his greatest need, God was there to help him.

But He hadn't.

Carlton was barely conscious. He kept mumbling something but Josh couldn't understand him. His concern for the older man completely blocked the pain in his groin, the continual aching of his head, the infected sores on his feet. They were nothing compared to the disaster that was befalling them now.

He reached over in the dark and groped around for his book. When he found it he stood and went to the hole in the wall to see if there were any words that might be used to convey what he needed. He flipped through the pages and in the bleak pinpoint of light he found it. 'I need a doctor' 'Daktar lagbe'. He went to the door and started hammering on it, pushing away the knowledge of what they might do to him. But they didn't answer. As if they knew it was only him and not Carlton demanding to be heard. He returned to the still body, took the Swiss army knife from the shoe and using the end of it banged on the wall.

The hatch finally opened. There had been a change of guard. It was Genghis.

"Daktar lagbe," Josh said and pointed to Carlton.

"Na!" The guard began to close the hatch but Josh shoved his shoulder against it.

"Daktar lagbe!" he repeated, managing to keep the hatch open.

Genghis stepped backwards, his curses shrill as The Wrath came running. Genghis pointed into the hut.

"Daktar!" Josh shouted. "His heart." He pointed to his chest. "He needs help, daktar."

The Wrath moved away murmuring something to Genghis, then he ran into the adjacent hut. Thank God, he was going to do something. Genghis tried to push the hatch closed, catching Josh in the shoulder. The guard screamed again, lifting the machine gun square to Josh's chest. He held his hands in the air, stepped back meeting the guards glowing, fanatical eyes. The spatter of gunfire made him drop to his knees as the bullets splintered a corner of the roof, flinging shards of wood into the air like feathers from a broken pillow.

The door slammed. He returned to Carlton, hands shaking as he took the man's wrist in his. He put his ear next to the still mouth and listened for the rhythm of breath. Yes. Faint but steady. Was it a stroke then? How was he supposed to diagnose correctly? Heart failure? How could he know? He hadn't wanted to learn medicine, had lost interest in it after he'd met Bekah and she'd encouraged him to do what he had really wanted. Had she been wrong? Had his fate ultimately brought him here to show him that to turn from his family's desires and his religion would bring him disaster?

He moved his bedroll next to Carlton's, looking into the blank darkness. Stillness engulfed him. He wished there was something he could do, someone he could turn to for help.

He closed his eyes and then remembered the rabbi, by his side, in the Laundromat. He had prayed then to no avail. But it was all he had left.

"Dear God," he whispered. "Won't you listen to me this time when I need you so. Dear God. Please help me, in this time of need." He began rocking as he had been instructed to do on his bar mitzvah, to make his praying more convincing; rocking because it was the most comforting thing to do. "Dear God, please help us. Dear God, you who are meant to guide us, your people." He found suddenly that there were tears streaming down his face and his body was swaying like a weight hanging from a string, caught in the wind. Over and over, "Dear God, please guide me and forgive me."

Through the interweaving of tears, he could see Carlton's chest barely rise with breath. He wiped his eyes, discouraged and then angry. What was he doing? God wasn't going to help him. He hadn't managed to do it before, why should this time be any different? And how many instances since his marriage to Bekah had his mother assured him that he was breaking every commandment Jehovah had set out for his people.

His people! Who were they? Lambs to the slaughter. A race the world hated. Hated with such a vengeance that they created new and better ways in which to exterminate them. He hated being one of them. Didn't even know what it was supposed to mean. And yet now, in his heart, he needed someone, anyone, to pray to and he knew of no other God, so fearful, so monstrous, so capable of granting some small mercy.

Carlton moved his hand and groaned. "Josh?" His voice was feeble.

Josh put his hand on Carlton's shoulder, "How are you feeling?"

"Better. What the hell happened?

"Just rest for a while, Mr. Ramsey."

"I'm damned thirsty," the old man said. "Is there anything to drink in this dump?"

Josh reached over and grabbed the can of pop.

"Let me help you sit up." He gently propped Carlton against the wall then opened the can.

"My arms are like lead," Carlton said.

"I'll hold it for you," and Josh put the can to the older man's lips and let him sip it.

"You're a pal," Carlton whispered and then shut his eyes again.

The late sun came in the peep hole like a torch beam of holy light as the silence interwove with the steam and heat of the humid prison. Josh wanted desperately to take the older man's hand in his to give reassurance, but he couldn't do it. It might be misconstrued.

Had God answered his prayer? Or was it just a fluke that Carlton woke up when he did? Would it help if he prayed more? But now that the direct emergency was over, the anger and revulsion to the superstition that religion brought stopped him cold. Besides he didn't want the old man to see him pray. It would be too great a sign of weakness.

"You know my wife thinks I don't know I've got this condition. My father had it. Dropped dead the week after he retired. Probably happen to me too."

"You're not retiring are you?"

"Sure I am. Bastards are kicking me out."

"That's crazy, you're one of the best people they have."

"That's good of you to say son. But it's true. This is my last assignment and you should know it. You're the one who brought the papers."

"I had no idea. I never looked at those papers."

"You would say that." Carlton's words sank in. Is that why the older man had been aggravated with him?

"Do you think I was sent out to replace you?"

"It doesn't matter anymore Josh. Don't worry about it."

"Shumacker sent me out because I needed the experience. And I do. That's the only reason. I swear to you I never looked at those papers."

Carlton grinned, a flash of white teeth in the pinpoint of diminishing light. "Is that why you think Shumacker sent you out, son?"

"What other reason could he possibly have?"

Carlton didn't reply. Left Josh to ponder the inexplicability of it.

"What are you going to do?" Josh asked.

"What, you mean if we live through this?"

"Now who's being pessimistic?"

Carlton chuckled. "Josh, do you mind helping me with that soda again?"

Josh lifted the can up to the man's lips and let him drink.

"I've been an asshole to you, haven't I?" Carlton said when he had finished.

"It's been a real difficult situation, especially if you thought that I –"

"Don't cut me a break for Christ's sake."

"Okay, you're a grouchy old bastard. Is that what you wanted to hear?"

Carlton laughed feebly, but he laughed nonetheless. "I'll be honest with you. I didn't want you on my patch. If it hadn't been for Shumacker someone else would've been sent."

"I've got that now. Nonetheless, I'm grateful to him," Josh replied.

"Don't be. Shumacker was only using you, son. Don't ever forget that. He'll be the one responsible for getting us out of here. Why do you think we're not free yet? The bastard doesn't want to pay the money. It won't look good on his record."

"You're kidding!"

"Think about it." Carlton fell silent.

Left to his own thoughts Josh felt like a ship who'd sprung a leak then hit a storm. Was Carlton saying there was no hope for them?

"Josh?"

"What?"

"Would you help me with that can again?"

Josh raised the drink to the man's lips but this time Carlton managed to lift his arm and grasp the soda, helping himself. "You want some?" he said.

"No thanks, I've had mine."

Carlton put the container down by his side. "I'm supposed to be taking medicine for the old ticker." He patted his chest and winced.

"Maybe we can convince the guards to get us some aspirin. It's supposed to prevent clotting. Do you want me to try?"

"No thanks, son. They won't have any. I either live through it or I don't. Teach Maribel a lesson anyway."

"What are you talking about?"

"Oh nothing, forget I said it," Carlton sighed. "You see that cigar of mine anywhere?"

Josh brushed his hand along the floor looking for the cigar. He found the aluminium container, handed it over and then continued searching for the rolled leaf, accidentally knocking Carlton's hand. He pulled away, murmuring, "Sorry."

Carlton said, "That's okay son. I appreciate you making the effort."

Josh found it in the corner. "I think it's pretty muddy." He handed the cigar to Carlton then returned to his side of the hut, listening to Carlton sigh with pleasure. How could someone get such satisfaction out of something as inconsequential as a cigar, especially in circumstances like these? Josh couldn't understand it and wondered what it was that he found as pleasurable.

Solace perhaps. In his work. With Bekah. But pleasure? Hard to think of pleasure in all this pain. Didn't let him touch the essence of it. He leaned his head back gently. Pleasure? Yes, those moments on the drilling rig, the smell of the oil, listening to the mud pumping through the pipe. The cold air on the Rocky Mountains. Skiing down a rugged slope. Yes, there was pleasure in that. Bekah. No, don't think of her. Not now. It brought him too close to the truth of this hut and what they'd done to him. But he couldn't stop the run of her in his mind. His hand along her dark skin, the silk of her... No! Don't! Don't do this! Her face in laughter, wiping the juice of New York pizza dribbling down his chin...

Happiness. Ephemeral. That wasn't what this life was about was it? He should ask Carlton what he thought. The older man would probably tell him it was a stupid question. Maybe it was. Somehow he didn't really feel that he deserved to be happy. Thought he should suffer. Isn't that what all this was about? But he could examine it no further. There were no clear answers to his questions.

Discouraged, he wanted to reach out to Carlton but couldn't trust the older man not to make him feel worse. He tried to sleep but closed eyes brought images of his mother. If he listened to her now, he'd lose all hope.

"Josh!" Carlton called out. Josh crept over. Carlton was breathing heavily and smelled of stale sweat and the lingering odour of the cigar leaf. "Talk to me, son. Please, I'm going crazy."

"What would you like to talk about?"

"I don't care. Tell me about your family or your travels, just anything." He was gasping for breath.

Josh moved closer. Was Carlton having another stroke?

"Ramsey?" he found then lifted Carlton's wrist to feel for his pulse.

"What the hell are you doing, boy?" Carlton pulled his hand away.

"I'm checking your pulse. What do you think I'm doing?"

Carlton didn't answer.

"Look, I'm sorry, I was just trying to help," Josh said.

"Forget it, Josh. Didn't know what was going on."

Josh crawled back to his spot and put his hand up by the hole. The air was cooler at the interface than inside the hut and he wished he had a straw to suck more of it in.

"What'd you do your Master's thesis on?" Carlton persisted.

"A study of modern and ancient beach sands. I did a comparison."

"Really!" Carlton's voice sprang with interest. "That was one of my favourite subjects too. You study Manheim?"

"Of course. I even did a field trip with him in North Carolina one summer."

"Manheim's a good friend of mine. Knew him from the old days in Java."

"When were you in Java?" Josh was conscious again of changing the subject. Conscious of letting Carlton do the talking. It'd make the older man feel better and it would take the spotlight off himself.

He listened to Carlton's adventures. Some of it was interesting. Most of it was about people whom he didn't know or would never meet. He wondered if he'd be the same way when he was older. Living in the past, finding so much enjoyment in the recollection. He yawned. Carlton stopped abruptly.

"I didn't mean to bore you." Carlton's voice was gruff, the happiness drained quickly away.

"You're not," Josh answered but the words couldn't cover the real feelings.

Threads of tension hung between them. Josh regretted his callousness, wanted to reach up and tug them down. A little effort on his part would have made the man so happy.

Carlton rustled against the wall and then Josh heard him lie down. He held his breath. He should apologise but he couldn't bring himself to do it.

Carlton's voice sounded very tired as he spoke. "Does an old man good to talk about his past."

Josh nodded and let the guilt wrap around his emptiness.

11

BEKAH DREAMT THAT SHE WAS FLYING, like Superwoman, over the hills crowded with jungle foliage, her baby tightly held in one arm. Below her were native straw huts, some in clusters, others separated in ones or twos away from the others. Children were playing in little clearings near the river and she swept down to take a closer look. As each child became distinct she saw bursts of light flash in front of her and she realised that the children were now shooting at her. She panicked, feeling one of the bullets hit her. The baby started crying and as another bullet hit her in the arm she lost her grasp and the baby tumbled perilously to the ground.

Maribel's hand was on her shoulder shaking her hard. "Bekah?"

Bekah opened her eyes. Was she still on that sofa? How long had she sat there? Her arm was bruised. Where she'd been hit. She touched the spot. "I had the most terrible dream."

"Yes, the whole house could hear."

Bekah leaned her head against the back of the sofa. This dream? Was it only a reflection of her waking anxieties? Or was it trying to tell her something deeper? About her baby? About Josh?

"Habib is serving dinner in fifteen minutes. Are you hungry?"

"Not really." She rubbed her eyes.

No, nor am I. But you ought to eat something," Maribel said nodding her head towards Bekah's midriff.

Bekah pushed herself stiffly from the chair, stretched her arms. Why did she feel as if she'd been stuffed into a dark little box? So confined. Was it only Shumacker making her feel this way?

Maribel opened the door to the dining room, waiting for her.

"I suppose I owe you some sort of explanation." Maribel placed the cloth napkin primly on her lap.

"You mean about Shumacker?"

"Yes, how did you know?"

Bekah shook her head and grinned.

"It was that obvious was it?"

"Yes."

Habib placed a portion of curried vegetables with rice in front of Bekah. She met his eyes and smiled. He grinned back, quickly served Maribel who gave him a cold thank you.

"Why do I always feel you're judging me?" Maribel suddenly scolded.

"I'm not," Bekah answered quickly but even for her the answer was too flippant. Yes, it was true, she was judging her. Continually.

"Well I don't believe you."

Bekah put her fork down, smiled. "Good," she said. "I'm glad you don't believe me because you're right. I'm watching every move you make."

Maribel lifted her chin, a little movement which said a thousand words: 'you see, hmmmph I was right' and 'how dare you'. But she spoke none of these.

"You see, so far I'm only at the judgement stage." Bekah lifted her fork and tasted the vegetables. The sauce was sweetish and spicy. She didn't know if she was up to it.

"I suppose I should know what you mean by that," Maribel answered indignantly.

"You seem to have already decided on me, Maribel."

"What impertinence!"

Bekah grinned. That wasn't the first time she had heard that word applied to her.

"Well I have to admire it I must say." Maribel pushed her plate away. "I can't bear to eat."

"I give up too," but she was sure it was for different reasons. Habib magically appeared and swept away the plates, putting in their place strange looking yellow balls. Bekah raised an eyebrow.

"They're yoghurt," Maribel said. "It's a local dish. Goat's milk and honey."

Bekah lifted one and touched it with the tip of her tongue. Yes, it was nice. She could probably swallow that. She put it back on the plate and cut it in half with her spoon then lifted it to her mouth, noticing Maribel watching her.

"Carlton hates those. And no matter what we say to that young man," she indicated to Habib. "He always puts them in front of us.

I think his mother sends them as a gift."

"But that's so charming." Bekah put the other half in her mouth as Habib came in smiling and fluttering about her. "From your mother?" she asked and Habib nodded enthusiastically. "Please tell her that I send my thanks. They are delicious!" With the praise, Habib glowed then just as suddenly scowled at Maribel's untouched portion, shook his head, and carried her plate away.

"We'll have our tea in the staff room." Maribel scraped her chair away from her as Bekah put her napkin on the table. She was glad to go and sit on something softer.

"You were going to tell me about Shumacker," Bekah said as she eased herself into the sofa that had brought the dream.

"Yes, I was, wasn't I?"

"If you'd rather –"

Maribel waved her hand dismissively, "It happened so long ago. You'd think everyone would have forgotten about it by now. But you know it lingers like shrapnel in a wound never healed."

Bekah leaned forward slightly. Listening and then trying her hardest to hear beyond the sound and semantics. Maribel had fallen silent.

"Did Carlton know?" Bekah asked.

"I suppose he must, though we never talked about it."

Bekah sighed. The words now taking shape. A marriage of silent misunderstandings. "What happened?" she finally asked.

"I can hardly remember."

Bekah doubted the truth of the words and it pushed her boldness. "Shumacker obviously does."

"Yes, someone told his wife a few years after and she left him. He never married again and he thinks it was me or Carlton."

"Lord," Bekah groaned to herself.

"As if you're so innocent," Maribel snapped.

"What have I got to do with this?"

"You and your saintly husband!"

"What?" Bekah pressed her fingers against her eyes. Why couldn't Maribel just give her answers instead of... accusing, turning it to mean –

"Mr. and Mrs. Innocent," Maribel continued. "As if your Joshua had nothing to do with this trouble."

"No, he didn't!" Bekah protested again.

"As if your husband wasn't gloating like some carrion crow on the wing, just waiting for Carlton to fall."

"Don't be ridiculous."

"Don't be ridiculous," Maribel parroted.

"Oh for Lord's sake, will you stop this!"

Maribel's lips compressed. "As if you had nothing to do with Callahan's enmity."

"Uh, uh." Bekah stood. "I'm not taking this bullshit from you."

"No, the truth is too unpleasant for you is it?" Maribel shut her eyes, closing Bekah out.

She wasn't going to let Maribel do this to her, wasn't going to take responsibility for this trip. "Let's get some thing straight." Bekah moved closer so as not to raise her voice.

"We have everything perfectly straight," Maribel replied, her eyes still shut.

"I don't think so. First of all, Josh and I know nothing about you or your husband's plans, career ambitions and personal or marital disintegrations. Is that clear?"

Maribel's eyes snapped open, surprise widening them.

"Secondly, if you have a grievance against me or my husband, you let me know that grievance in a civil manner or not at all."

Maribel leaned against the back of her chair closing her eyes again. "Go away," she flapped her hand dismissively. "Go away and talk to the servants in that tone of voice, not me."

The words shocked Bekah into immobility as the clock in the hall chimed a reminder: another hour lost, you must do something soon.

12

JOSH SAT UP GROGGILY as Carlton hammered on the door with his shoe. He hadn't wanted to be woken. Fought it, in fact. Hadn't wanted to come back to the reality of the situation. Even when he heard Carlton stirring he had ignored it. He wasn't feeling that well. Needed to be sick during the night but somehow managed to hold it down.

The hatch opened, the glare of light made him squint. He grabbed his glasses and clambered up to help Carlton out of the hut, then climbed out himself and urinated against a tree. Genghis and the Wrath were still on duty and they were restless and irritable.

Carlton looked bad. The stubble on his chin made his face haggard and his skin hung loose under his eyes.

"What I wouldn't do for a dip in the river," he said and Josh agreed. They both stank.

Carlton walked up to the guard who backed away angrily, clutching onto his weapon. Then, yelling something, he raised the gun at the older man, who smiled.

"Pani," Carlton said and then made a washing movement.

The guard lowered the machine gun, a smirk creasing his face. He shook his head.

"Come on," Carlton said. "Let us have a wash."

The guards looked at each other and then looked towards the river.

"Na!"

Josh jolted forward. Had they actually understood Carlton? Had they understood all along? Had they known what he had been saying, what he had been feeling when he had pleaded with them?

If he moved now he would do something that would get them both killed. 'Remember,' his uncle Chayim's words rang in his head, 'don't give them the satisfaction.' His hands trembled with keeping himself still. How could people be so cruel?

He looked over at Carlton who had started to walk towards the river. He tried to call out to stop him but his voice stuck in his throat. Genghis started running after him. He grabbed Carlton by the arm. But Carlton managed to jerk free, continuing down the path, a slow amble as if he were on holiday, going down to the river.

The guard shrieked as he lifted the weapon, seeming to relish that moment as he had done the night before. He aimed at Carlton's back, then pulled the trigger. The sound ripped through the jungle, echoing against the distant hills. Carlton fell to the ground.

"No!" Josh broke into a run — in his mind bones shattered, skin broken, blood oozing into molten ground. He dropped to the man's side, his vision blurred with rage.

Why had Carlton done it? Why had he just walked off when he knew what the consequences would be? He could see nothing but the death of the man before him. He reached his fingers out to touch the blood. The spot was dry. He pulled at Carlton's shoulder to turn him over.

"Mr. Ramsey?"

Carlton slowly rolled over and grinned. "I move pretty good for a guy with a bum ticker, don't I? You don't think they'd kill me this early in the show, do you?"

Josh was speechless.

"Give me a hand up for Christ's sake, son."

Josh helped him to his feet. Carlton was covered with mud from head to toe. He looked pleased with himself. Josh had to admire his guts.

"You shouldn't let those bastards get to you." Carlton prodded Josh in the chest before he turned to face the guards and return to the cell.

Carlton climbed in first and then Josh. They went to their respective corners, the mud on Carlton's body beginning to dry and flake off onto the floor.

The hatch did not close behind them, remaining open, inhibiting Josh from saying what was on his mind though now he desperately wanted to talk.

"I wonder why they haven't shut us in?" he asked.

"Don't question it son. Enjoy it while you can."

But Josh didn't want the guards to overhear what he said, even if they might not understand.

"How's your foot?" Carlton changed the subject, gathering the remaining leaves from the corner.

The bandage on his foot was filthy and had disintegrated. Josh gently tugged at the strips, some of it sticking to the yellowy pus underneath. Carlton crawled over and took a look.

"Does it still hurt as much?" Carlton asked.

"I don't think so."

"I'll stick some leaves on it again and tie it up with some clean cloth."

"I can do it. I mean…" Josh hesitated as Carlton faced him, the expression in the older man's eyes, a challenge. "I mean I really appreciate what you're doing for me."

"That settles it then." Carlton returned to his corner and started chopping and squashing the leaves, then he tore the other sleeve off the bloodstained shirt and moved over to dress the foot.

"Thank you," Josh said, unsure how to handle the kindness, unable to understand what motivated Carlton. He always did the opposite of what Josh expected him to do. Why would anyone in their right mind challenge the guards when they knew they would lose the struggle? The man was from another planet, upon which Josh was sure he would never be welcome to land.

"Hey, Josh," Carlton whispered as he stood to look out of the door.

One of the guards shouted a warning. Carlton sat again, his back to the open hatch. "I'm getting bored just sitting here. You know it's against my nature doing nothing. What say you we play an old oil game. You and me."

Josh's suspicions rose. Games. He'd never been good at losing himself in other people's 'fun'. Always found it mindless and destructive. Games were for jocks and good time people. He'd never been flippant enough.

"What kind of game?" he asked cautiously.

"You still have those coins on you?" Carlton's breath was close, mingled with the smell of mud.

Josh dug in his pocket and pulled out half a dozen nickels and dimes.

"Right," Carlton said, "we'll use two nickels as dice and the dimes as players. Don't worry son, you'll enjoy this. A bunch of us used to play it in the desert in Saudi. Remind me to tell you about that sometime." He shook his head at the memory and chuckled, took the knife and drew a circle then divided it into equal segments.

"Okay, here are the rules. South of this median line," Carlton etched a thick line in the centre of the circle, "all the acreage is yours. That is, you're the government on this acreage so you decide which slices of your pie contain oil and how much. But don't tell me! You also decide what kind of deal you want from me as an oil company to explore and then produce the oil.

"Remember, your country's economy is desperate for this kind of income. The more money you get from your oil the more you or your people benefit.

"North of the median line is my land, i.e., I'm the government here and you're the oil company and desperate for profits so you can pay yourselves and your shareholders. Each piece of pie is a different country and a different deal but the same oil company. Shake the coins. Not that way. You're gonna have to toss them in the air. That's it."

Josh threw the coins. One head and one tail.

"That's a no-play throw, Josh. I'll take a turn and show you how it's done." He threw the coins. Two tails. "If this had been the middle of the game, I would have already been sitting on your acreage. Throwing two tails means that you as the government can decide to nationalise your oil industry and kick me out. I lose all my investment. That can hurt... Your turn."

Josh threw the coins again. Two heads.

Carlton said, "Two heads means you move one space. Now's your chance to bid on this plot. It just so happens that there is oil here. What do you bid for it?"

"How much oil?" Josh asked.

"Now that's my business and I'm not about to tell you. That's the whole point of the game. You know there's oil but you don't know how much. You also don't know if it's economically viable to do a deal. You have to decide what the gamble is."

"That's ridiculous. I don't have any data. Nothing to base my decision on."

"Well now, that's the kicker, son. You have to follow your guts."

"How do I know you won't change the numbers after I bid?"

"You've got to trust me."

Josh pushed the broken glasses back onto the ridge of his nose. The last thing he'd ever do is trust Ramsey. "Do I get to know what part of the world we're in?"

"Sure, let's call this South America."

"So my chances of finding something worthwhile are good."

Carlton nodded.

Josh rubbed his chin thoughtfully, "I'll give you twenty percent of profits. That means that all my suppliers, workers and taxes are paid."

"That's fine, but let's say in this country, I'm a son of a bitching dictator and I want ninety percent of all profits plus paybacks into my own pocket."

"We're talking corporations here, not individuals!"

"Uh, uh." Carlton shook his head. "Wake up Josh, you're in the real world now. I want a numbered Swiss bank account set up for me by your company."

The old man was driving him crazy. That was illegal and he wasn't going to be made into a cheater.

Carlton said, "No one's to know. You put eighty percent profits through the government books and ten percent through my numbered account. In fact, I'll make it easy for you. You put the whole ninety percent through my account and I'll be responsible for distributing it downwards.

"No deal," Josh said. "It's either legal and above board or we don't do business."

Carlton started laughing and the laughter forced him to clutch at his chest falling sideways for a moment.

"Son!" Carlton gasped. "How the hell do you think we've gotten into most places? Do you honestly think that your company, your employment, is based on one hundred percent ethics? We're a profitable business, Josh. Think about it!"

Josh refused to listen. "Well, I don't have to work that way. Go on take your turn, there's no deal here."

Carlton picked the coins up and threw two heads. He rubbed his hands greedily then moved onto Josh's acreage.

There was oil there, but not much. Slim chance of profits, but Josh wasn't going to let on.

"Right!" Carlton said, ready for action. "Where are we? What have I got? Let's get the show on the road."

"You're in the Gulf of Mexico."

"Probably deep water, eh? Hell, it's high risk and not necessarily high return. Tax regime's stable, I know the politics and there are virtually no environmental restrictions. Okay son, I'll go for it. I'll shoot some seismic and drill a well."

"That's not good enough."

"Sure it is. No one else wants to have anything to do with it. Let's face it, you're stuck Josh. Your government's got a mounting foreign deficit and increasing reliance on Middle Eastern oil. You're laughing if I supply you with in-house reserves."

Josh saw the point and relented. He said, "Okay, you find ten million barrels."

"That stinks Josh. I would have lost money on that deal. After exploration and production costs, the expense of a deep water platform, pipelines, even at twenty dollars a barrel it's not cost effective. You understand what I'm trying to tell you?"

Josh threw the coins and moved onto another portion of Carlton's acreage.

The older man said, "This is the Arab Emirates and remember." Carlton winked at him, "You haven't made any profit so far."

"I'll give you your usual production taxes and build local amenities such as desalinisation plants and schools, but only after production. Until then you give me tax rebates for exploration."

"Hey, that's good thinking son. You're catching on. I'll make an oil man of you yet." Carlton looked anxiously over his shoulder at the open door. "With a bit of luck."

They threw another round of coins until Josh was back on the crooked acreage.

"Same deal Josh," Carlton whispered.

"I just won't bid if those are the terms. I don't need your oil!"

"If that's what you want to do. But remember there are only a limited number of places where you can explore successfully. You have to find profits somewhere or you lose your shirt. It's up to you."

"I still don't want that acreage."

"In that case, I can always find some hack to put the exploration money up for me. That's what I'll do... Hey! What do you know! I've just found a hundred million barrels of beautiful crude!"

"You can't do that!"

"Sure I can."

Josh pushed away from the circle. The old man was a liar and cheat amongst other things. Carlton picked up the coins. He was clearly winning the game. What was the use of continuing? He couldn't out negotiate Carlton. The older man, despite his infirmity, was as cunning as he was crooked. What chance was there in making an honest buck? None as far as Josh could tell.

"Come on Josh, You'll learn more from this game about oil deals than you will in your pretty little office in Houston. Where am I?"

"You're in Kuwait and the neighbouring country has just invaded, setting all the oil wells on fire. What do you do then?"

Carlton laughed. "I go in there with my military and bomb the hell out of them then go back in with new contracts at a better deal."

"There's no stopping you, is there?"

"Not when there's oil to be found." The acreage was all taken. Carlton had won hands down.

"I admire your motives, Josh," Carlton said, "but you're in the wrong business if you feel you can't bend the rules. Why do you think the stuff is called black gold?

The game had left Josh emptied. Defeated. What had he expected when he'd joined Standex? Surely he had never been stupid enough to feel that he was accomplishing anything for humanity working as a geologist. What had he been trying to do? Just fulfil himself. Did that necessarily mean ripping others off?

He got up and went to the door. There was no one there.

"What are you looking at?" Carlton asked.

"I think the guards are gone."

"You're joking!"

"Look for yourself!"

Carlton hurriedly struggled to his feet. He poked his head out of the opening, looked left and right. "Damned if I can see them."

"What should we do?"

"Look out that peephole... Jesus, they might be waiting for something like this. Hoping we try and get out then shoot us."

Josh looked out of the hole. "I think they're gone!"

"Christ!" Carlton paused. "Let's get the hell out of here."

Josh climbed out of the hut, holding his hand up to keep Carlton in, signalling that he would have a look around first. The place had been abandoned. He quietly made his way to the other hut. There were ARM cartons piled in one corner other than that it was completely empty.

He returned to the hut and signalled to Carlton who climbed out of the hatch. Carlton gestured, this way, towards the river. They moved quietly and quickly. Past where Carlton had been knocked down earlier in the day, past where Josh had dug holes for the toilet. Just behind them there was a sudden rustling of leaves.

"Carlton!" Josh grabbed the older man's sleeve. They stopped to listen. Carlton put his finger to his lip approaching the sound. If it were the guards, if they were caught just then, what was going to happen? Carlton bent over the large leaves, poised to swing out if necessary. He raised his arm smacking into the air leaf and soft wood branches. There was nothing there.

"Just an animal," Carlton whispered. "They're not here. Come on."

"Why don't we take the track?" Josh whispered close to the older man's ear.

Carlton shook his head and pointed his chin in the direction of the river, then quietly waded in. Josh followed pushing through the water, the liquid tugging, cooling his skin.

They were escaping! His breath came in heavy gulps as he swam behind Carlton across the fleeing river. They rested for a brief moment on the opposite bank. Away from the huts. It was steeper on this side. The jungle denser.

He looked back for an instant. It reminded him of the story of Lot's wife. 'Don't look back Mrs. Lot,' his father used to say, 'or you'll turn to salt.' The bank seemed peaceful, hard to believe anything menacing had ever been there.

He climbed out then offered Carlton a hand, pulling him upward. The action brought a sharp pain through his abdomen. Carlton's hand slipped. He fell backwards thumping into the water.

"Son of a bitch!" Carlton hissed. Josh reached out again. "My stomach. I don't know what –"

Carlton clambered out more quickly this time. "Come on, let's get a move on."

They pushed themselves into the entanglement, Josh trapping himself in the trailing vine which wove the shrubs into a net. Another pain thrust itself through his abdomen forcing him to grab onto a branch just to keep himself upright. Carlton came alongside, pulling the tangle aside. The older man had a knack of moving through the bush with the minimum of effort as he signalled for Josh to follow.

Animals scurried in the brush, water rushed behind them. A small waterfall splashed somewhere nearby. Carlton halted and looked around him like an animal sensing his game. He narrowed his eyes as if he could smell something and then shook his head and indicated to Josh to carry on.

Josh was moving faster now, picking up Carlton's technique. Step and sidestep, use the forearm to sweep aside large leafed plants. With each step, the rag on his foot disintegrated, the pain jagging at him until he had to stop and pull the bandage off, in the background the panting of his breath, the leaves whisking against his glasses, splashing him in the face, his intestines hissing and growling, threatening to burst if he dared to stop.

Another tumbling river lay in front of them, this one younger and steeper than the one they had bathed in.

"This is it," Carlton whispered. "This is where they took me that first day. Jaintipur is maybe two, three miles from here. We should make it by nightfall if we hurry."

He stepped foot into the flowing river, its ferocity knocking him down. Josh hurried in to help.

"We'll have to go upstream." Carlton retreated to the bank. "It'll bring us closer to Jaintipur anyway."

A bird called. A loud cackling sound. Or was it a bird? Carlton's movement broke as the sound repeated. Then he started climbing the coarse white sandstone, pebbles gritting against the skin.

Josh was better at this than rushing through the tangled weed. Liked the feel of the rock beneath his fingers, though the jagged matrix cut into his infected foot. Here he was free and natural and easily passed Carlton. He paused to look below him, saw Carlton slumped against the stone. He made his way down again.

"Just resting," Carlton gasped. "Don't think for a second I'm gonna give out just yet."

Josh nodded taking the opportunity to look around, soak in the fact that they had truly been let go. The kidnap was over. All they had to do was walk a few more miles and they'd be safe.

"Come on, Josh." Carlton got to his feet. "This is probably the best place to cross." He stepped into the beating water. One step at a time. Too fast and you tumbled against the rounded boulders which glistened like bobbing balls of silica crystal.

Carlton was over first, hanging onto a slender tree which bent itself in the water. Josh was just behind him when the bird called again, first faintly then coming closer. Carlton stepped onto the opposite bank and pulled Josh over. The bird settled in a nearby tree and scolded. Perhaps they were near the nest. It didn't matter. They'd be moving on. But the bird persisted, broadcasting their position. Carlton tugged at his sleeve. "We'd better get going."

A crack of thunder in the distance rolled through the hills, washing over the ground they were moving against. Josh felt the sonic wave under his feet. Lightning streaked closer to the canopy. They were in the wrong place for a storm. Just on top of a wet rock. They'd be hit if they didn't go downstream and fast.

The rain began to spatter. First lightly, then, with another bang of thunder, in large cool drops. Mountain rain from the mountain gods. It ran down their bodies and melded with sweat and rivulets of blood from thorn-ripped flesh.

Sudden flashes of light crackled, sizzling through the undergrowth, followed by the hammer stone of thunder. "We should move downhill," Josh called out. But Carlton vetoed it.

"It's the lightning or Genghis and his buddies Josh. Take your pick."

Josh climbed after the older man until they reached a clearing where they could see the jungle and waterfalls and a large spread of huts in the distance scoured into the hillside.

"Jaintipur, my boy," Carlton panted rubbing his chest.

"You okay?" Josh covered his eyes in the sudden flash. This was no place to stop.

"I've got to rest." Carlton crumpled to his knees. "Jesus, when did I get so unfit?"

Josh knelt beside him.

"It's the bloody good life, Josh. Don't let it ever get you." He pressed his chest and grunted with pain. "Jesus!" he said again and lay his body across the slab.

"Ramsey?" Josh put his fingers to the older man's neck.

"Stop trying to declare me dead boy!" Ramsey growled at him. "I'm just taking a breather. That's all!"

Josh sat beside the resting figure, concerned about Carlton, concerned about the storm. Trying to figure out the next move. How was he going to get Carlton into Jaintipur if the older man couldn't walk? Why did everything in this country try and break you down, shatter everything you believed about yourself and others?

Carlton sighed, his eyes still closed, oblivious to the falling rain and crackling electric. Josh considered building a temporary shelter but when he got up to collect sticks and leaves Carlton stopped him, so he sat down again. There was so much to admire about Carlton. So much to emulate. He reached out to touch his arm.

"Hey, I ain't dead kid, so bugger off."

"We should be moving on," Josh answered pulling away. The unapproachable bastard would always be the same. He got to his feet.

"I gotta rest some more. You go on. Bring back help."

"No way. I'm not leaving you behind."

Carlton grinned and closed his eyes again as another bolt of lightning sizzled under the swamp of blackened clouds, raising the cackling call of the angry bird that seemed to follow their every move.

13

THE STORM POUNDED AGAINST THE WINDOW of the
bedroom, the wind howling and rattling a staccatoed arhythmic
gospel. Bekah watched the lightning with its flash of sudden faces only
to disappear into the nameless murmur of falling rain. Count the
seconds between light and sound to tell the distance. Ten, fifteen,
twenty. The eye of the storm was a long way away.

She hadn't brought any books with her, thinking that there would
not be any downtime. Time with nothing but worry and helplessness
on her hands. So she had looked around the few scattered bookshelves
in the staff room. War, crime and badly written romance novels —
nothing with heart or soul. She flipped through a romance —
victimisation and rescue with no poetry or crafting. Why were women
always so desperate for the sweeping away of what they were?

She always thought of herself as the rescuer. Another syndrome but
with different consequences. She was sure that was the reason she had
done her Master's degree in social work and sociology. But did she
understand any better how to help people? Not by the look of things
as they stood today, with Maribel hiding from her in her bedroom.

Between the flashes of lightning, darkness slid into the room. The
electricity had gone down for the second time and Rashid had started
tinkering with the back-up generator. The lights blinked on and off
and on and off, undecided. Did they want to stay or not? Then one
light flickered and held. Bekah reached under the bed for her bag,
pulled out her wallet which contained a small photo of Josh, his face
captured as long as the paper retained its strength and colour and the
light continued shining.

She closed her eyes as she held the image between the fingers of both
hands. Josh. She could feel now an imagined breeze on his face. Where
are you? But the answer was shrouded by a frightened garble. Get past

that, she scolded herself then opened her eyes. The game she played refused to work in fear.

There was a tapping at her door. She hoped it would be Habib, sure he had more to say once out from under the domination of Maribel and Rashid. But it was Maribel, tear streaked and clutching a silk robe. "May I come in?"

"Of course. Please have a seat." Bekah gestured coldly to the more comfortable of the two chairs in the room.

"I've been thinking about what happened before." Maribel sat. "I'm sorry. I have no right to take my troubles out on you."

Bekah felt a melting slip and slide from her face, past her shoulders. A melting and a disbelief. "No, it's me who should apologise. Sometimes I mouth off without thinking."

"Anyway, it's irrelevant," Maribel said. "We must try to think of ourselves and our husbands. We must try to win Shumacker to our side so he will put a little more effort into helping us."

Bekah sighed. She didn't see any way of convincing Shumacker, not with all the complications.

"I thought perhaps we could invite him for lunch... or tea," Maribel said.

"You're kidding."

"Of course I'm not. You don't think it's a good idea?"

"Do you think he'd come? What would we say to him? Oh Callahan, come have tea and crumpets with us so we can discuss the ransom?"

Maribel looked offended again. "You think of something then."

"What about this Khalig person? He hasn't answered our fax. Let's send another one."

"No, no, we really ought to stick to the rules. Let Callahan deal with this. Oh I know he seems awful but he isn't. Well, not really. At least he –"

"At least he what?" Bekah shook her head incredulously.

"At least he came to Dhaka."

"That's a great comfort."

"Yes," Maribel said and Bekah for a horrified moment thought Maribel meant it. She waited for clarification but none came.

"Well I think we should contact Khalig again. We're not going over Shumacker's head. We're just getting in touch."

Maribel looked doubtful.

"I'll do it. Neither of you will have to know." Bekah went to the door. "I don't see how it could hurt." She left the room in search of Habib, thinking about the best way to word the fax so this time they received a response.

14

CARLTON SAT UP as another dark cloud extended its long tentacles of mist and touched his face. The bird called again moving back and forth in the trees. Then another similar bird answered.

"We'd better get a move on." Carlton slowly got to his feet. There were two birds now calling to the third that hopped in the trees above them.

Carlton started to move up hill again. "We haven't got that far to go." Every movement he made seemed an effort.

There was a break in the wind. The clouds lingered, flashing, yellow corners around dark weeping stains. There was a shuffling movement on the floor of the jungle, just to the right of them. Another bird called or laughed or screamed. Josh could not tell — sounds were beginning to merge, to become menacing. Carlton gripped his arm.

"What is it?" Josh whispered.

"This isn't right." Carlton pulled at him. There was another scream, then an echo of laughter. First behind, then in front. The leaves suddenly smacked apart. A body hurtled towards them, waving the heavy gun, the head covered with a bright red balaclava.

Behind them another scream and another masked guard jumped out.

"Don't do anything stupid." Carlton knelt down.

The first soldier leaped towards Josh butting him in the guts, bringing him to his knees beside Carlton, boots kicking, networks of pain spreading through his body as the boot came in again and again.

When they finished, Josh opened his eyes but didn't move. Carlton was lying sideways on the rock. The guards had taken off their ski-masks and were laughing gently as they passed a cigarette between them. It was Genghis and The Wrath.

He slowly moved his hand, inch by inch, to where Carlton lay. Genghis jumped up brought the tip of the gun-barrel to his mouth. He waited. Carlton had not moved. The Wrath bent down and tugged at Carlton's still form which didn't respond.

"Let me," Josh said, getting to his knees. He inched towards Carlton until he reached him, despite Genghis' threats. He leaned over the older man and checked for a pulse. He was still alive. But for how much longer? He tried to get Carlton to sit up.

"Bloody hell," he heard the old man say, "I was having a fine dream."

"I bet," Josh said, bringing Carlton's arm around his shoulder, and despite his own infirmities managed to lift him up.

They shoved them into the hut but left the hatch open so the mosquitos could come in and have their meal. But Josh needed to be closed in now, invisible to the guards' gleaming, hateful eyes. Wanted the darkness as if it would ease the assault of pain.

Despite the wetness of his clothing, he was sweating heavily. There was a fever lingering over him, as the storm had done hours before. A pain in his gut jolted him forward and he gagged, river water coming from between his lips.

"Why don't they close it?" Josh wiped the acid from his mouth.

"Because they're spooking us, it gives 'em pleasure."

The pain pulsed again as Josh pushed his fist into the soreness of his stomach.

"Take it easy, Josh. Don't lose it yet. We've got a ways to go."

Josh rolled onto his side, losing track of the last wisps of diminishing light, the gusts of rain that blew in.

Something whacked against the wall over his head.

He sat up, startled. It was a can of soda. Genghis dropped another one by Carlton's feet along with two food trays. Carlton pulled the food over. He opened the box and stared at the contents with disgust then pushed it over to Josh who ignored it.

"You gotta keep your strength up Josh," Carlton said weakly.

Josh shook his head. "Can't do it."

"Look." Carlton dragged the tray closer. "I'll eat if you do."

Josh looked over at the older man. He'd cut his lip — when he'd hit the rock. That was all. The guards hadn't even touched him. Maybe that was good. Maybe Carlton wouldn't have survived the punishment they were giving to him. Maybe Carlton knew a way around it and wasn't letting on.

"Come on Josh, eat up." Carlton's voice was getting stronger as he drank the soda.

Josh lifted the tray, his hand shaking. He saw Carlton notice then turn away.

"What do you think they'll do next?" Josh asked.

"I don't know what their plan is." Carlton opened his food tray. Using the spoon, he took a mouthful. "Well, the bloody food's not getting any better. They need a new chef." He put the box on the floor and pushed it away again.

Josh stared at his companion. How could he still make jokes? He forced the food into his mouth using his filthy fingers. Carlton looked at him again, this time his mouth twisted in disgust. What was he thinking? As the food slid down Josh's throat he choked, feeling the vomit rinsing into his mouth. Carlton had picked up his own tray again and took another taste of the rice.

'You should eat it,' Josh heard his mother's voice, could feel her standing over him, her fingers interweaving into his throat, reaching into his sinews and twisting. 'Eat! Look what's happened to you. Look what happens when you marry out of your faith, try and go your own way. When you turn away from your God. Fallen. Fallen angel, separated from the one you love.'

But the one he loved wasn't God. It was Bekah. She was more real. The image of her overwhelmed him. Bekah? Where was she? He closed his eyes, let the pain ease as he imagined her. She felt so close. So close. He snapped his eyes open. Carlton was staring at him.

Josh shivered as if the temperature had plummeted. The inside of the hut became a blur. Insects buzzed near his ear, landed on his nose. He could barely move his arm to push them away.

Carlton reached over, grabbed both trays and tossed them out the door, then he came back and sat in silence — darkness and a slight breeze mixed with a new sound: the faint intoning of prayer from the guards outside.

"One minute they're kicking the stuffing out of you," Carlton said angrily, "the next they're praying to their God to have mercy. What a bunch of idiots."

To Josh's ear, the rhythm was much the same as in the synagogue: that rocking and moaning. He crossed his arms, hugging himself, trying to get the warmth back into his body. Against his will, the rhythmic moaning drew him in, compelling him to join soundlessly.

"You ever pray?" Carlton stretched his legs out.

"Why?"

"I'm just asking. I don't believe in it myself. My wife, she says she prays, but to tell you the truth I don't think she ever gets any answers."

"That's because it's all wishful thinking."

"I don't know. It's probably a good thing to do. As a Jew you should be real close to your God, aren't you?"

"Fuck off Ramsey!" Josh lunged forward, clutching his stomach.

"What the hell did I say? Jesus, you sure are one of the most touchy kids I've ever met!"

Josh staggered to his feet. The praying outside had reached a lamenting intensity. He leaned out of the hatch gasping for breath. There was a candle lit inside the other hut, the light gleaming out of the door. The prayer abruptly ceased replaced by a murmur of voices as the candle was snuffed.

"Well what did I say?" Ramsey insisted.

"Nothing, forget it."

"No, I won't forget it. You've got a chip on your shoulder. There's no room for that b.s. here."

"Take a look at your own life Ramsey before you criticise mine."

"I don't know what you mean by that," Carlton groused back.

Genghis appeared, leered into the hut then slammed the door.

"What I mean is that you're a bigoted old bastard. Do you get it now?"

Carlton didn't respond as Josh leaned against the bolted hatch.

The older man sighed sadly.

"I didn't mean that," Josh murmured. "I apologise."

"You said what you felt kid. I can take it."

"I haven't got any right to talk to you that way." Josh slumped to the ground.

"You do have the right. Hell, in this hut, we're total equals."

Josh shook his head. They weren't equals here or anywhere. What illusion of denial was Carlton living? Sweat dripped from his face pouring down his neck. Words could no longer make a difference. He stretched his legs and reached for the can of soda, pressing his fingers into the metal to try and abate the pain. His stomach churned as the fizzy sweet syrup ran down his throat.

Something slithered over his hand then scuttled onto his leg. He jumped up, crying out, hitting his head against the rafters.

"Calm down son!" Carlton shouted.

Josh threw himself against the hatch.

"Josh!" Carlton shouted again.

He smashed against the hatch again.

"Sit down." Carlton gripped his arm dragging him downward.

Josh heard himself whimpering like a wounded animal. Carlton's voice went on and on. He was saying things that Josh couldn't understand. Josh closed his eyes and shivered again, felt a hand on his shoulder biting into his muscles.

"It's okay Josh," Carlton was saying. "It's okay. Those lizards are helping to keep us alive. They eat the spiders and the mozzies. That's a good thing."

Josh pushed the caring hand away. "I'm not feeling too good," he sniffled, wiping his running nose on his hand, then pushed his back against the wall trying with everything he had to suppress his anguish. His intestines churned violently, forcing an uncontrollable strain in his bowels. Clutching his stomach he got up and again began to pound on the wood.

Carlton too started hammering on the wall with his shoe, shouting for them to open up.

Another spasm lurched through Josh's intestines. He heard his voice join in with Carlton's begging the guards to let him out. He didn't hear the bolts scraping. When the hatch opened he fell over, found himself crawling in the mud, heard the sound of laughter again.

He managed to get his trousers down, grasped at his underpants. The liquid was hot and burning. It poured out of his ass and spewed from his throat. He grabbed at a branch to steady himself and threw up again.

He heard the laughter, knew they were trying to shame him, make him lose his dignity. He grabbed at some leaves, wiped himself and then felt the torrential filth pour from him again.

15

THE MORNING CAME SADLY, another night passed without a word. Interminable time. Just before breakfast, Bekah went to sit in the staff room. Habib brought her a fax. It was worded succinctly.

"I have been ordered by a higher authority not to have any contact with you. My apologies. Khalig."

No contact from Khalig. No contact from Shumacker. Should she now write to Ershad? Dear President, please find my husband for me and rescue him. Please, please, someone help me. She hadn't been brought up to believe that someone miraculous would suddenly appear to help. She had to do it for herself. That's what Momma always said. 'Get up and do it yourself.'

But what to do? And who to ask? Only Maribel and Shumacker held any of the answers to her questions and she had successfully alienated both of them. Maribel had been right. She was a fool and couldn't help it.

There were voices in the hall. The distinct southern twang of Shumacker's belligerence intermingled with the consoling tones of Habib.

"Mrs. Felstein." Shumacker strode into the Staff Room.

"You have news?" She stood to meet him.

"I'll wait for Mrs. Ramsey if that's all right with you," and he indicated for Habib to go and fetch her.

Within moments Maribel hurried in.

"Callahan, I'm so grateful you've come."

"Look ladies." Shumacker ignored the woman's gratitude. "I've now had the chance to consult with all the authorities. We're going to have a country wide search for the two men. With the floods coming there are only a number of places they can be discreetly held away from the general population. We're going to target those areas first."

Thank you Lord, Bekah whispered to herself, then realised what the man hadn't said. "And the money?"

"We're still negotiating."

It was something. They were doing something.

"I wish there was something that I could do," Bekah exclaimed.

"I've tried to be candid with you Mrs. Felstein. Nothing seems to get through. You can only cause trouble if you do anything. Just sit still and wait."

"He's right," Maribel chipped in. "Callahan, I'm sorry if we said anything yesterday to upset you. You must realise –"

He interrupted her. "Forget it Maribel. What's past is past."

"Yes, but –"

Shumacker strode to the door. "I've kept my part of the promise ladies. I expect you to keep yours. Sit tight, your husbands will be back sooner than you think."

His footsteps receded, from the marble hallway onto the slabs of stone in the front garden. The door swung shut and Habib appeared to guide them into the dining room. But neither were hungry as they sat across from each other.

"Why do you apologise to him?" Bekah pulled at her napkin angrily.

"We were rude. Apologies are a necessary social custom," Maribel replied.

"Not in these circumstances they're not."

"Habib." Maribel lifted her hand. "I just want coffee, that's it."

"But Missis, you not eat for two days. Eat something."

Maribel looked at him coldly. "You heard what I said."

"Lord's sake Maribel," Bekah leaned over as Habib dashed out of the room. "The boy is being kind. Why do you treat him this way?"

"What way?"

"You're kidding!"

"Habib is a servant. You don't get chummy with servants. Learn girl. This is expatriate life!"

"He's a person," Bekah responded.

"An employee. Is that better? We pay him."

"You don't pay him enough to treat him that way."

Maribel turned her face away, sighing in displeasure. Then she clasped her hands together and looked to the ceiling as if that would give her guidance. "This is not your world, my dear. Therefore you cannot impose your own moral or personal codes on it. What you think of as right may very well turn out to be wrong."

"So you're saying that there are certain situations where you can be rude and abusive to other people and it's socially and morally correct?"

"I am not being rude to him."

"But you are."

"I am merely letting him know the rules of employer to employee. He appreciates it."

Habib entered carrying coffee. He poured Maribel a cup. "Thank you," she said sourly.

Habib moved over to Bekah's side and offered her a cup of coffee.

"Do you perhaps have any juice or herb tea? Coffee's not good for baby," she asked apologetically.

Habib bent close to her, his voice low in her ear. "You no worry Missis, Habib takes care of himself."

"I beg your pardon," Maribel interrupted.

Bekah couldn't help but smile. Habib was like she was, but more tactful with it.

"Only telling Mrs. Josh what tea we have." He smiled and left the room.

"Insolent boy." Maribel sipped at her coffee but her eyes showed a dislike that went far beyond the situation.

16

CARLTON WATCHED as the morning finally crept in through the gash in the wall as the sun broke through heavy monsoon clouds. Josh stirred again, groaning. He was passing wind and the stench was sickening. Carlton wanted to gag in the stifling of the hot air, getting closer every minute.

At least the pains in his arms and chest had finally subsided. The fresh air must have done him the world of good since it hadn't finished him off. Don't get too optimistic, he grumbled, there's still more good times for the guards around the corner. He'd have to be more cautious next time, neither he nor the kid were weathering this match too well.

Where's that cigar? He searched around for it. The thing was covered with mud so he wiped it on his shirt. It tasted foul but he didn't care. It gave him something to do.

He'd had a rough night. What with the sweeping rain along the roof, Josh knocking the pain of his gut against the walls, and his own heart intermittently racing and slowing making him feel that this was the bloody end for sure. Not even getting the chance to say goodbye to the people he loved.

Maribel. It was his heart aching for her. She was a part of him and it had taken him this long to realise it. She'd had no right to abandon him. And look where it had landed him. Half dead and nursing a sick boy.

The bolts scraped easier. They must have oiled them. The hatch swung open. Genghis and The Wrath — this time without those absurd woollen ski masks. He longed for the comparative relief of Tweedledee and Dum. Genghis signalled him to stay put.

He smiled determined to show them his strength. "Good morning fellas," he said. Let them think he was feeling great. Enjoying himself. What a holiday.

A voice behind the guards startled him. It sounded like Khalig's! He stood up slowly, warily, accustoming himself to the glaring light.

"Out! Both of you!"

Carlton tried to see the speaker but the voice was hidden behind the guards. "I've got to wake the boy." He stalled for time.

"Now!" He ignored the command and stiffly knelt by Josh's side. "Josh get up. We've got visitors."

Josh stirred. His face was sheet white and feverish. "What?"

"I can't lift you Josh, you've got to try and stand on your own."

Josh tried to sit up and swayed backwards, his breathing heavy and irregular. He tried again, managed to get onto his feet. Carlton grabbed his arm and ushered him to the door, but no sooner was the boy out than Genghis knocked him down, tying a blindfold over his eyes.

Carlton was next. There was just a glimpse of the man before Genghis wrapped a cloth around his eyes too. He was dressed as an officer and it wasn't Khalig!

"I am told you have been giving my men trouble."

Carlton willed his eyes to see through the cloth. "Just a few health problems is all. Nothing serious that death won't solve."

Josh suddenly groaned.

"And, what is your problem, young man?"

Carlton broke in, "He's got cholera, or dengue. What does it look like to you?"

The officer dropped his voice. He said something to the guards. Carlton strained to hear what was being said, perhaps he could catch a word or two.

"A little cholera never hurt anyone, Mr. Ramsey," the officer said. "You've got more pressing things to worry about."

"Surely you must have some salt solution you can give him! I've given away enough of it."

The officer mumbled something again. Carlton heard the shuffle of feet.

Moments later the officer said, "Drink it!"

Carlton heard his charge fumbling with a bottle, then the sound of gulping.

"And you, Mr. Ramsey? Why do you need a doctor?"

"I suffer from heart trouble."

"You are surviving."

"It seems so."

"Your people are not as eager for your release as they should be. Perhaps we will encourage them with a small token."

Carlton froze.

"What do you suggest?" the officer asked.

"Why don't you negotiate with them?" Josh mumbled angrily.

The officer laughed. "Yes, twenty percent off for every finger."

Carlton swore under his breath willing Josh to keep his mouth shut. They were doomed. Josh's foot was bad enough. In their condition any amputation meant certain death within days. "Why don't you send them our clothing," he suggested calmly, knowing if he showed fear they would be goners. He heard the rustle of a well starched military uniform.

"Clothing?" the officer mocked him. "A bit soft, don't you think. What about the boy's ear? It's an artistic touch and we are an artistic people."

"I would say our clothing is more dramatic, more insidious. It would have greater impact," Carlton countered.

The officer laughed. Carlton had always got along with this type. Thought he had enjoyed them.

"A finger from the boy then," the officer suggested.

"You're a fool if you do that."

"Oh yes?"

"What use are we to you dead?"

"The boy is incidental."

"He keeps me alive." Carlton felt every muscle in his body twitching as the officer consulted with his men.

"We are not a cruel people you know Mr. Ramsey. Of course we would prefer not to harm either of you but we are in desperate circumstances. Had your company not nourished the dictatorship of Ershad you would not be here now."

Carlton didn't want to argue politics. He just wanted to keep them both alive. Ershad had replaced a dictator and would be replaced by the same. "You've got to give them time to go through their bureaucracy," he said. "It's a big company they need to do a lot of talking."

"Yes, bureaucracies are always cumbersome. I'm in a charitable mood... for now." The officer continued, "We will send them your... shall we say, your trousers... yes, but let us make it a little more dramatic than that."

The guards were moving.

They grabbed Josh! The boy was struggling!

Carlton lunged forward grabbing in the blindness, catching hold of someone's arm. He was knocked backwards and shouted, "Leave the boy alone!"

He heard the laughter, then the ripping of cloth.

Josh screamed out! They were stabbing him! Jesus God, they were murdering him!

Carlton charged forward again, yanking at his blindfold. Something smashed down on his head. Under the blindfold, he caught a glint of light coming from a dagger bearing down on him!

Involuntarily he cried out.

The voice came closer. He could feel the warmth of the moist breath tarnishing his skin. "Tomorrow will be more serious."

The voice pulled away and said something to his guards and then in clipped English, "If you will gentlemen. Undress!"

Carlton was yanked up. He unbuttoned then unzipped the trousers, letting them fall to his ankles. He strained to hear what they were doing to the boy. Then he heard material ripping again.

"Well done," the officer said sarcastically. "I'm sure your wives will be glad to receive them."

"Wives?" Josh called out.

Jesus, Carlton slumped with relief. The boy was still alive!

"Yes," the officer continued. "I am informed that they are both in Dhaka campaigning for your release. Let us all hope they are not as foolish as they first appear.

Carlton was shoved into the hut as he pulled his blindfold off. He fell on his arm. They bundled Josh in and he tried to stop the boy's fall. The hatch was bolted.

"You all right son? Did they cut you bad?"

"It's…"

"Where are you cut? Damn it, I can't see!"

"My thigh… It's just superficial… Shit!"

"Jesus! How bad are you, son?"

The boy was sighing, catching his breath in gulps which sounded as if he were weeping. It was terrible!

"Now look Josh, you've got to fight it. If it's only a cut we can take care of it. Physical pain is nothing if you can keep your spirit strong."

The boy seemed to stop his panting.

Carlton took the leaves out of his pocket and broke them between his fingers. He touched Josh on his foot.

"Take these leaves. Spread them over your cut. Let them sit there awhile. Are you bleeding badly? Josh? Answer me for Christ's sake!"

"Hurts pretty bad," the boy whispered, the voice a child's.

"Damn!" Carlton searched around for the remains of the shirt. He pulled at the material, ripping a strip. "Take this and bind it real tight. Do you hear me? You rest now but let me know if it doesn't stop bleeding."

Carlton sat in his corner. He couldn't keep his heart from storming against the cage of ribs. The words of the officer revolved in his head. Maribel was in Dhaka. And the bastard said wives, wives instead of wife? Wasn't Josh's wife about to have a baby? Is that what he meant about foolish?

He looked over at his companion, could make out the forlorn silhouette slumped against the wood. Poor kid was taking the brunt of the punishment. Relief and guilt were becoming all too common bed partners. He wanted to comfort Josh but he didn't know how. What if he just talked? Maybe that would help clear the misery.

"Josh, have I told you about the time I was held hostage in Karachi in '79 when the locals broke into the company building?"

"No," Josh responded dismally.

"Damnedest thing! I was in the loo when it happened and I had no idea what was going on."

Carlton rubbed his chest again and prodded himself on. "I was walking back to my office and there were dozens of Pakistanis running through the hallways. Crazy looking they were, picking up everything that wasn't nailed down. They ignored me though, as if I wasn't there."

Carlton paused. Was the kid conscious? "Josh?"

"Then what happened?" Josh whispered.

"I walked past a few offices, you know, looking around. There was no one about. Well there should have been a whole office full of people.

"Another group of Pakistanis ran by, some were armed. This was no joke. Something had happened. You know it was about the time the Ayatollah's people were holding those Americans in Tehran. The rescue Carter botched up so badly."

He heard Josh sigh. The boy probably wasn't interested but he continued anyway.

"I went back to my office to try and find out what was happening, but just as I got inside this young punk smashed the door open waving a rifle. You know the kind of big shot kid that's never touched a weapon before in his life and he thinks its a broom stick. So he forces me out of the office and pushes me into the conference room where the rest of my buddies are being held.

"The secretaries are bawling their eyes out. This crazy kid, he starts shouting something about CIA agents, as if we had anything to do with politics. You know, the one thing I've learned in my days as an oil man is that oil exploration is not just another business, it's a venue for politicians and rabble rousers. That's why we're here." He stopped speaking. If the kid really wasn't interested he wouldn't continue.

Josh moved his leg brushing Carlton with his foot, "How did you get out?" he said, so low Carlton could only just hear it. The kid had been listening!

"Damnedest thing! The Pakistani starts shooting into the room and we hit the floor, secretaries and all. He lets out one round after another shooting at the windows, the walls, anything he can hit. Glass is crashing everywhere, wood's splintering and then the rifle is empty and he runs out of the room.

"Tim Howard, you'll probably meet him one day, was the first one up. I was close on his heels. He grabs a chair and bolts it under the door handle, then we start stacking the tables and every damned thing against those doors. It was a miracle no one'd been killed."

"How long were you in there for?" Josh's voice was stronger. Now Carlton was getting somewhere.

"Two hours."

"So, it's not like this?"

"No son, it's nothing like this."

"So, you don't know if we're going to make it?"

"We'll be fine." How could he make it sound convincing when he didn't believe in his own words? "I'll tell you what. Why don't we build a catchment area for the water that's running through here. That way we can use it to dress your wounds or wash our hands if they don't let us bathe. What do you say?"

"I don't know."

"Come on it'll take your mind off the pain." His insistence took on a desperate note.

Josh sighed. What was the kid thinking? Was he gonna give up this easy? Sure he'd had some knocks, some pretty bad ones. Was he yellow bellied, like Carlton's own son? Giving up at the least bit of pain?

"Look kid, you learn to fight your corner or you're nothing. You understand me?"

Josh didn't answer.

"Kid?" Carlton reached out, ready to shake some sense into him. "Joe!" he shook Josh's shoulder. "Joe do you hear me?"

"My name's not Joe." Josh pushed him away

"What?"

"It isn't Joe and it isn't Kid."

"I didn't call you Joe." Carlton sat back confused, his hand on his heart.

"That's your son's name isn't it?" Josh said softly.

"You must have heard wrong Josh," Carlton mumbled then started scraping a hole in the floor where the water could collect whenever it rained.

17

THE PACKAGE ARRIVED at the front door wrapped in ARM cardboard and fishing line. It was Habib who found it. It was addressed to Mrs. C. Ramsey.

"Begum!" Habib ran up the stairs carrying the box. "Begum. Big box for you!"

Maribel rushed out of her room onto the landing. She knew instinctively after one look where it had come from.

He handed her the box. It stunk of sweat and excrement. She choked, dropping the thing onto the floor. Her knees gave way and she grabbed hold of the railing, staring at the package, knowing what might be in it. A finger, or an ear...

Bekah put a hand gently on her shoulder. But it didn't help. She couldn't stop shaking. That dreadful box. Did it mean that Carlton was dead?

"What is it?" Bekah whispered.

"I can't bear it!" Maribel wailed. "What if they've..."

Bekah stared at the package, "We'll get Shumacker to open it." She knelt down to pick it up, shuddering as the odour hit. She grabbed the string and straightened slowly, stiffly, letting the box dangle lopsidedly by the fishing line in her hand.

They went downstairs and put it on the table by the phone. The package seemed to have a life of its own. A horrible, horrible life, as if it were about to spring open, splattering them with the thing that caused the awful smell.

Maribel lifted the receiver to dial Shumacker's number. Her hand trembled violently. Bekah took the phone and dialled.

"Mr. Shumacker?" Bekah's voice shook.

"What do you want?" Shumacker's answer was loud enough for Maribel to hear.

"We've got a package from the kidnappers."

Three was a pause on the other end. Then he said, "Have you opened it?"

"No, we can't bear to."

"Well what does it look like? What size is it?"

"What difference does its size make?"

"Look, you. Answer my questions. Do you understand?"

"Why can't you just come here and see for yourself instead of your stupid –" Maribel grabbed the phone.

"Callahan! Please come over and deal with this!"

Callahan Shumacker arrived with an air of authority which, despite herself, immediately made Maribel feel safer. The parcel was sitting on the staff room coffee table. He went over to it and pulled at the string to untie it. It wouldn't open and he commanded Habib to bring him a pair of scissors.

Before cutting the string, he looked at Maribel. His eyes were troubled and bloodshot. For a moment she detected a hint of compassion. Then he glanced at Bekah. His expression hardened. As the string was cut, the parcel fell open. Shumacker's face contorted with disgust.

"Carlton!" her husband's name flung itself from her mouth. They were just his trousers. She couldn't bear the relief. "Callahan, please bring him back to me!"

Callahan lifted the trousers, rummaging through the pockets, scraps of leaves falling out.

"There's no note," he said.

"They are the note," Bekah whispered hoarsely. She reached out taking hold of the ugly checked trousers Josh's mother had given him. She ran the material almost dreamily through her fingers, remembering what she had told him before he'd left. 'Ruin them.' Lord why had she said such a stupid thing. A stain on the material caught her eye. What was it? She looked closer! "No!"

Shumacker grabbed at it then he too recoiled. Agitated, he hurried to the window, pulled the curtain aside and stared outside.

"First the trousers," Bekah chanted, "Then something more valuable. When are you going to pay the money?"

Shumacker's face was haggard as he turned to face her tears. He said, "Standex has been advised not to give into the kidnapper's demands. It sets a precedent. I'm sorry."

From somewhere inside but somehow beyond her, Bekah felt a contempt which came out undisguised. "You mean Ershad's threatened

159

to kick you out of Bangladesh if you supply his enemies with funds."

"Not now Mrs. Felstein," Shumacker replied.

"We know what you're up against, Shumacker," she continued. "If you pay, you lose your contracts and if you don't we lose our husbands. Is that right? Don't you think their lives are worth more than some stupid fucking oil field?"

Shumacker glared, "You have no idea what this is about. No idea and so you should keep your mouth shut until you do!"

"I'm not planning on keeping my mouth shut, or staying put while you sit around on your fat Southern ass doing jack all!"

"Look you!" Shumacker menaced.

"Callahan!" Maribel rushed between them, fingers tight on the man's arm.

As he stared down at her, he said, "Belle, try and explain to this, this... how things work out here. She seems not to be able to comprehend even the simplest things! Maybe you can make her understand!"

Maribel looked up at him. "I don't understand either Callahan. Explain it to me."

"This isn't only about your precious husband. It's about the company! What they want! And I can't win! It's my reputation, my career too!"

His own reputation! That's what he was concerned with! She had not realised what depths the man had sunk to in his jealousy and the need for his petty revenge. But it had little to do with him anyway. He was right. It was up to the Company to pay, not him. But what was she to do?

"I demand that you pay that ransom!" Bekah pushed Maribel aside.

"Shut up!" he lunged towards her. "I've told you before. Any more scenes from you and you're on the next plane."

"That's what you think. I step foot back in the U.S. and every newspaper between here and New York City knows about it."

Shumacker smirked. "That's fine. And we'll bring your husband's mutilated body back in a bag for you."

Bekah gasped.

Shumacker turned to the window again, brushing the net curtains aside as if there were someone watching or waiting outside. When he faced them again he seemed calmer. "This is a terrible situation for all of us. Let's try and put our best foot forward. The army have swept the south of the country and are moving into the Dhaka area,"

Shumacker said with a kinder assurance.

"But everyone knows they're in the north!" Bekah exclaimed.

"Now she's an expert on military matters as well!" Shumacker clenched his fists. "Get her out of here before I do something I'll regret!"

"But Callahan," Maribel said. "She's right. They were taken in Shylet, the faxes came from Jaintipur. Do you think they've moved them around in this weather? Surely they're on high ground."

Shumacker paused for a moment as if he saw the sense in what she was saying. Then he shook his head. "We have to do it the army's way. They're the experts."

"You don't want them rescued do you?" Bekah shouted. "You don't care. It's nothing to you. You'd be happy if they were dead. You're nothing but a –"

Maribel grabbed her sleeve. "Shut up. You don't know what you're saying. Callahan, she's hysterical. Please do as you think best. Just find them!"

Callahan pressed his fist into the palm of his other hand as Bekah slumped into the chair, wrapping the bloodied cloth round and round her fingers, tears mixing with the brick red dust.

"You don't understand how the Company's operating these days Belle. You've lost touch. We're all expendable now. It's hire and fire at a whim. Not like in the old days. One wrong move and you're out."

Maribel didn't answer. She knew of the phone call he had made to Carlton, knew how he had broken the news of his retirement.

"You'll have to live with this for the rest of your life Callahan. You make the best decision for yourself," Maribel answered, kneeling by the girl.

"But this time it'll be me making those choices," Shumacker answered.

Maribel looked up at him startled.

"You self pitying bastard!" Bekah spat through gritted teeth. "You're willing to see two men die just because some woman jilted you over twenty years ago?"

Callahan jumped forward, his hand swinging downward, but instead of hitting Bekah he thumped the back of the chair. Bekah made no move — except to fix her eyes on him in a cold steady stare.

"Callahan please!" Maribel jumped up, "These are extraordinary conditions. No one is acting normally. Forget what's been said and done. Please help us! I beg you!"

Callahan drew back, his breath shallow and frequent. "If you want help, Maribel," he said, now turning to the door, "then call the Rottweiler off."

Bekah pressed her face into her hands. What kind of idiot was she, losing her cool like that? Pushing Shumacker beyond his capacity? Not in all the days in University, not in all the times that she had stood in front of an all white, all male exam board, not when she had gone to battle with Josh's mother had she ever stumbled so often and so badly.

"I'm so sorry dear." Maribel's warm hand rested on her shoulder.

"You're right, I don't have the experience to handle this."

"I know it sounds terrible but the best thing to do is leave it to the men. They're much more experienced in these things."

"I'm sorry I just can't believe that."

"You must. That's the way of the world."

"Your world. I just hate this passivity, this waiting for something terrible to happen!" Bekah banged her fist against the chair.

Maribel picked up her husband's trousers feeling the material between her fingers. Her eyes filled with tears. "There's nothing we can do," she said and when Bekah didn't respond, left the room.

Bekah rested her head against the back of the chair. She was so tired her whole body ached. Why was it so wrong to fight for Josh's life? To want to be pro-active. Wasn't that the normal way of behaving?

Was Shumacker so filled with hate that he had to attack her? A Rotweiler. A vicious black bitch. Didn't she have enough strength of character to ward off such attacks?

She lifted her chin, extending the taut muscles of her neck to ease the tension. 'Joshua,' she whispered and tried to sense him. No matter how she concentrated, all she could see was darkness.

She tried to visualise him now. So helpless, so vulnerable. Her man. Her sweet helpless man. What have they done to you?

How she wished her mother were there to advise her, to guide her through the labyrinth of politics and personal grudges that seemed to motivate all that Shumacker did and said. She had never felt so discarded. What a silly child she had been, convinced that she had already met the real world and conquered it. Momma, she cried to herself and felt the baby shift.

Her eyes closed, the tears fell as they would. There was nowhere she could turn, no one who could really advise her.

'Now Bekah honey.'

"Momma?"

'You've got to keep fighting! Keep fighting...' The words echoed and were gone.

But how? How could she keep fighting? It was like punching into air. She made no contact. There was no one to turn to, no decisions she could take on her own. But... Wait!

She sat upright! Of course! Money talked the whole world round! She would phone Josh's family. They'd wire her enough money to start. And she would drain her own savings! Maribel might raise quite a bit. They could buy information, find out where Josh and Carlton were.

She stood up, panting with excitement. Of course! Oh Lord, that's crazy. Calm down. Think it out. If she could get Khalig on her side he would know what to do.

She rushed to the phone, dialled his number. Miraculously it rang through and Khalig answered it.

"Look," she said. "I know you're not supposed to talk with me. But nothing's being done here. What if I raised a lot of money? Couldn't we buy information?"

Khalig sighed on the other end. Even with the bad connection, Bekah heard the inner argument. Then he said, "How much can you raise?"

"Ten, maybe twenty thousand dollars."

"I see," his voice became stronger. "Yes," he paused thoughtfully. "But you mustn't let on to Shumacker or any Company representative that you've approached me."

"That's not a problem," Bekah said

"Well then, I think we can do business."

"What are you doing?" Maribel appeared as she put the phone down.

"I've got a plan. But you don't have to have any thing to do with it."

"What plan? What are you suggesting? Oh my goodness, you are the most obstinate –"

Bekah walked away.

"Stop!" Maribel called. "I insist you tell me."

Bekah faced the opposition. "You must promise me that you won't mention it to Shumacker or anyone else. If you can't promise me that, don't ask."

"You foolish girl, this isn't a child's game."

"No promise, no information." Bekah started walking away again.

"I promise. Oh God, what are you getting up to now?"

Bekah took a deep breath then faced the older woman, "I've just talked to Khalig. He may be able to buy information."

"But we've been forbidden!"

"Tell me, what have I got to lose?"

"All that you have. These people are not what you think."

"Who? Who are these people? Shumacker? Standex? Who are these nameless demons you keep referring to?"

"Not us. Not them. These people."

"Garbage," Bekah answered.

"Bekah, listen to me. You must tell Callahan if you're going to use your own money to buy information," Maribel pleaded.

"No way!"

"You must!" She reached out to the wall, holding herself up.

"He won't do a damned thing. You know that."

"You're wrong. You misjudge him. He has his hands tied."

"That's right, he does, so it's time we took some action. How much money can you raise?"

"You're mad!" Maribel pushed herself harder against the wall.

"I'll do it myself."

Maribel crept away from her as if she, Bekah, were a mad woman and must be escaped from.

Bekah hurried after, scolding, "What's the alternative, Maribel? Do you want to wait to see if Shumacker is going to do anything for us? Do you think he's in a great rush?"

"You don't understand anything!" The older woman stopped running.

"Oh I do. I do understand and I'm not going to sit on my ass waiting for someone who doesn't give a shit!"

Maribel gasped then ran up the stairs slamming the door of her bedroom.

No matter. Bekah was past the point of caring. She phoned her brother-in-law over and over again until finally she got through. No, he too didn't agree with her. But he had no counter argument. It would seem as if he was signing his own brother's death warrant if he didn't give her what she asked for.

She faxed her own bank, emptied her savings. She'd raised enough to start her own campaign. It was a beginning. She phoned Khalig again. He suggested she come north and she went upstairs to pack her bags.

18

JOSH'S FEVER CAME BACK IN THE NIGHT.

The rain had stopped and the hole they had dug and sealed with a food container was almost empty of water. They should have saved more. The hut was moist and warm. Too warm. The skin under Carlton's arms had broken out in a rash. He yearned for the relief of the river. If only Tweedledum and Tweedledee would return.

Carlton chuckled despite himself. Maribel used to recite to the children when they were young:

> *Tweedledum and Tweedledee*
> *Agreed to have a battle;*
> *For Tweedledum said Tweedledee*
> *had spoiled his nice new rattle.*
> *Just then flew down a monstrous crow,*
> *As black as a tar-barrel;*
> *Which frightened both the heroes so,*
> *They quite forgot their quarrel.*

"Ramsey?" Josh's feverish voice called out. "Got to go again. I don't think I can get up."

"All right son, just hold on. Let's see if I can get you out."

Carlton grabbed a shoe and started pounding on the wall closest to the guard's hut. Josh tried miserably to crawl towards the hatch.

Poor kid! Carlton stooped down and helped Josh to his feet and then pounded the wall again. He could feel the heat of the fever rolling off the kid. He hoped to hell the guards would bring in more of that salt solution before it was too late.

The hatch opened. It was Genghis and he was nasty faced. Josh climbed out and fell to the ground. Genghis kicked and cursed him.

"Hold on, can't you see the boy's ill?" Carlton shoved himself through the hole and stooped over Josh. The boy had shat himself. Carlton could smell it through the underpants.

"Christ!"

"I'm sorry!" Josh struggled to his feet.

"Forget it kid." Carlton looked at Genghis. Wrath of Khan was nowhere around. If only there were some way to grab the weapon without getting them both killed. Genghis seemed to sense his thoughts. He gripped the shaft of the machine gun tighter, twisting his shoulders sideways. He spat some words and Carlton assumed he was telling them to move.

"I need water," he said, "Look, pani, for Christ's sake!"

Genghis called over his shoulder and Wrath of Khan appeared. Then Genghis screeched out something else and the Wrath disappeared into the shadows returning some moments later with a bucket and a cloth. He carried it to the side of the hut and pointed.

Carlton grabbed Josh's arm, dragging him upward.

"I'm sorry!" Josh repeated.

"Come on boy, don't let the side down now. We've got water and a towel. What more can a guy ask for, eh?"

He dragged Josh to the side of the hut and propped him up against the wall.

"Don't," Josh begged. "Please! I can do it myself!"

"Forget your pride, Josh."

"I can do it!"

Carlton pulled the soap from his pocket and stuck it in the boys hand then he moved away and listened as Josh sloshed the water around. He looked about him. The leaves were dripping with moisture and they were thick and fleshy. Good enough to chew. It was such a relief to get in the open air. The hut had begun to smell of vomit and infected flesh and he was gradually yielding to the belief that it was becoming more like a coffin. His and most probably Josh's.

These moments of reprieve were a blessing. He never thought he'd be so easily pleased with a gulp of air and a drop of cool water on his face. Maybe tomorrow Tweedledee would be back and they'd be allowed to return to the river.

At least there was something to look forward to.

Josh, holding on to the roof of the hut, made his way to the front. He was still wearing his underpants.

"Have you washed?" Carlton asked.

"Yes," Josh said weakly.

"That's good son." But Carlton wished the boy had stayed away longer. What he wanted more than anything else in the world was to postpone the time he had to return to the cloistered cell. But Genghis grew impatient as soon as Josh appeared and beckoned them to return. They handed Josh another bottle of water with salts. Christ that was something!

He reluctantly climbed in first and then helped his charge stumble back to his mat. The hatch was bolted and without warning the sudden darkness gripped Carlton with fear. He had to get out. The place was choking him to death. He fought the feeling as hard as he could but the harder he struggled against it the larger it loomed. It was the fetid air; his limbs screaming out with stiffness, the lack of movement, couldn't bear to be locked together with this boy who, in his pain, brought the guilt of his own inadequacies rushing up to meet him.

He pushed himself downward. Hard against the floor. Groped around for his cigar. Found the case and rolled it back and forth, the warm aluminium against the parched fingers.

After some time, Josh fell asleep again. Carlton crept over to him. What was it about this boy? Kept wanting to call him Joe. Had to stop and think. In the dark he was sure it was Joe sitting there. Wanted to shake some sense into him. Listen to your father, he wanted to shout. Listen to me. But in the light. There was no doubt. It was Josh. Lanky, dark, humble looking Josh. Joe was tall and blond like himself. But not so broad in the chest. From not playing quarterback. And he would have been good at it. If he'd only tried.

Carlton crept back to his own corner, an anger bubbling from somewhere inside of him. 'Get rid of it,' he scolded himself. 'Try not to think about it.' But the sweltering warmth pressed in against his throat, his face, forcing him to succumb to what he had always been able to escape from before.

Memories cascaded against him as he closed his eyes. It was the night he had come home from a trip overseas. They had been stationed in Houston at the time and he and Maribel had been holidaying in Switzerland. Joe had not been expecting them back until the following evening and they had thought nothing of surprising him.

The lights were on in the house. The door was unlocked. They called out when they entered and heard something drop upstairs.

"Joe?" Maribel had put her hand on the banister. Joe appeared without a shirt and was just zipping up his trousers.

"Mom! Dad! I wasn't expecting you!"

"We decided to come back a day early, sweetheart." Maribel's voice sounded with concern and then she cocked her head. "Is there someone there with you Joe?"

Even Carlton could see the guilt that passed over his son's face when he said, "No."

Carlton knew he was lying. What the hell was his boy up to? And then he relaxed. Joe was old enough to have girls. In fact, he was pleased. His son, a man. A virile strong man.

Carlton heard metal clattering at the side of the house and opened the front door to check.

"Dad!" Joe hollered at him but it was too late. Carlton saw a boy running across the lawn to the road. He looked back up the stairs. He wanted to vomit. Their eyes met and then Joe lowered his and slunk away.

He would have been happier if it had been drugs. He couldn't even talk to Maribel about it he was that angry. He couldn't talk to anyone about it including Joe. His own son. It was more than a betrayal.

"Dad!" Joe was standing in the doorway. He'd come back from college for the weekend. "Dad, we've got to talk."

Carlton looked up blankly. Since that night the year before he hadn't said more than a dozen words to the boy.

"Dad, please. You can't close me out forever."

"What is it?" Carlton forced himself unsuccessfully to be civil. He wanted to be able to cut himself off completely from Joe and couldn't. His son was a reminder of how he had failed. Failed to provide a normal home for his children. He blamed himself, or he blamed Maribel for mollycoddling the boy, giving him too much time and attention just because he was sickly.

"Dad, I just want you to know that I'm sorry."

"What about son?" Carlton's voice was cold.

Joe hesitated and Carlton wished he would go away and leave him alone. He felt dirty being in the same room as a fag.

A sudden cry from Josh jolted him. "For Chrissakes, kid, what the hell's the matter with you? Josh?" Carlton calmed himself as he called again into the silence. Jesus, he had nearly lost it. He had to remember that he was responsible for Josh.

But then, he had been responsible for Joe too and he had let him down, abandoned and rejected him. The pitch of anger rose in his head, but again he wasn't sure if it was toward himself or his son.

He tried to doze. What was the thing he had wanted most in his life?

He had no idea. He had just carried on and done what he wanted at the time the desire arose. A normal life, a normal family. And what did he want now? To be free? To be with Maribel? If he died now and had one wish before he left what would it be? He stirred as the answer came to him. To be able to accept his son for what he was.

"Damn!" he murmured as a solitary tear rolled down his cheek.

19

BEKAH STOOD AT THE DESK of the Sonargon Hotel, surreptitiously watching for Shumacker. It was imperative that he didn't see her. Didn't see what she was doing. The clerk handed her a package and she exchanged five hundred dollars worth into taka.

As she hurried out of the hotel an army officer brushed by her, accidentally knocking against her bag. The look in his eye as he apologised gave her the creeps. Hadn't she seem him somewhere else?

She returned to the Company villa, rushed to her room and collected her bags. Maribel was waiting for her at the base of the stairs blocking her way.

"You shouldn't be doing this!" Maribel protested.

"I need to. I can't just do nothing!"

"You don't know what you're getting yourself into!"

"I have to Maribel. Please let me pass."

Maribel refused to step aside. "I must stop you from going there. It's so dangerous. You may not even accomplish anything."

"I'm going. Please!" Bekah pushed her way past.

"I can't let you do this!"

"Oh, cut me a break!"

"No! I know this is wrong!"

"Wrong for you Maribel, but not for me. Now please move."

"Must you be this way?" Maribel beseeched.

Bekah nodded.

Maribel wrung her hands, trying to decide what to do.

"I haven't got much time," Bekah interjected.

"All right, I'm going with you!"

"You'd better pack quickly," Bekah replied. "I'm leaving in ten minutes."

"My bags are in the hall." Maribel handed Bekah a large brown envelope. "Here, add this to your funds. If you must do this, then we're in it together."

The journey to Shylet was thankfully short. Bekah had no patience for any more argument. Maribel was with her or she wasn't. It hardly mattered. This felt right. But when they arrived Khalig was not there to meet them. They waited for him along one wall of the arrivals room. Bekah stood heads above the crowd watching as throngs of men paused to stare and then moved on. It was as if she was wearing a huge sign, 'American!'

Back home, in University, she had often stood out as one of the only brown-skinned women amidst the sea of beige and blonde. But here, the difference was even more obvious.

Maribel seemed quite at home. Perhaps it was because she had never belonged to any one place, she obviously was easy in all of them.

Two armed officers approached them.

"Are you waiting for someone?" one asked Maribel in broken English ignoring Bekah.

"Yes, thanks. He'll be here in a minute," Bekah responded but the officer pretended not to hear.

"We can take you to where you are going," the officer said.

The women exchanged glances. There was something wrong. Bekah could smell and taste the wrongness as if it had been bottled and the contents thrown in her face. Something sharp stuck in her side.

"Move," the officer said.

They walked slowly just slightly in front of the officers, Maribel's expression frozen. If she was frightened, she did not reveal it. No one else seemed to notice what was happening. Even if they had, would they do anything about it?

Bekah felt the sweat trickle between her breasts. The gun pressed insistently into her backbone. Her knees wobbled. Suddenly Maribel's voice filled the hall,

"Khalig! Khalig!" she lifted both her arms, waving them wildly before the men could stop her.

Khalig strode up to them, all smiles, his arms held out towards Maribel as the officers slid away.

"Those men!" Maribel pointed to where the officers merged in with the crowds. Khalig rushed after them.

Bekah leaned against the wall, her knees were shaking so hard she could barely stand. Surely only Habib and Khalig knew they were coming to Shylet and she was sure Habib wouldn't tell anyone. She looked suspiciously at Khalig as he came back but Maribel was enthusiastically clasping his hand, looking so pleased to see him. Surely she of all people must know who to trust!

"I'm so sorry I'm late," Khalig was saying. "I've just received information that might bring us closer to the kidnappers. I've set up a meeting in Jaintipur. There's a chance that we may be able to make contact. If nothing else, we can try to send them food and clothing. Do you have the money?"

Bekah nodded.

"Good. What we don't need today we can leave in the safe at my house. Are you feeling all right?" His look showed concern.

Bekah put her hand on her stomach. Was that the baby or her stomach jumping up and down like a frog?

Khalig's house sat like a palace amidst the terrible squalor that lay outside its gates. It made Bekah even more suspicious. He stood over her as she reluctantly lay the envelope containing her money in the safe. The money Maribel had given her in Dhaka she kept to herself. Khalig needn't know about that.

When he introduced his English wife, Myra, Bekah liked the situation even less. Myra was dressed in an immaculate powder blue silk jacket and skirt and her accent matched the cloth. But she had generously prepared two baskets of food: one for their journey to Jaintipur and one for Carlton and Josh if it was possible to make contact with their captors. Bekah looked inside the men's basket: there was food, cake, clothing, candles and medications. She wanted to drop with gratitude. Was it really possible that these supplies would reach their destiny?

The road to Jaintipur was bumpy. Bekah stared out of the window. The dirt track went on and on, interrupted only by pockets of water that ran across the road. Every now and then she caught a glimpse of faces peering out from the foliage, sometimes a little hand would suddenly wave and disappear. Who lived back there? Did they know where Josh and Carlton were? She tried to penetrate the fog of green. Somewhere in that endless jungle was her husband. He was that close and that far away.

They arrived in the shanty town of Jaintipur. Khalig pulled up outside a long row of low lying shelters with corrugated steel roofs held up by bamboo poles.

"Wait here," he said as he disappeared into one of the buildings.

They waited ten, twenty minutes. It was getting too hot to sit still. Bekah opened the door.

"You must stay in the jeep." Maribel touched her arm.

"I'll just walk around a bit. It can't hurt."

"You stupid girl! Listen to me!"

Bekah walked slowly towards the busy river. Everywhere people sat under black umbrellas chopping stones with little hammers. Every container, boat and barge was filled with the broken stone. From the river, young women with baskets on their heads brought up loads of larger cobbles to be crushed by the squatting people on the banks.

Bekah looked into the distant hills. The glint of a waterfall against white stone caught her eye. Silently she whispered, "Josh, are you there?" She sent her love on a puff of breath, hoping that somehow it would reach him.

She turned back to the jeep not quite registering that all the doors were now swung wide open. As she approached, she realised that Maribel was no longer there.

She broke into a run.

"Maribel?" she called. There was no answer.

"Maribel?" she called again, turning to the lean-to that Khalig had entered earlier.

It was empty. She went out and looked in the back of the jeep. Both hampers were gone.

She must calm herself. There had to be some explanation! Lord, Lord, Lord! She tried to communicate with a man standing near but he spat at her feet. She pointed to herself and then the jeep. He couldn't understand. Or maybe he just wouldn't. Maribel!

"Does anyone speak English!" she cried out. People only stared. "English! Oh my Lord. Maribel? Khalig?"

Children came running, surrounding her, tugging at her shirt and her trousers, pointing to something behind her. What were they telling her?

She let them pull her down the road, around another long row of shanty huts. They chattered at her then abruptly left her at the dark entrance of a lean-to.

She walked into the enclosure. She could see nothing in the dark.

"Maribel?" she called.

"I'm so glad you could join us."

"Khalig?" Her eyes adjusted to the darkness. It wasn't Khalig. The face was hidden but she could just make out the military uniform.

"Where is Mrs. Ramsey?"

"She is somewhere secure."

"What do you mean secure? Where have you taken her?"

"That is not your concern."

"Who are you? What it is you want?"

"Your people are not cooperating with us. We are tiring of your petty bargains."

"I have no say in corporate decisions. Surely you can be reasonable. We are no different than you are; run by corporate politics. Look, I have ten thousand dollars here in Shylet. I'll give you that. No strings attached. Just release your hostages."

"You insult me."

"I can raise more but not as much as you're asking. And I can campaign on your behalf in the U.S. I've done that kind of work. Surely if you have a grievance international pressure is worth more to you than money?"

The man laughed.

Bekah continued, "The people you are holding are innocent. They are not party to these politics. What you're doing is wrong!"

"Tell your Company that we have changed our terms."

"Thank the Lord. So you'll take my help. I'm sure we can work together to change –"

"Tell them that we hold the woman as well and we will not hesitate to kill her."

"What?"

"You have three days"

"No! Lord! Exchange her for me! I'm younger. I can take the conditions. I beg you!"

"You are of no significance. Go back to your people and tell them that we now demand three million United States dollars."

"We can't raise that kind of money! Don't you realise the Company won't pay that! Isn't there any compromise? Any settlement? Please let Mrs. Ramsey go. I won't even tell them I've given you my money. Please!"

"You have three days before she dies. Now go!"

Two shadows suddenly grabbed at her.

She struggled against them. They shoved her hard and she landed on her knees outside. She jumped up and ran back into the lean-to. Her way was barred and she was thrown out again. The two men stood over her, rifles pointed at her head. She heard the clatter of a car engine and they suddenly ran, dissolving into the shrubs and trees.

She ran back to the jeep. The keys were in the engine. She grabbed them and started running from hut to hut calling for Khalig. But the more she called the more people gathered round her until she could no longer move.

"Help me! Can someone help me! Please!"

A young man pushed his way through the crowd. He looked shyly at her then pointed in her direction, touched her hand then pointed at himself.

"Do you know where they are?" she asked.

He pointed to her and then to himself again and began to push his way through the crowd. She followed. He led her down the hill away from the village into the jungle.

'Where is he taking me?' she sobbed to herself, but instinct told her to follow. Perhaps he even knew where Josh was. The man stopped suddenly and pointed again. By the side of a stream, Khalig lay bound and gagged.

She rushed over to him untying the ropes, removing the cloth from his mouth.

"Khalig are you all right?"

"Yes. They have Maribel."

"I know." Bekah wanted to sob but she didn't. Now was the time to be strong. She helped Khalig up and turned to thank the young man but he had disappeared. Khalig hobbled back to the jeep. There was no one there.

Khalig started the engine and pulled away noisily. "I'm not sure who they are yet but I have my suspicions," Khalig said as they stormed away along the bumpy track. "How much of that money are you willing to use?"

"Use all of it. If that's what it takes. I don't care. Just find them!"

20

THE NEXT MORNING, Tweedledee opened the hatch and handed in another bottle of salt solution. Josh sat up, his face grey and strained. He drank the fluid.

"How're you feeling?" Carlton asked.

"Better, I think." Josh shuffled to the exit. Carlton followed. It was raining and in the distance lightning flashed on the horizon.

Carlton looked askance at the cut on the boy's leg. Miraculously, it didn't look infected. It was a nasty gash and Josh was limping with it but to his credit he never complained. They were led down to the river to bathe, Josh lagging behind, stumbling every now and then, letting his glasses fall to the ground and then groping for them.

The water was moving rapidly. Carlton couldn't wait to get in and quickly waded in up to his waist. It was ridiculous to get such pleasure from the simple act of bathing. But it felt like the rushing of the water took with it the discomforts of aching.

He found the soap in his shirt pocket and began washing himself. How he had taken everything in his life for granted, if this is what his ultimate pleasure had come to be. He dipped down and immersed his head under the water, washing his hair. If he was to meet his death, it would have to be in the solace of this river. He emerged, gasping from the effort of holding his breath.

Josh was just standing there. For a moment, Carlton longed to be free of the responsibility of caring for him. If the kid's too stupid to take advantage of the short time he has left then let him suffer. Nevertheless, he made his way over and handed him the soap.

He moved away from Josh into the deeper water. But the boy still didn't move. He was wasting valuable time! He waded back over.

"You need help, son?"

Josh nodded. "Can't keep my balance. World's spinning."

Carlton extended his hand. He led Josh into the water and left him again. From a distance he watched as Josh cleaned himself stiffly, getting no joy, no pleasure from the sensuality of the running water. What did he expect, considering the state of him?

The guard shouted something. It was time to return and Carlton hadn't finished washing. God damn it! He was angry when he should be feeling sorry, but the more guilt he felt the angrier he became.

He pushed his body through the water, pulled himself up the bank then helped Josh out. At least he smelled better. Tweedledee ran up and threw a bright blue rolled cloth at him. He unrolled it. It was a lungi, one of those skirt-like things the men in the villages wore. He stepped into it, took his underpants off, tied the material into a knot and tucked it in. Josh did the same.

"Thank you," he said nodding his head. He heard Josh reluctantly say, "Asalaam alaikhum."

The kid was learning fast.

They dragged back to the prison site. But instead of being shoved into the hut, they were directed to an area about five feet away. Carlton made eye contact with his compatriot. What were the guards up to? Tweedledum pointed at the log and motioned for them to sit.

Carlton sensed Tweedledee behind him. What was the man doing? He tensed. First the trousers, then the... What had that English educated asshole said to them, the one that had sounded like Khalig? First the trousers and then what?

The hand behind him tugged at his scalp. The sharp blade sliced through his hair. Fine, if it was only the hair, he could live with that. It'd make life easier. He wished they'd give him a shave too. Poor Maribel, he thought, when she receives this she'll have a fit. In a perverse way, it cheered him up.

Tweedledum jerked the gun upward. Carlton got to his feet and watched as they did the same to Josh, cutting off his dark curls, putting them into a brown paper bag. With his hair in patches, his face drawn and sickly, Josh looked both wretched and comical. Carlton couldn't help but smile at the boy. Josh grinned back.

They were both going crazy.

Carlton expected the guards to shove them back in the stench and dark but they didn't. They just milled around casually. Were they giving them another chance to escape? Would he take it? Carlton walked to the back of the hut but Tweedledum came chasing after, pushing him to the front.

"How you feeling, Josh?" he murmured to the boy.

"Much better, that bath really helped."

"I was beginning to wonder about you, son," Carlton said.

"Must have been something I ate." The boy grinned again.

Carlton laughed and slapped Josh lightly on the back.

"What do you think they want us to do?" asked Josh.

"It looks like boys day out. Might as well enjoy it."

Josh slowly stretched his arms and sighed, then he stiffly bent down, his fingers reaching only as far as his knees. He cranked himself back up and moved his neck to and fro.

Carlton did the same, gently. His chest felt tight and he was afraid to upset the equilibrium.

Tweedledee appeared with what looked like a broom: reeds strung together and attached to a stick. Then he produced a bucket with hot water and soap and pointed to the inside of the hut making mock sweeping gestures outside the door.

"I think he wants us to clean our little cottage." Carlton took the broom from the guard and climbed into the hut. Josh followed with the bucket. They didn't slam the hatch. Carlton started sweeping the floor humming a tune, then he broke into a quiet song... "Could you coo, could you care, for a cunning cottage, we could share?"

Josh picked the mats up and shook them outside. He returned, reaching out for the broom,

"I'll do that Mr. Ramsey."

"No thanks, son. I'm fine. Feels good to get the old arms moving again." He pushed the broom around then stopped. "Though Christ knows what it is I'm trying to accomplish."

"I think we have to put the water down first."

"What the hell will that do?"

"I suppose it's to get the top layer off."

"I'm all for experimentation if it means cleaning the place up some."

Josh dropped to his knees and started scrubbing at the ground. Carlton swept up behind him until they came to the edges of the hut.

"Jesus!" Carlton said, "That's a hell of a sight better. You can breathe in here now."

They climbed out of the hut again expecting to be shoved back in, but the two guards were still milling about. Tweedledee left for a moment returning with two food trays and some fruit, soda and salt solution.

The guard smiled. At the sight of the fruit, Carlton wanted to go up and hug him. "Damn!" he said overcome with emotion. Then he sat on the log and opened the tray. There were pieces of cheese with bread and some of Khalig's wife's cake. Carlton stopped dead. This was too much. Khalig knew where they were. He must do. He was sickened by the thought. He looked up. Josh was staring at him.

He suddenly felt like a very old man. He and Khalig were friends. Sure they'd had their disagreements but, no. He couldn't face it. "Shit," he murmured. He set the tray aside and then noticed that Josh hadn't touched the food either.

The guards looked confused. They said something to him but he couldn't understand a word. They urged him to eat but he shook his head. Tweedledee ran to the hut and climbed in. A few moments later he came out holding Josh's guide book. He searched through the pages and triumphantly found what he was looking for.

"Bhalo," he said and shoved the book in front of Carlton, pointing to the word.

Carlton nodded. The man was saying, 'good'. Yes, good food. But where had it come from?

"Roti," Tweedledee said desperately, "Roti, bhalo. Khabo!"

Josh whispered, "What is he saying?"

"He's saying that the food is good and that we should eat it."

"This is Myra's cake, isn't it?" Josh asked hesitantly. Tweedledee was pointing at the book shouting,

"Bondhu, Bondhu."

Josh took the book from Carlton and looked down the list of words. "Bondhu means friend."

Carlton nodded while Josh asked, "Does that mean that Khalig knows where we are?"

"I don't know." Carlton was drenched with weariness and he heard the sound of his own voice echoing his disappointment.

"Then we're saved, aren't we?" Josh's expression was full of hope. Like the hope he had heard in his own son's voice the day he had left for California and was trying to repair the rift between them. The wound that Carlton had refused to let heal.

Carlton lifted his head and closed his eyes for a moment. He had to give the boy hope. He nodded and looked at Josh, forcing a smile, then lifted the tray and said, "Eat it son. It's the only decent meal we've had in a long time." And then he collapsed inside himself.

21

BEKAH RUBBED THE GLITCH of discomfort that ran its way through her abdomen. The jeep was rocking back and forth, banging over ridges in the road, bumping her head against the roof one moment and her shoulders the next against the metal of the door.

Stop. Think. Try to work it out. What am I going to do? Oh why hadn't she listened to Maribel? How obvious it was to her now. This image of herself as a great hero. Save Josh from his kidnappers, from his mother, even from himself. Even now all she could think of was how to free Maribel. How to find out enough information. The opportunity to be passive was now lost because of her previous actions.

"Khalig? Isn't there anyone you know who can find her for us?" But he was deep in thought and didn't answer, or perhaps she hadn't even spoken aloud.

They should have stayed in Jaintipur. Surely they should have stayed there. Bought information. People would have seen something. But somehow it seemed more appropriate to flee. She glanced out of the window. Little children were scattered at the edge of the perpetual jungle. They waved but she didn't wave back, her hand weighted down. When would this endless journey cease?

Finally, the gauze of undergrowth split apart to reveal a cluster of shanties. Livestock and the milling crowds swarmed in front of the jeep. She wanted to shout at them to get out of the way, but she kept quiet. Khalig's expression made sure of that.

Inside Khalig's house, Myra's voice echoed from upstairs and Khalig ran to her, leaving Bekah to her thoughts. She paced the hallway, lost. What was she going to do? How could she bear to live with herself now?

"Where is Maribel?"

"What?"

Shumacker had come up silently behind her. His presence filled her with ice.

He asked again.

No, she couldn't tell him. Couldn't say to him that Maribel was in danger, that he had been right all along. She should have let him do his job without interfering. She bit her lip.

"Where is she?" he took her arms and shook her.

'Don't be a coward,' she told herself. 'Tell him. Face up to what you've done.'

"She was taken in Jaintipur," she said.

"Taken! What does that mean? What the hell have you done?"

His hands bruised her but she had no spirit to fight.

"No. I can't believe she would have followed you! She knew better than that!"

Bekah drooped in his grasp.

"But you!" he suddenly let her go pointing his finger in her face. "You! Why didn't they take you?"

She held herself upright.

"Tell me you stupid -"

"They sent me with a message," she stepped away from him. "They want... another million..."

His eyes bulged with anger. He took the few steps towards her.

"They've given us three days." He had every right to attack her now. What an idiot she had been.

Unexpectedly, Shumacker groaned letting his arms fall to his sides. He collapsed into a chair.

She didn't expect this from him.

Shumacker put his hands to his face, rubbing his forehead repeating Maribel's name. Then he lifted his head and looked at her, a look of such deep hatred it shocked her back into her self.

She said, "They're going to kill her if you don't get them the money!"

Khalig suddenly appeared, as if he'd been standing outside the room, listening in. Bekah warily caught a glimpse of the envelope containing the money she had brought in his jacket pocket.

"And you, you son of a bitch," Shumacker shouted, "What the hell were you doing driving them around!"

"Ah!" Khalig said calmly. "My duty is to perform requests made of me."

"When this is over Khalig –" Shumacker growled.

"Yes?" Khalig challenged. Shumacker was unexpectedly silenced.

Khalig handed a small brown parcel to Bekah. "This was delivered a few minutes before we arrived. It's addressed to you."

Bekah examined the package recognising the scrawl of handwriting. Who were these people who seemed to follow her every move?

She looked up at the two men. They were as still as statues. Her shaking fingers tore at the paper. There was a note. 'Three days,' was all it said. She handed the message to Shumacker, tugged further into the brown paper. It fell apart. Black curls and white twigs of hair scattered onto the bare floor.

Josh.

"It's going to get worse," Shumacker said angrily, turning away.

She knelt and picked up the dark strands, scooped together the scattered hair, staring at it in her hand, dissolving the men out of the room.

"Mrs. Felstein." Shumacker's movement flung the hair upwards.

She grabbed at the floating wisps then gathered more and more in her hands.

Shumacker knelt down and dug his fingers into her shoulder.

"Leave the girl." Khalig's voice was near but Shumacker ignored him.

"Mrs. Felstein. You're going to have to tell me what happened. Of course I have to report this... Mrs. Felstein, do you hear me?"

"What is it you need to know?" Khalig interrupted.

"The facts from her, not from you."

"Perhaps she is not the one who has all the facts."

"And you do?"

"Of course not." Khalig checked his watch. "And this isn't the time to argue about them either. Anyway, I must leave. I have some business to attend to."

"Business about what Khalig?" Shumacker glared.

Bekah got to her feet clenching Josh's hair in her hand. She looked to Khalig who was standing in the doorway, wondering what he would say.

"It's personal," he answered. Bekah's eyes met with his. He gently patted the pocket with the envelope and shook his head glancing for a moment at Shumacker. She nodded. Khalig was right. Shumacker didn't need to know about the money.

Bekah held on to the sound of Khalig's foot fall, wishing that he wasn't leaving and dreading the moment when she was alone again with Shumacker.

"I'm waiting," Shumacker said.

She started slowly. Always expecting him to blow. Always cautious of what she said. Leaving out as much as she could. But he waited till she was finished before he spoke,

"You'll return to Dhaka with me. From there you can fly back to Houston. I want you out of the way."

"No!"

"Yes, Mrs. Felstein. You're going home."

"No, no I can't go now. I'm begging you. Please let me stay."

"I don't give a damn what you want. You're trouble and I want you out."

"Callahan, let the girl be," Myra swept in.

"Keep out of this Myra."

"We all make mistakes. Let the girl stay. I'll make sure she's no more trouble."

Shumacker glared at the woman and then sighed, muttering under his breath. "I'll hold you responsible then."

Myra shrugged.

"Well, I doubt that you could fuck things up any more than you already have," Shumacker said, "don't you?"

Maribel was sure that she had been taken into Shylet. She'd been there enough times to recognise the sounds and the smells. The ceaseless traffic of passing feet. The door opened, a young man entered.

"Begum," he whispered. "I have food for you."

"I don't need food."

"You must eat. Not good thing to waste."

"You eat it then."

The boy set the plate in front of her.

"I leave for you. You get hungry later."

She shook her head. "I cannot eat. Here you have it."

The boy looked closely at her. He couldn't be more than nineteen. Twenty at the most.

"Tell me. What is your name?" she asked in Bengali. It caught him off guard.

"My name is Bashir. You speak Bengali?"

"A little," she responded. "Bashir, can you tell me why you are holding me?" she continued in his language.

"Begum, I am sorry but it is necessary to our cause."

"This cause? What is it?"

"To own what is ours. To have freedom and democracy."

"And you're willing to hurt –"

Something knocked against the door.

"Bashir!" a man's voice called.

"I must go now Begum. I return later." He hurried out of the door.

She sat motionless, alone in the dimly lit room. An immense calm forced its way into her. Or was it resignation? Carlton's fixation on his career had finally led her to the place she had always tried to escape from. Her aloneness. Yet now she didn't have the spirit to fight it.

She wondered what her children would think if they knew that their mother was a prisoner. Maybe Joe would fly out. Join up with Bekah to get her out of there. They wouldn't have enough time. The feeling was too strong. Time was running out for her and Carlton, but they would be together in the end, no matter what.

The door swung open. Bashir entered. "Begum, I have book for you. This will help you to understand what we are doing."

"A book?"

He handed it to her. "It is the work of our national poet, Nazrul."

"Nazrul? My father knew him. Such a tragic life," Maribel said.

"You have met him yourself?" Bashir asked.

"Only once. But by then he was very ill."

Bashir's eyes widened. "You have read his poetry?"

Maribel nodded. "Yes. I have read *On the Song of Students* and *Rebel*. They are very strong. I can see why you feel he represents you. Have you read his other works?"

"Of course. In University."

"So you know that he wrote some beautiful poems, of love and the sorrow of tragedy, the importance of Muslim values. Didn't he?"

"Yes, Begum."

"Only a few of his works spoke of violence."

She leaned towards the boy.

"Sometimes it is necessary," he said.

She gently shook her head. The boy seemed charming, innocent. There was something about him she had instantaneously liked. Bekah would be astonished.

"Begum, can I get you anything to drink? I can make you some tea."

"Yes, Bashir. Tea would be lovely. You are very kind."

Bashir left the hut. The sweetness of the boy's manner reminded her of her own son, Joe as a child. If only he had girlfriends instead of... It

184

wasn't to be. She had accepted it long ago. No grandchildren from her only son.

Bashir came in and handed her a cup of steaming liquid.

"Thank you Bashir." She sipped the tea then put the cup down on the table in front of her. "I…"

"Yes, Begum?"

"No, I suppose…"

"Please tell me what you are thinking."

"It's… Well, I just cannot understand how someone like you could become involved in this."

"It is people like myself who must do this work."

Maribel sighed and picked the cup up again. "Tell me Bashir, you said you studied Nazrul in University. Are you still a student?"

"No, Begum."

"Have you graduated? You look too young."

"No. I was not able to finish my studies. I became involved in protests against Ershad. Now the University is closed."

"But that's such a shame. You seem so bright. There are other Universities. Why can't you go to them?"

"No Begum. There is no possibility. Now I fight for my people." He sat earnestly across from her.

"But you can help your people more by returning to school."

"It is too late. I have said," he shook his head sadly.

"It needn't be."

For a moment Bashir looked into her eyes, his young face hopeful.

"I am working now for all my people."

"But what does that mean?"

"It means that I accomplish what we set out to do."

"But will you? What if you're wrong? What then?"

"I have faith in our movement."

"You have faith enough to kidnap me? To threaten my husband?" She looked into his eyes. They were warm, intelligent. "Bashir, if they kill me for nothing, you'll live with the burden of my death for the rest of your life… I just know you will."

"But we will not have to kill you. Your company will pay. We will release you."

"No, no. You must realise by now that the oil company will never pay your ransom."

The young man looked dismayed. "How do you know this?"

"It is not Company policy to give in to terrorists."

"I am not a terrorist! I am a freedom fighter!"

"You will be a murderer of innocent people, Bashir. Very soon."

Bashir fell silent.

"Bashir, what were you studying at university?"

"Political policy and economics," he fumbled with the book.

"But those are such important subjects! You could do so much good. Someone like you."

"No, Begum. I have told you, the university is closed. I cannot return."

"But what about your family? They must be very disappointed."

"Yes. My parents have worked all their lives to send me to University."

"Oh, my!" Maribel finished the tea. "You know, there could be another way."

Bashir shook his head. "It is too late."

"Dhaka is not the only place that has a university."

"I can go nowhere else."

"But there you're wrong. Why not go to university in America or England?"

"That is impossible."

"Bashir, I've already sponsored several young men like you."

He shook his head. "I would be betraying my people."

"No, no. You would be helping them. I have lived in this world long enough to believe that education is far more important than joining causes."

"Begum. I cannot think about it right now."

"Why don't you speak to your parents. Find out what they think. I would need their permission if you were interested anyway."

"All right, Begum. I will."

"Bashir!" The voice outside called.

"I must go now." Bashir went to the door. He paused, came back into the room and picked up Maribel's cup. He seemed expectant as if he was thinking about something. Then he went to the door. As he opened it he said, "Yes, Begum. I will speak with my parents about this."

"Bashir?" Maribel's voice stopped him.

Bashir closed the door again.

"If you are going to accept my offer," Maribel whispered. "I will need your help."

"Yes, Begum, I realise that." With that he left.

Maribel heard his voice outside, could barely make out what he was saying. The sound died away leaving others in its wake — the voices of women passing by, the whirring of rushing wheels. Perhaps if she screamed someone would help. But the guards would get there first.

"Excuse me, Begum."

Bekah's eyes opened. She hadn't been feeling all that well and exhaustion had caught up with her. She had fallen asleep on a verandah chair with the cup of tea that Myra had made for her in her hand.

A young man stood anxiously on the steps. "I have message for you."

"How do you know who I am?"

"You are not hard to recognise from description."

"What do you want from me?"

"I have a message –"

"Wait a second I'm just going to call –" she began to rise.

"No Begum. I speak with you alone."

"Is it about my husband?"

"No Begum. I am guard to Mrs. Maribel. She is saying that I will tell you where she is."

"Oh come on. You don't think I'm going to fall for that after all I've been through? Why would you come here if you're her guard?"

"Here is note. She explain everything but you come quickly."

Bekah read the note. The handwriting was small. Tidy. It could be Maribel's. Whose else would it be?

"Please come quickly."

Bekah ran into the house and grabbed her bag. She should write Khalig a note, tell him where she was going, but the young man called to her again and she raced out of the door.

He led her through the twisted dishevelled streets, away from Khalig's. Landmarks to guide her return were scarce. This post. That shop. Finally the river and a bridge. A park and colonial houses, then back into a scatter of corrugated iron roofed shanties.

The young man stopped.

"Begum is at end of street. I call my mother now. She will take you there."

"Wait!"

"Yes?" he asked.

"Tell me your name."

"It is Bashir." He slipped into the shadows of a hut and then called to her. She entered the hut.

"Begum, Maribel said that you would have money," Bashir whispered.

"Yes," Bekah nodded. "But first I must see Maribel."

"No. No. I bring Maribel this." He was holding a long black skirt and square of black cloth. "You go with mother outside. As you walk to end of road you give money to children. Make much noise. You keep them busy. I bring Maribel out."

"But how do you know that will work? Where are these guards?"

"You give money."

This was just a con. Shumacker had underestimated her. She could fuck things up worse than she already had. "Wait a second."

"No time," Bashir said. "We must hurry. Soldiers come soon. They hurt Maribel."

Bashir's mother took her hand and led her out. She followed the woman down the road. There were two men sitting lackadaisically outside the long row of huts at the end of the road. They wore civilian clothing. Too young to be guards. She could see no weapons. Bashir's mother was calling out to the children who came running. The woman urged her to open her bag. To give them money.

Bekah reached, unwillingly into her bag, felt the notes brittle against sweat-cold hands. She tugged releasing a bill, let it slip into the air and the waiting, excited hands that were now in commotion around her.

The crowd surged around her, lifting her off her feet, making her dizzy, starting up pains where the child lay in her stomach. She cried out, trying to get them to let her be, when the crowd suddenly parted, dropping her.

The young guard who had been sitting outside the hut where Maribel was supposedly being kept was cursing at her. He grabbed her arm.

"Jan!" he shouted in her face.

She put her hands up, shaking her head. "I don't understand."

"Jan!" he screamed jolting her into the crowd of children. She held a bill out to him.

"Na! Na!"

Where was Bashir's mother? She searched the crowd. The woman was gone and the guard shoved her again as the children chanted, tugging at her clothing. She stumbled to the ground, scraping her knees. Hands tugged her upward.

She pulled several bills from her bag. Held them out to her aggressor. "Take it."

He paused, staring at the money. Considering it. Then looking round suspiciously he grabbed the notes and stuffed them in his pocket. The other guard was now pushing at her, tugging at her bag. She clutched onto it, pulling out notes one by one.

Over their heads she could see Bashir enter the hut. A few minutes later he left it, followed by a woman in a long skirt, her head, face and shoulders draped by a black cloth. They hurried down the road. The woman could be a Bangladeshi. Or it could be Maribel. There was no way of telling.

The guards began moving away from Bekah. She must stop them. She offered more money. They grabbed it from her and started pushing at the children to get out of the way. With a last searching look at Bekah's empty hand the guards returned to the hut, slumping against the door.

Bekah wanted to run. Break loose of the jostling crowd of women and children and flee as fast as she could towards Bashir's hut.

Above the cries of confusion she heard the sound of a vehicle approaching. Bashir and the woman were now out of sight. She frantically tried to push her way out of the crowd. Suddenly his mother appeared and taking her by the hand, led her through. As the vehicle screeched around the corner into the road, they ducked into a nearby hut.

The jeep stopped. Sounds of the excited children diminished. She heard men talking. Someone shouted. An argument broke out close by. Something was smashed. Broken glass and cries of pain. She wanted to vomit. Surely they would come looking for her next.

Bashir's mother beckoned her quickly to climb into what looked like a storage box under a bed. It was full of cloth and household goods. She lay down in it and the lid was shut firmly.

There were men's voices just above her. Women's answers. Then an argument. Bekah heard them moving in between the two small rooms. Smashing things apart. The baby suddenly lurched in her stomach, forcing gasps of pain. The men stopped moving. They had heard her. The pain came again. Ripping into her.

Footsteps came closer. The board sagged above her head pressing against her. She mustn't breathe, mustn't let... Another contraction forced her to clench her teeth.

The men left. She heard them as they went from hut to hut. Heard

Bashir's voice and then the sound of the engine starting up again and moving away. The lid opened. A woman she didn't recognise beckoned to her, reaching a small hand in, helping her out. Another contraction forced her to clutch her rescuer's arm. The woman then draped a large cloth over her, pushing at her to hunch her shoulders, to make herself smaller. Somehow she followed the other out, moving as quickly as she could.

There was a rickshaw standing close against the door of Bashir's hut. She was pushed into it. Bashir and the darkly clad woman were already in. At once, the rickshaw pulled away from the hut and as it hurried around a corner she heard the sound of an engine coming close.

She covered her face and hunched herself into the most shrivelled person she could be as the baby ripped at her from inside.

The sound of the vehicle faded away.

The other woman suddenly grasped her hand. She looked down. It was a petite hand, well manicured, and it was white.

"Bekah!" Maribel whispered.

"Oh Maribel! I'm so glad you're all right!" she gasped.

"I'm fine and better for it."

Bekah shook her head. "I don't understand."

"You were so right, Bekah. So right about this."

"How can you say that? I've done nothing but bludgeon my way through things I don't understand."

Maribel squeezed her hand. "I'm glad you did. I really am."

The baby tore at her again, an oozing dampened the inside of her thighs, running into her panties.

"I don't think I've ever been so frightened in all my life," Maribel whispered close, still holding her hand.

"You were incredible," Bekah suddenly whimpered.

"Are you all right dear?" Maribel reached up with her free hand and pushed back the hair on Bekah's face, looking deep in her eyes.

Bekah nodded. This was not the time to panic, despite…

"Oh dear. Lean against me if you'd like. Here put your head on my shoulder."

For a few moments the pain subsided, though the tears that streamed down her face refused to pause. Bekah pressed her head deeper into the woman's shoulder letting herself drop into the strange comfort of French perfume and Bengali dust.

"Can you imagine what Carlton would think if he saw me dressed like this?" Maribel patted her hand.

Bekah grinned and nodded, rubbing her chin against the dark shawl. She could well guess, even if she hadn't met the man.

"Please, no more talk," Bashir whispered urgently. "There are soldiers everywhere."

The rickshaw went over the bridge and turned another corner finally rushing into the large drive leading to Khalig's. As they drove up, Khalig came out onto the verandah. He looked puzzled. Bekah was the first to climb out. He hurried to her.

"Where have you been? We have been anxious –"

He saw Maribel.

"Thank Allah! I cannot believe it's you!" He hurried them into the house, shutting the door in Bashir's face.

"Bashir!" Maribel ran to the closed door.

"What is this boy to you?" Khalig stopped her.

"He has saved me." Maribel swung the doors open and pulled the boy in.

"Khalig!" Bekah gasped as the pain of another contraction hit her. "You must contact Shumacker. Bashir knows who the kidnappers are!"

"You, Bashir. Come with me." Khalig signalled to the boy. He hurried out of the room and Bashir ran quickly after.

Bekah cried out again. She leaned against the wall, feeling the gush of warm fluid soak through her panties and run down her legs.

"Bekah!" Maribel was upon her. "Are you all right, dear? Oh my goodness. It's the baby, isn't it? We need to get you into a hospital! Oh dear! Just hang on sweetheart. I'll find Myra."

Bekah doubled over as Maribel fled the room.

"Joshua!" she called to the air. "What have I done?" The contraction hit her, bringing her to her knees. Her hands were flat on the floor, the tiles cool. Sweat ran down the skin of her face and dropped in tiny splashes onto the floor.

"If you cannot save my baby, Lord…" she murmured. "If you cannot save me, Lord. Then please, please, save my husband."

Maribel and Myra were tugging at her.

"We must get her to a bed." Myra's clipped accent made her sound so efficient.

Somehow the two women pulled her up the stairs, cajoling her, making promises she knew they could not keep. The baby wasn't going to be all right.

"I've sent for a midwife," she heard Myra say.

At first, Bekah managed to lie down on the bed. Maribel tugged at her clothing, the warm air pressing against her skin as she was stripped bare. The contractions heightened, pain compressed through her, so total, so consuming, forcing her to sit upright. Then it melted to liquid, splashing up against her, changing again, hardening, steely fibres twisting into her, tightening then breaking. Faces moved in and out of the room. Whiffs of perfume that made her want to scream.

Maribel's voice.

Her hand squeezed reassuringly.

Bekah smelled the musty odour that hung on Maribel's clothing. The same smell of that box she had hidden in. The light in the room dropped, a cloaking darkness altered by the tepid gleam of lamps.

The baby came in the morning hours. It shot out suddenly after eons of merciless agony. Maribel laid the tiny child on Bekah's breast, it was gasping for breath. It refused to suckle. The midwife tried to coax it and coax it. But by the time the sun broke in through the bedroom window, the baby lay lifeless in Bekah's hands.

22

MYRA'S CAKE DIDN'T SETTLE WELL with Carlton. It made him feel crazy and uncontainable. First he was lying down in the dark and then he was sitting up and couldn't remember doing it. He saw light coming through the peephole in the wall. He was dizzy and then the light blurred and plunged into darkness again.

They were trying to poison him now. Kill him slowly. Dying without dignity. That's what they wanted him to do. But he wouldn't let them. He'd fight them every step of the way. Josh had started talking to him about Khalig and he wanted to shut out the boy's questions. The stupid kid, why couldn't he figure out what the truth was. That Khalig had betrayed them both for a cut of the ransom.

"You don't know what you're talking about," he suddenly shouted at the darkened blur in the corner. It continued murmuring at him but the noise sounded more like water running through a narrow stream, so he ignored it. Then the stream increased in volume, rushing through his head. He put his hands to his ears to stop the roar but it only intensified.

He had to get out. He was going mad. Had to get himself into the fresh air. Back to work, back to Maribel. He looked about him. Didn't know where he was. Stuck in some kind of dark room. He went over to the hatch and started slamming his shoe against the wall. Over and over again, hammering at the son of a bitching wood.

No one came to the door. Where was he? He continued slamming the shoe but he couldn't understand why he was doing it. Then he remembered where he was and felt himself imploding. He banged on the door again, shouting at the useless wood,

"You stupid bastards, let me out!" Those son's of bitches. He'd kill them with his bare hands if they'd only let me near.

He heaved himself against the door striking his shoulder and feeling the pain of the impact run into his chest. He struck it again. The cabin rocked, but didn't give. The guards were shouting outside and hitting the wall with their weapons.

Good, he thought. Get them riled up.

Someone's hand was on his shoulder. He spun around, squinted at the face. He didn't recognise it. It looked strange. Jewish. The eyes were dark and imploring, the face contorted, a creature with black curls hanging at the side of the ears, a prayer shawl, long white tassels, swaying, though the air was still and stale. He jerked around, hit the monster with his elbow catching it in the chest. It absorbed his arm and rocked and moaned back and forth.

"Blessed God, Beloved Hashem."

"Get the hell away from me!" he yelled, but the arms were back and reaching. Long thin tentacles wrapping around him. He deflected with a blow from his right, but it caught his wrist.

He screamed and the monster's face became the boy's, then Joe's, then an old man's blank, dying expression, his own face, staring at him, grey hair, fading sick eyes, his own eyes, watery, staring back.

The monster caught his wrist. He wrestled with it to no avail.

"Ramsey!" a voice was calling. It was from somewhere above him. He couldn't see it. The face came back. The Jew, with features contorted, the nose growing, large and bulbous, changing shape, expanding. Black hair twining and reaching out like vines wrapping themselves around his throat, choking him. The silken shawl brushed against his face, the smell of dusty books rushed through his nose, leaving dust spattered against his skin, the wretched sounds, the rocking and the moaning.

He yanked his hand away and suddenly, awkwardly struck out with his left. The thing ducked and his fist hit the sloping roof of the hut.

"Filthy Jew!" He was being pinned against the wall. "Bastard! Bastard!" he cursed, fighting with everything he had left.

"Mr. Ramsey," the monster shouted over and over again. Now it was leaning against him, trying to violate him. The nose growing larger and larger, spreading across the face, the top of the head flattening. The body pushing against his. He was helpless, diminished.

His arms were suddenly released and he swung again as the Jew stepped back, revealing its ugly face. He hit it square on, sending it reeling backwards through a dark empty space, then penetrating the walls of the hut, spiralling upwards, screeching an eerie scream of death.

He sat up. The air was like glue. He could barely move his arms. He rubbed his chest. Was he awake or asleep? There was spittle around his mouth. He was foaming. Like a rabid dog. Wild dreams. Dreams of childhood. Dreams of University days.

He reached over and touched the boy's foot, which didn't move.

"Josh?" he whispered but there was no answer.

He felt alone and frightened. Didn't want to be alone. Not now. He reached over in search of the fragment of cigar and found it with the Swiss army knife in his shoe.

His clothing was soaked in sweat. He took his shirt off, then the lungi which had wrapped itself around his thighs. He played with the Swiss army kit. The utensils pulled open stiffly. There were two small knives, one spoon, a pair of scissors, a file and a corkscrew.

He ran his finger along the twisting shape of the corkscrew and wished for the comfort of a wine glass against his lips. Could practically feel it, the thick dark claret which would rub the skin of his tongue. He'd swirl it in his mouth, cherishing the moment and then slowly let it trickle down his throat, drop by blessed drop.

"Drink to you, Josh," he lifted his hand to the boy's silent figure. Then he picked the knife up, crawled over to the sleeping form and started wildly chiselling away at the little hole in the side of the wall.

As it grew larger, more air filtered in. He put his eye to the outside world. The sun was rising, a spectacular fire behind a massive bank of low-lying dark clouds. Then he moved his head away from the hole and returned to his gouging and scraping, barely conscious of what he was doing.

His face was wet but he couldn't quite remember how it had got that way. The air from the gap cooled his skin. Was it raining outside? Had water splattered without his realising it? He lifted a dirty hand and rubbed his cheek, feeling the smear of grit against his skin.

He was tired. Tired and useless. He crawled back to his corner and lay down on his mat but every time he closed his eyes the image of the grotesque Jew in his prayer shawl haunted him, as if he were the angel of death.

23

IT WAS RAINING OUTSIDE. Carlton sat up, trying to remember where he was. His head spun and he lay down again. His chest tugged at him, reminding him of something. Why couldn't he remember? He lifted his hand to his hair. The spikiness jolted him. He sat up again and looked over at the light.

He closed his eyes, heard himself groan but could do nothing about his own suffering. Suddenly, Josh was shaking him. He opened his eyes. Grateful to see the boy. His head pounded.

Josh looked angry.

"I've had a terrible dream," Carlton said.

"It wasn't a dream."

"What? What wasn't a dream?" he was so confused.

"Do you know me?" Josh asked.

"Of course I know you. Have you gone mad?"

Josh crawled back to his corner. What was the boy on about? He felt frightened. His left hand was all scraped and bloody, his shoulder ached. Had they beat him?

"What happened to me?" his voice shook.

"You're all right now," Josh said coldly.

"I can't remember anything." As if a fire had burnt through him leaving a charred shell. He rubbed his chest. It was just about the only thing that didn't hurt. Had he fallen? But where? The last thing he remembered was the guard slicing his hair off. What had happened after that?

"Josh, please. Talk to me."

"Just leave it alone."

He wasn't going to beg. Why was the boy torturing him so? He lay down on his mat, curling up into a foetal position. But he couldn't rest. His right side ached too much. He sat up again. He felt so alone. Even though Josh was just there, within touching distance, he had been completely abandoned now.

It was the summer of 1955. He'd just got out of Yale. Top of the world he was and they sent him to Jakarta to train with Joseph Hornsby.

Him and Joe Sr., good friends until the old man's death. What a great father-in-law to have had, but Maribel didn't get on too well with him. Said she was tired of moving every few years, could never make friends. Guess she didn't get a much better deal after their marriage.

Josh stood up and moved to the door, bent down and picked something up. It was his shoe. What the hell was it doing there? The banging sounded like thumping on saturated bog wood but the door finally opened, flushing the place with the smell of damp air.

Josh climbed out and Carlton tried to scramble to his feet. But he must have been real slow because Josh was back at the door before he got there.

"I could use a piss," he said meekly, but Josh just shrugged.

Carlton struggled to climb through the damned opening. Had they made it smaller in the night? Josh just stood there. What was the matter with him?

"Now come on son, why don't you give me a hand?" his voice was gruff but he felt helpless and embarrassed. The kid helped him out and he tottered to a tree and pissed against it. It felt good. He lifted his face to the dripping sky and let it refresh him. The guards were stalking him warily. He couldn't figure it.

"Din!" he called out to them and Tweedledee disappeared for a minute, then returned with a lit candle. Josh was waiting, took the candle and helped him back in. The door closed.

Carlton stuck the light in the centre of the room and watched with satisfaction how the breeze from the hole in the wall flickered the flame. They were getting some fresh air. That was something.

He looked at Josh who was sitting cross-armed in the corner.

"What's eating you, son?" The boy's animosity intimidated him. He wanted it to go away.

"Leave it, Ramsey." Josh's voice was crusted with anger.

"But what did I do?" Carlton pleaded.

Josh refused to answer.

Carlton returned to his mat and lay down again. Closed his sore eyes. Felt like they were gritted up with the sands of the Sahara.

There was Maribel. Dressed up in that beautiful white wedding gown and there was a rim of pink silk around the headdress. He hadn't noticed that silk before. He lifted his fingers to touch it. It was smooth like her skin.

She looked up at him. She was so tiny, so frail. He wanted to protect her from the world. And he promised himself that he would shelter her from any danger.

The priest stood before them, all dressed in black with a white collar. Beautiful New England church. Fall of '59 with the leaves turning red under their heels.

He looked back. His parents were sitting in the front row holding hands. He was so happy. Another step in his perfect life.

Joe Hornsby was giving Maribel away. He'd asked Shumacker to be his best man. His other buddies hadn't been around. The bastard! Always tried to take what wasn't his...

Carlton was on the rig with his father in law who was hollering something at him. Maribel was in trouble. He'd heard it over the radio. Something to do with the pregnancy. They were just getting into the oil zone. Damn! He'd called for a chopper. The weather blocked anything 'til the next morning. 'Maribel!' He heard himself shouting into the rain.

Josh was shaking him. He struggled to his feet. The boy's face was in his. It was frightening, reminding him of something else, recently, something very disturbing. What was it?

The boy pushed the food tray into his hand. The hatch was open. He hadn't even heard it. What was happening to him? He looked at the food and started weeping. It was rice and yoghurt. Khalig hadn't been there after all. He couldn't remember what had upset him so badly.

Josh's hand was on his shoulder pushing him down.

"I don't understand," he said, his voice echoing in his head.

"Sit down," Josh said gently, and he hung onto the smoothness of the boy's voice like a rope which he held as he eased himself down. Josh was squatting in front of him, opening the spoon out of the knife kit.

"You have to eat something," he was saying. He looked up at the boy, trusting him, and he was no longer a boy but a young man with a kind face and concerned eyes.

"Damn, I wish there was something to drink," he said.

Josh handed him a can of pop but his hand shook too much to open it, so Josh did it for him, held it to his lips and he wondered if he was travelling down the last stretch of his own highway.

"What happened to your eye?" he asked innocently.

"You punched me."

Carlton was stunned into silence.

"I don't remember," he faltered.

"It's okay, Carlton. Don't worry about it. You were sick during the night."

"I'm very sorry. I really do apologise."

"It's okay. Forget about it." Josh went back to his own mat and, breaking the edge of the food tray, made a spoon and fed himself the sickly mush.

When they finished eating, Josh picked the trays up and flung them out of the door.

The boy returned to his mat and started tugging at the bandage on his foot, the leaves falling away damp and mouldy.

"I'll do that," Carlton said as he inched his way forward.

"You just rest," Josh answered.

"I'm fine. Really." He couldn't even convince himself of that.

He picked the boy's foot up awkwardly and was dismayed that he couldn't stop the tremors in both his hands. The pus had dried and there were scabs surrounded by inflamed skin. He touched the cuts lightly.

"How does it feel?"

"It doesn't hurt."

Carlton pressed harder on the wounds forcing himself to concentrate. "How's that?"

"Okay, I feel it now." The boy smiled.

Carlton then examined the wounds on Josh's thigh. They were healing nicely.

"You're gonna be okay now, son. That herb's done the job."

"Thanks." Josh reached over and clasped Carlton's arm. He squeezed it tightly then let it go. Carlton felt embarrassed but, oddly enough, pleased as hell.

Tweedledee ordered them out of the hut. Today was a river day. Carlton was having difficulty getting to the bank. He stumbled and Josh grabbed his arm. "Can you walk?"

Carlton nodded wearily. His left side was numb. He wasn't moving right. The riverbank was too steep. Damn if they didn't make the slopes more difficult during the night! He didn't want to ask for help. He wasn't that far gone. But Jesus, take a look at the kid's eye, all black and swollen. He still couldn't believe he'd done that! He felt bad about it. But then again... He chuckled weakly. It gave him some degree of strength, he'd been chipper enough to do some real damage there.

He lost his footing and fell into the water, couldn't get out for a minute. He gulped for air and went down again. Josh dragged him upwards.

"Nothing like a belly flop," Carlton said, trying to cover the indignity.

Josh just nodded but he didn't even try to make him feel better. It was like facing the truth all the time with this boy. No light relief. All knees and honesty.

They washed quickly, then walked back to their prison. The area around the huts had been cleared of the logs and all the food boxes. It looked as if the huts had been abandoned.

The guards were in no rush to lock them back. Tweedledee lay on the ground with his weapon against his chest. Tweedledum squatted against a tree looking bored. It seemed they were waiting for someone or something.

Carlton wondered if they were going to be moved. He leaned against a tree. Hadn't even the strength to stretch. Josh was shuffling about, bending down to touch his toes while his broken glasses slid along the rim of his nose, thumping gently onto the ground.

Those glasses. Carlton wished they had some tape to fix 'em with.

In the distance, Carlton heard a sound start up. A sound that he instantly recognised. He'd been on enough drilling rigs offshore, off enough coasts around the world to recognise the distant clipping sound that a chopper made.

He signalled to Josh. Now was the time to overcome the guards. Josh walked over to him looking into the horizon, the direction of the noise. Tweedledee jumped up suddenly. He ran towards them shouting. Carlton put a hand on Josh's arm. "Stall 'em," he said.

Josh put his hands up and side-stepped away from the hut. Tweedledee charged him, pushing him with the gun against the hut. Tweedledum thrust himself at Carlton. The hum of the bird was fast growing into a roar. Tweedledee let off a round of ammunition at Josh's feet while Tweedledum came running over and pushed Josh into the hut. They grabbed Carlton and shoved him in then slammed the hatch shut, scraping the bolts across the wood.

Overhead, the noise grew louder and louder.

"What is it?" Josh shouted.

"It's a chopper for Chrissake! It's a goddamned chopper! That Shumacker! I didn't think he had it in him. Damn it! He's bloody found us! Quick, stick something out of that hole. Let 'em see us. For Chrissakes, hurry up!"

Josh scurried around in the dark. He found nothing that would do. The roar filled the hut, as if the plane were landing just on top of them.

"Jesus, we're gonna get out!" Carlton smacked his shoulder against the hatch, trying to break it open while Josh pounded on the roof with his fists, shouting, "We're in here!"

The hatch didn't budge, but Carlton, in his excitement, continued throwing himself at it, calling out, "We're gettin' out of here boy! Jesus! Come on, hurry up. We're out of here!"

The roar of the chopper suddenly lifted.

"Stop 'em from going, son!" Carlton hollered, but his voice was swallowed by the din of the engine. "We're in here!" He shouted impotently at the roof. "We're in here!" His whole body shook with the effort.

The clamour of the chopper lost its intensity as the rotating blades began to diminish in the distance.

Carlton slumped to the floor. He put his head in his hands, trying to contain the bitterness, the disappointment... It inundated him, making him gag. He looked in Josh's direction. The boy was completely still. He mustn't show the kid his despair, mustn't let him see his fear.

"Josh, you all right?"

"They're coming back I know it," Josh whispered, so young, so full of hope.

"Don't count your chickens –"

"When I was a boy," Josh interrupted him, "my father used to take me and my brothers to the local heliport. He'd make us all a picnic, we'd watch them take off and land. Spend the whole day there. My dad, he always wanted to fly his own chopper... Always dreamt... He knew everything about them..."

"Son?"

"I mean when they hover like that, they can see everything. They would have seen the –"

"There are hundreds of huts like this one on these hills Josh. Don't get too hopeful."

"But I'm sure they know it's us."

"You get your hopes up too high, they get dashed." Carlton thought of Standex. Then Shumacker. He wasn't naive. He knew what the score was. But even so...

"Are you saying they won't know where we are?" Josh persisted.

"I couldn't tell you," Carlton answered wearily.

"But don't you think Shumacker paid the money?"

"No, I don't," Carlton answered. He'd already asked himself that same question. Told himself the same stupid lies. All those years of service... If they had paid the money, the chopper wouldn't have to search. They'd know.

Damn them! The double crossing bastards. It hit him hard. If the kid weren't here as witness he'd probably... Probably what? Blast them. He wasn't gonna let them break his spirit. His anger propelled him into action. Positive action. He was a winner, always had been, and nothing and no one was going to stop him fighting this round too.

"Josh!" he called out.

"What? Do you hear it coming back?"

"Forget the chopper."

"But I've thought of something. If they were hovering above us, maybe they couldn't land. They could have found somewhere nearby which was more open or flatter. My father –"

"Josh! We've got to think of other things right now. If they're looking for us, they'll be back. Okay? Meanwhile we've got to get our minds on something else."

"But we should make a plan of action. If we listen real hard. Maybe they'll be on foot. If we take turns listening, we can call out."

"That's a good idea son, but I think it'll end up driving us crazy with hope."

"But if we don't. My father always –"

"Your father! He must have been an interesting man!"

"What?"

"Your dad. He wanted to fly did he? How come he didn't?"

Josh was silent.

"He would have been real proud of you turning out the way you have."

"Are you shitting me?" Josh yelled.

"Why should I do that?"

"I don't want to talk about my father!" Josh slammed his fist against the roof. "When do you think the choppers will come back?" Josh began rocking from side to side against the rafters. "Shouldn't we prepare a message the next time they come over?"

"Sure," Carlton said sarcastically. "You go out there and write in big letters 'Hostages here'. How 'bout that?"

The boy stopped his rocking. "You don't think we're going to make it, do you?"

"I didn't say that." Though he damned well felt it.

"You shouldn't give up so easy," Josh said.

Carlton smiled, leant over and patted Josh on the leg. "That's good, Josh. Never give up hope. That's good."

Carlton sat back and wished for a fresh cigar. He wouldn't give up hope with a Havana. "I'll tell you what, son. If we're going to be rescued in a few hours time, fill me in on some details. If you don't want to talk about your dad, fair enough. Tell me something about the rest of your family, your grandparents for instance. I'm always interested in that sort of thing."

Josh didn't respond.

"Hey, I won't bite."

"It's not interesting," Josh replied.

"Sure it is. Come on, give me a break. You let me be the judge of that."

The boy hesitated but Carlton could wait. He said nothing more. Josh sat down. Carlton could hear the boy scratching at himself. Finally Josh said, "All right, I'll do it your way. What do you want to know?"

"You must have come from somewhere, tell me about that."

"My mother's grandparents are from Russia. They fled in the pogroms of the early 1900s."

Carlton interrupted. "My ancestors came over on the Mayflower in 1620. Can you imagine? My family's been living in roughly the same place for all this time."

Josh was silent.

"We were immigrants too," Carlton said defensively. "Nearly didn't make it."

"You see what I mean? You're not interested at all," Josh accused.

Carlton chuckled. "Okay. You win. So your grandparents came to the States from Russia. Is that right?"

"They were abandoned by the captain of their ship in the Black Sea and were left to die. My great grandmother and two uncles didn't make it."

Carlton shuffled his backside against the hard ground. Why didn't he feel any compassion? Josh must have sensed it, because he didn't continue.

"What'd your grandfather do after he came to the States?" Carlton asked.

"He sold horse brushes."

Carlton lost interest. These people were losers: pedlars, hawkers. He said, "I thought all Jews went into the professions."

"That's a generality," Josh snapped back.

Carlton couldn't blame the boy for snapping at him, but he couldn't help himself either. Josh's history made him itchy.

"You're the first Jewish person I've ever spent any time with. I never had anything to do with your people..." He was rambling, letting out some kind of pent up antagonism or discomfort. "You get the impression you're all lawyers or bankers. You know the kind of thing I mean," Carlton laughed.

He peered at his charge. Josh was sitting very still.

"Come on, Josh... I'm just kidding, boy."

Suddenly Josh blurted out, "Bastard! You think I'm some kind of freak because I'm Jewish?"

"No need to name-call, son," Carlton retorted.

"You hate me because of it, don't you?"

"I don't hate you." How could the boy be so direct?

"Bullshit. You've hated me from the first moment you laid eyes on me. Do you think I couldn't tell?"

Carlton was too stunned to answer. It wasn't his fault the boy was Jewish. "Whatever it is you are," he said, "you should be proud of it."

"Crock!" Josh growled.

"You're an individual, not a whole race," Carlton lied unconvincingly.

"That's crap and you know it. Every individual represents something."

"Okay, fine. What's your problem then?"

"It isn't my problem it's yours."

"I can't agree with that."

The comment silenced the young man.

"Josh?"

"I don't even understand what it means to be Jewish. Don't understand what makes me so different, from say you or someone else who isn't and yet –"

"Yet?"

204

"You know the difference."

"Josh you're right, I'm an asshole."

"Don't fob me off like that."

The absence of sound hung around them. Gave too much meaning to their own destiny.

"It's like wearing your identity on a name plate. That's what you said that first evening. Like I was some sort of advertisement."

The boy was being emotional, just like his own son was.

Josh continued. "It was okay in New York, where I grew up I didn't even know there was anything different about being Jewish. Then I went to North Carolina." Josh hesitated, as if he were considering his own words, or remembering his experiences. "I knew someone." The edge in his voice grew more brittle. "We were friends for over two years and then one day he found out I was Jewish. I had let out that I was going to my nephew's bar mitzvah. I hadn't even thought it would mean anything, thought it was normal!

"My so-called friend jumped out of his seat, urging me to stand up, turn around. I didn't know what he wanted. 'You don't have a tail!' he said. A tail and horns. That's what he was looking for."

"Oh come on son, you're exaggerating things."

But Carlton could tell Josh wasn't listening.

"I became paranoid," he continued. "I didn't want anyone to know I was Jewish. But they just seemed to. And then when I went home, the things I'd cherished as a boy I hated now. The cloistered view. The expectations. That's when I transferred from medical school to geology. Needed to break away from what everyone expected me to be."

Carlton squirmed uncomfortably. He tried to understand what Josh was saying but it was so foreign to his own experience of life.

The heavy air tumbled between them and as the wind changed direction outside, splashes of water spattered through the hole.

"Like I said, I've never had any dealing with Jewish people." Carlton wished he could say more to the boy to make him feel better.

"But what is it?" Josh pleaded and Carlton searched within himself to try and give his companion some honesty.

"I don't know. I guess it's what one is brought up to believe."

"And what were you brought up to believe?" Josh's tone was bitter.

Why couldn't the boy realise that he was trying to help him? "Just general impressions I guess. Nothing I can specifically put my finger on."

"Yeah, I bet."

"Now look, son." Carlton was getting tired of the boy's accusing attitude. It cut too close to the core and he couldn't really take the pressure. "You'd better come to terms with yourself. No one else can do it for you."

"You don't know what it's like."

"Don't presuppose what it is I know or don't."

"It's pretty easy to tell," Josh growled, but Carlton wished they could be at peace with each other. Wished the boy would forgive him.

"You are what you are, Josh. You've got to learn to live with it."

"Yeah," Josh answered angrily and Carlton sensed the boy shut himself away from any further conversation.

24

ALL THROUGH THE NIGHT, choppers flew by, sometimes shining their lights so that small beams of yellow would break against the wood and enter the hut.

Josh alternated helplessly between despair and hope. Every time a helicopter would near he'd shout and bang on the wall, hoping someone would hear him. Carlton finally told him to stop his yelling. He should save his voice for when it really mattered.

How could he sleep? He sat up listening. Listening for the sound of engines, new voices, sounds of rescue. The cacophony of the wind replaced the chopping blades. Then Ramsey started snoring. How could the man be so relaxed at a time like this? He was so full of contradictions. Josh would never understand him.

Time dragged, splashed against his face and smeared his skin. Dropped into the stubble of dark beard which he scratched with dirty fingers.

He needed to think things through. Needed to understand exactly what was going on. Maybe tonight, maybe tomorrow they'd be rescued. Maybe Bekah would be there. The thought of her jolted him. He had to get out. He had to see her, touch her.

He gasped for air.

Try and think. All the fears that surrounded his life confronted him now. Carlton had become a mirror reflecting back to him his own inner thoughts, his own anti-Semitism.

"Ramsey," he called, but the older man just snuffled and started snoring louder.

The sweat dripped from his face. Now that the sickness had lifted, every muscle ached with inaction. He desperately needed to get up and run.

Bekah.

His body craved hers. That comfort. He reached out in the darkness.

Imagined that he could touch her. Imagined what she would say to him.

'Everything has meaning, Josh.'

'No. Bekah, no. I can't think...'

'Meaning, Josh... '

He scrambled over to the corner. Groped around for the knife. Started working on the hole. Next time the chopper came round he'd stick the blade out, turn it round, maybe the light would catch it. His dad had taught him SOS. If only...

The wind gusted against the wall. There, in the distance, he thought for sure he could hear his father's voice, then Bekah's. He was getting like Carlton, hearing things that weren't there.

Damn the old man! He'd called him a filthy Jew! Flung back at him what he most wanted to avoid. Jew! But what did it actually mean? He searched within himself and found only images of candles. Endless candles. Burning, flickering through his childhood. Candles and blessings. Candles and miracles. Candles for the dead. His father lying on the floor of the Laundromat. Candles and prayers.

No!

It was all illusion. There was no God. No beneficent Old Man sitting in the heavens. No Cosmic Father. Science was better. That's what saved him. Things he could touch and feel. Measurements, observations. You could try to prove that God existed but in the end you couldn't. It was all based on belief and he was too sceptical to believe in anything he couldn't see. No, that's not right either. What about love? Kindness? Faith?

Faith in what? His mother's shocked look fell before his eyes. Like a malevolent spirit, a dybbuk come to haunt him. She'd be horrified if she heard him deny God, deny religion. But he had. There, he had thought it and nothing worse had happened.

He couldn't understand why there was even one Jewish person left believing, when God had failed to prove himself time and time again. Then he shook his head and reminded himself. As dark as his own child would be and despite Bekah's Catholicism, another Hitler would remind them and their grandchildren that they were Jews: fodder for a murderous god.

He stretched his leg and grazed Carlton, who stirred. The older man hadn't even remembered what he'd said in that nightmare state. Didn't even remember punching him. Josh put his hand up to his eye. It was swollen and bruised. Another insult to the injury of his face.

And when Carlton had finally come round, the left side of his mouth had looked dragged down and didn't move when he spoke. Josh hadn't said anything, hadn't wanted to frighten the older man.

It'd be easier to hate Carlton. The gulf between them was gaping. Too large for any real understanding. Too deep for any true crossing. But he couldn't bring himself to hate him. If anything he was feeling the opposite.

Carlton groaned again in his sleep, calling out his son's name, 'Joe!' But was it Joe or his own name? They sounded so alike in the garbled emotion of sleep.

The choppers hadn't returned. The wind had fallen and the jungle was silent. Even when he put his ear to the hole, Josh could hear nothing but the dripping water on the bending leaves.

He drifted. Back into his childhood. The praying in the synagogue, his father in a dark suit, rocking back and forth, reaching up and kissing the Torah. The wooden bench was hard. Uncomfortable. He couldn't keep still. His mother was on the other side of the room behind a curtain. He dropped to the floor to peer through the legs. She always wore the same black shoes.

His father yanked him back up. Scolded him silently. When the prayers started again, he crept from the benches and ran outside where the black kids that hung around the steps of the synagogue smoked cigarettes.

But Abraham, his older brother, always came looking for him.

He was finishing his Masters. One night he and his buddies decided it was time to celebrate. Get drunk. Only two more weeks to the Thesis Defence. They all staggered down to Woody's. A few beers and onto Huck's for a party.

They were throwing eggs or something. One smashed against the wall. Someone jumped him, grabbed his hands behind his back. Another guy shoved bacon rolled in cheese against his lips. Shrieks of laughter…

Driblets of sweat lined his upper lip. He hadn't told Carlton about that. Couldn't admit the impact that it had on him.

The next morning there were no longer sounds from the skies, nor from the guards outside. Carlton sat up. He stretched his arms out then ran his fingers through his spiky hair. "Why don't you convert?" he asked.

"What? Conversion? Conversion to what?

"To Christianity. Get yourself baptised."

"I can't do that."

"Why not. You're not happy as you are."

"But it's the Christians who have persecuted us all through history. How could I become one of them?"

"So many of your brethren have."

"I couldn't."

"So become a Buddhist then, or a Taoist."

"That won't change anything. You can't hide your past. Anyway, I'm not a practising Jew. What difference does it make?"

Carlton shook his head. "I don't know son. It was just an idea." Carlton dipped his fingers into the small pool of collected water and rubbed his eyes.

"You're Protestant, aren't you?" Josh asked.

"My parents were. I've been christened, but religion? What does it mean? I don't go to church. My wife has more to do with that sort of thing than I do. I don't feel any affinity with any particular God."

"Then what are you so bigoted about?"

"I'm not a bigot!" Carlton protested. He patted some more water on his face. He looked up at Josh who stared at him angrily. "Well, I guess I might be some," Carlton mumbled.

The answer was a surprise. Josh had never expected Carlton to admit anything about himself. He was suddenly grateful and wanted to grab the older man's hand and shake it. But he sat still. Didn't move. Let Ramsey continue if he would.

"I've got these crazy notions," Carlton said. "You know, these images that come into my mind. And I don't even know where they come from. Images of ghettos with Jews dressed in black. You know, those black coats and hats and long black beards. Somehow they seem dirty. That's what it is." Carlton stopped speaking suddenly, as if deep in thought. "That's what it is... No. It's crazy..."

"What is?"

"It's not worth saying..."

"Tell me!"

"Those images. I don't even know where I got them from. Something about killers... That's right. Killers of Christ..."

Josh sighed. The sins of the fathers lasted longer than seven generations. It held on through all time, ran through the blood and resurrected hate.

"Is that what you believe?" Josh choked, unable to say anything about the age old belief, the age old hate that marked him and everyone like him.

"Who cares who killed Christ!" Carlton raised his voice. "If it hadn't been the Jews it would've been the Romans or one of his own. If he even existed. If he hadn't been martyred we'd probably all be practising Jews by now," Carlton chuckled to himself. "Besides, it's all a load of hogwash. Just another excuse to hate each other. It's in our natures."

"To hate?"

"It's all brainwashing," Carlton continued.

"What is?" Josh said wearily, didn't really want to find out what Carlton was referring to this time.

"This hating the Jews business," he laughed as Josh tensed further. "It's easier to hate than it is to love, isn't it, Josh?"

Josh let out his breath not believing the old man's words. Easier to hate. Didn't think Carlton was capable of such thought, of such depth. He didn't know what to say. Easier to hate. Easier to hate himself. Easier to hate others than extend love. Easier to hate his parents. Easier to hate Carlton.

"I hated my son." Carlton's words made Josh gasp.

"You're kidding?" What was he to say?

"He's a queer bastard, you know. Can you imagine what that did to me when I found out?"

Josh wanted to laugh. Of all the contradictions. Of all the great ironies. Mr. macho himself has a gay son.

"You think that's funny?" Carlton asked.

"Yes." There he had said it.

This time Carlton was silent. Waiting. But Josh wouldn't say anything. Not dig himself a hole.

"Well you're right. It is funny. Damned pitifully funny. And I've been a complete jerk about it!" Carlton reached out and grabbed a shoe and hit the wall with it.

Josh jumped. "What're you doing?"

"I've got to take a piss," Carlton growled and hit the wall again but there was only the refrain of silence in response.

"Give me your other shoe." Josh took the shoe from Carlton and started banging on the wall too. There was no response. Josh shouted. He put his ear against the wall and heard nothing but the rustle of monkeys or birds in the trees. He squinted his eye against the hole but saw no movement.

Carlton continued banging. "Damned sons of bitches. Listen Josh, if we both try to knock the bloody thing over."

"I don't know if that's such a good idea." Josh put the shoe down.

"Why? I feel fine. In fact, I feel better now than I've done all week."

Josh got up reluctantly. Was there nothing he could say that would stop Carlton?

"Are you with me son, or do I have to do this myself?"

"I'll do it."

"Hell no! Takes two for this job. It's teamwork son. You and me. Are you part of my team or not?"

"I am, but I don't –"

"Josh, are you with me or not?"

"I'm with you," Josh replied.

"Okay then. Let's do it. One, two, three," Carlton commanded and they both threw themselves against the wall. The hut didn't budge. They tried again and then a third time.

Carlton was winded. He leaned against the wall.

"You've done enough now Ramsey."

"Naah, I just need a breather."

"It isn't working anyway. What if we kick it?" Josh returned to his side of the hut. He put Carlton's shoes on his feet and aimed himself at the wall kicking it as hard as he could. The hut moved slightly.

"Hey, that's good," Carlton said encouragingly and Josh tried again. Carlton lay down beside him.

"One, two, three... Kick!" This time the hut shook appreciably. They kicked again. Josh kicked and kicked not paying any attention to anything but the shaking of the roof timbers and the rocking of the walls.

But Carlton had stopped. He lay still with his feet against the wall. Josh scrambled upright. "Carlton?" he shook the man's shoulder. "Carlton?" The hand was limp but warm. Josh searched for the pulse. It was weak. "Carlton can you hear me?" He lifted Carlton's legs, twisting the older man till he lay flat on the floor. He rolled him on his side. Felt for his pulse again. There was nothing.

He bent down and placed his ear next to Carlton's mouth. He could hear nothing. He checked one more time then rolled Carlton onto his back.

He lifted Carlton's chin upward, pinched the old man's nose as he gulped a breath of air and transferred it to his body. He watched the man's chest rise and then let it fall. Calmly, gently, he repeated the breathing, willing himself, in between breaths, to be able to see through the darkness whether Carlton's lips had changed colour.

He put his ear to Carlton's chest, feeling simultaneously for a pulse in his wrist. No. There was certainly nothing.

He positioned himself over the old man's chest and pumped against the lower half of his breast bone, one hand on top of the other, rocking himself forward with the compression and rolling backward in between. Fifteen times he repeated and then returned to giving breath.

"Ramsey? Can you hear me?" he shouted desperately. Carlton stirred slightly.

"Carlton!" he called again. But the still man gave nothing in return. Maybe the movement had just been his imagination. Josh groped for Carlton's wrist feeling for his pulse, then touched his neck. It was there! Hardly noticeable but there nonetheless.

He took his own shirt off, put it under Carlton's head and rolled him onto his side again. He checked Carlton's pulse again and leaned his ear against his mouth. He was breathing.

He crawled over to the hole and shouted through it for help. How could they leave them like that, without any food, any water? He stood and went to the door and hammered on it, shouting all the time until his voice grew hoarse. He banged on the walls with Carlton's shoes to no avail. Was there no one there? Had they truly been abandoned? Left there to die slowly?

He felt his bowels gurgle in response to the horror and clenched his buttocks. He had to relieve himself. Had to. He was shitting himself with fear.

He banged again on the wall and then lifted the lungi. He squatted in the corner. The odour was unbearable. The muck dribbled onto his foot. He took the lungi off and cleaned himself with it, then spread it over the gruel of shit.

Maybe Carlton was the lucky one. Going like that. Unaware of the situation they were in. Trapped and dehumanised beyond belief. Was this the horror that his ancestors had experienced, in the pogroms of Eastern Europe? In the death camps of Germany?

He sat by Carlton's side and leaned against the wall. The man's hand was cool, he took it in his own. Carlton jerked and suddenly moaned. There were gurgling sounds coming from his mouth and then total silence.

"Ramsey!" he called out again. Josh heard his words as if they came from above or beside him. They were a potion, they would somehow keep Carlton alive. He started telling Carlton about his family. His mother, how crazy she'd become after his father's death, about his brothers, the way they followed the religion without question. How, unlike him, they had never ventured away from the safety of New York.

His voice grew hoarse. He lay down beside the man and listened for his breath. It was scarcely there. He put his arm around Carlton, dragging him closer and started rocking him back and forth, their legs, their torsos touching giving Carlton the warmth, the comfort that he must need if he was to survive.

"Fight for God's sake!" He called out over and over again, the depth of his emotion coming not from inside him, but from a bottomless, fathomless pit that connected him to something greater, something deeper than he'd ever experienced before.

He sat up after an interminable amount of time. The last speck of light was just disappearing into an empty black hole. The silence was ominous. Carlton had been right. They hadn't been found.

Josh scratched his back against the wall. He pulled the old man toward him. The body was limp but still warm. He took Carlton in his arms and rocked him back and forth, tears of exhaustion running down his face then dropping and lying like pools of dried blood on Carlton's.

He held the dying man tight, trying to provide him with some shelter, to give him some of his own life force. He rocked and sang in a deep and saddened voice, and he remembered the prayers that he had sung every night as a young boy to shelter him from childhood fears. 'Baruch atuh Adonu, Baruch Shem Kavod. Oh God, please help us now that we are in such need of you, please dear God, please do not desert me yet again as you have deserted your people for all these centuries, testing us, trying us, your people.'

"You bastard! You stupid fuckin' lying bastard!" He shouted and resumed his rocking, his praying, holding Carlton in his arms.

Sometime during the night he fell asleep but was woken in the morning by the pinpoint of light against his eye. Carlton was still in his arms.

He felt for a pulse, lifted the hand. It was soft and supple. He bent his head and listened for breath. Nothing. He reached over and grabbed the shoe and started whacking the side of the wall. There was no one there. He was sure of it now.

He clutched at the old man beseeching him to live, to open his eyes. But he may as well be dead. He found himself begging Carlton to wake up. He clutched at the man's body and leaned back against the wall holding him. He closed his eyes and willed himself into unconsciousness, but found no release.

He couldn't breathe but couldn't let go of Carlton to go to the hole and find some air. His body was numb but his thoughts were assaulting him at every turn. All he could see was his father, in his dark coat with the prayer book in his hands, on the Sabbath, in the synagogue, praying to an inner rhythm, a rhythm, which he, Josh, could no longer understand or hear.

25

THE RAIN BANGED ON THE ROOF and flowed through the centre of the hut. Thunder echoed against the hills, shaking the wood and waking Josh. Carlton had slid onto his legs.

He leaned over, putting his hand against the man's face. It was cool and lifeless. He pulled his legs out, gently easing Carlton's head onto the ground. Then he knelt and put his ear to Carlton's mouth to listen for the absent breath.

He felt for a pulse. Demanded there be some life left in the man. Surely Carlton wouldn't give up so easily. The stench in the cabin made him ill. His own shit was the cause. He put his nose against Carlton's neck to smell for decay. Everything smelled the same.

He crawled to the hole and looked out. There was no one there. He had to urinate. He stood up, trying to wriggle his penis as close to the hole as possible to send the urine outside. The eaves stopped him. Miserably, he went to the corner, where the lungi lay wrapped in his excrement and urinated onto that.

All his life he had fought against being categorised, being put in little boxes with neat little labels on them and now he was going to end his life in just such a box. And it wasn't even because he was Jewish. This time his ancestry had nothing to do with it. He was too discouraged to smile at the irony.

He returned to Carlton's body. All he could think of doing was to rub the man's arms and legs, to try to get circulation going in them. But Carlton just lay there like stone.

Josh continued checking for breath, checking for pulse. He would make Carlton live. He would force him to. His emotions swamped him. He had let his father go but he refused to allow Carlton to.

He grappled wildly for his knife and found it in the corner of the hut. He cut a piece of Carlton's lungi, dipped it in the collecting, overflowing water in the floor and washed the older man's muddy face and then his chest and his hands. Then as the water renewed itself, washing through the cabin, he scooped it up and put it in his own mouth, the taste of it tantalising.

He was suddenly aware of an intense hunger and he hated his own body for its continual life. He was afraid of dying slowly, starving to death or from dehydration.

He collapsed exhausted and pulled Carlton's body upward, straining with the weight of it. A lizard scampered over his foot. He didn't react. That fear had become insignificant to what he had now become.

He pulled Carlton to him, lay his head against his chest and started his incessant praying. What did he care what God was out there listening? He would pray to every single one of them but all he could think of was his Hebrew prayers that he'd been taught for his bar mitzvah.

But there was no answer. No light flooding in. No candles everlasting. No sea parting. No miracles. He began to weep as the old man slid downwards, his head resting on Josh's legs. Something hard and intangible crumbled inside him. Carlton had reflected back to him his own self hatred and so he'd hated what was outside him in return. The realisation filled the emptiness with light. He pulled the older man closer, whispered to him, "If we get free, I'm not going to be afraid anymore."

The sound of the bolts scraping across the wood silenced him. A harsh glare broke into the darkness.

"Who's there?" he shielded his eyes.

"Felstein?" An American voice was calling him. "Jesus!" he heard, "It's like death in here."

"Who's there?" Josh called again, holding Carlton close to protect him.

"It's me son, Shumacker."

"Shumacker! Have you got a doctor with you? Hurry!"

Shumacker climbed in then bent over Carlton and searched for a pulse in his neck. He said, "He's still alive. Just hold on son. I've got a chopper and a medic coming for you any minute. Take it easy. You're in safe hands now."

Suddenly there were soldiers in the hut, rifles banging against Josh. Shumacker tried to get Josh out but he insisted on helping to lift Carlton from the hut.

"Drink this Felstein." Shumacker handed him a bottle of something to drink. It was sweet and syrupy and Josh gulped the liquid down.

"Those choppers! Were they you?" Josh panted as Shumacker handed him a lungi.

"They were us all right," Shumacker called to one of the soldiers to cover Carlton.

"But why didn't you come earlier?"

"Look Felstein. You've been through a rough time. Let's talk later."

"Tell me."

"We knew what area you were in. We just couldn't pinpoint you."

"So you paid the ransom then? That's how you found us!"

"Not exactly."

"Ramsey was right. He said you –"

"Listen son. Things are complicated all over. Don't you go getting ideas about –"

"Then how did you find us?" Shumacker muttered something then said, "Your wife... She –"

"Bekah!"

"Here comes the chopper, son. We'll talk later."

"Tell me! What about Bekah?"

Shumacker sighed. "Your wife found out where you were."

Josh could barely contain himself. Bekah? Bekah had somehow... "Where is she?"

Shumacker stalled. He lifted his hand to his eyes, searching the sky for the helicopter.

"Mr. Shumacker. Where is my wife?" Josh grabbed hold of the man's arm.

"I'm sorry son. She's in hospital in Singapore. She lost the baby. I tried to warn her –" he shook off Josh's hand.

"She's not... Tell me she's –"

"She's fine. You don't have to worry about that. Your wife's a real fighter. Nothing short of Hiroshima could stop her. Here it comes."

The chopper was nearly upon them sweeping the leaves around their heads.

"Stand back." Shumacker pulled Josh to the edge of the area as the helicopter landed. "Let's be quick about this," Shumacker shouted. "Felstein, you first."

Josh climbed aboard and watched as they carefully raised Carlton up. He strapped himself into his seat, emotions swirling about him. His baby was dead. Always, always there was a price for life.

He twisted around to look at Carlton. They'd put an oxygen mask on him, he could hear the breath pull in and release. He let out a deep sigh, thanked God for his mercy, then touched the wall of the chopper to make sure that it was real.

The craft lifted, Josh looked out of the window. Two little brown huts stood innocently amongst a canopy of jungle trees with a nearby river in flood. It was at once a place of intense beauty and hidden desolation.

26

CARLTON HEARD THE RUSTLE of material by his head, caught the scent of something familiar, enticing. Something that made him want to reach out and touch it: his wife's perfume. But he was dreaming or he was dead. He didn't trust his senses anymore, not after those terrible nightmares and whacking Josh in the face with his fist.

The soft warmth of a woman's skin lay against the roughness of his own hand. He was imagining it. Didn't want to open his eyes. Didn't want to know that the comfort he now imagined would disappear into the wretchedness of that prison hut.

"Carlton?"

He ignored the voice. Maybe it was the kid's but it sounded like Maribel. No, he wasn't gonna let this mirage go.

"Sweetheart?" Someone was gently shaking him. Forcing him to open his eyes. Maybe if he pretended. Kept his eyelids half shut. He'd be able to go back.

He was in a bed. In an ugly sterile looking room. And Maribel was just by him. "Maribel?"

She squeezed his hand and smiled. But he'd touched her hand before, smelt the sweet skin only to be pulled awake by Josh's concern. No, he couldn't trust his senses. Knew that if he reached beyond her he'd find the nightmare of the pressing darkness.

"Where am I?" he whispered cautiously.

Maribel bent over him, kissed him on the forehead. It seemed so real. "You're in the hospital in Singapore, sweetheart."

"Are you sure?"

"Of course I am. Here, let me straighten that pillow. How do you feel?"

"Pretty bad Mari... I..."

She leant closer. "What is it?"

"It's a crazy question... I..."

"Yes love. What is it?"

"Is this... Am I really here? The last time –"

"The doctor said you'd be disoriented. Don't worry about it. You're fine now and you're safe."

Carlton wanted to ask her a thousand questions but the thoughts slipped from his mind. He was so tired. So damned tired. Wanted to relinquish himself to it and yet...

"How'd I get here?" Maybe if her answer were credible...

As she explained, he found himself drifting, sometimes into her voice and then away. Could it be true that Josh had kept him alive? The rhythm of his breath brought images that sparked across his closed eyes: the choppers that kept flying away, Josh bending over him, the solace of his care. Maribel's voice saying that she'd been held... Held where? There were voices above him and then the sensation of floating...

"Dad?"

His eyes flew open. He was still in the same room but Maribel was gone. "Joe?" He couldn't move his head. "Joe, is that you son?"

"It's me dad." Joe walked around the bed and sat where Maribel had just been. Carlton reached out finding his son's hand. He clasped it weakly. "Joe is that really you? No, I know it can't be. But it doesn't matter, I need to tell you something, son. Josh!"

"Dad it's me, Joe."

"Jesus, son I need to let you know. What you are, it's nothing to me... Come closer boy I need to tell you –" Before the guards busted open... It was his only chance. He looked as hard as he could — seemed like it was Joe — trying to convince himself this was no illusion. The boy was a softer version of himself. Softer even than he'd remembered from before. "Damn!" he clutched at the other's hand.

"Dad?"

"Josh, I just want to say."

"Dad. It's Joe."

"Yeah, Joe. I want to tell you something."

"Hold on dad, I'll go get the doctor."

"I don't need a doctor. Godammit boy, give me a chance will you?"

"Sure Dad, anything you want."

Carlton moved his head to get a better look. The boy had tears running down his face. Jesus, why did he have to go and do that for? "For Chrissake! Pull yourself together." Carlton tried to sit up. The lights seemed to flicker as the room spun. Must cling on... He sank back into the pillows.

"Just rest pops. I'll go get Ma."

"No, don't leave me yet. Please. I was wrong son. Stupidly wrong. You gotta believe it. I didn't understand before. But I do now." He clutched at his heart expecting pain, but there was none. Then he was dreaming. He hadn't got his chance after all. Either that or he really was dead and it was too late.

The door swung open. Maribel floated in, chattering away like chimes in a wind storm. How that used to aggravate him but now it was angel's music. But who's that? "Josh?" Confused he looked at the young man beside him, "Joe?" Crazy dream this was. And who was Josh holding hands with? A black girl in a white hospital gown?

"Carlton, look who's here." Maribel took the girl's other hand. "I want you to meet the most wonderful person I've been telling you about. This is Bekah Felstein. Josh's wife."

Josh's wife?

The girl came over to the bed. Carlton peered at the dark, oval face.

"I'm so glad you're all right." Bekah leant over him.

"My wife says..." but Carlton couldn't go on. There was no use reiterating the fantasy that he had concocted about an escape which may not have really happened. He closed his eyes let himself begin to sink away.

"Carlton?" Josh's hand was on his wrist again. He opened his eyes looked around. Not the darkness of the hut but this strange sterile looking room. The characters of his dream had all remained as if they were waiting for him to tell them something. Haven't they got what they wanted?

"Josh?" Carlton reached out, drawing Josh towards him. "Josh, you've got to tell me," he whispered. "I know I can count on you to give it to me straight. Am I dreaming? You know what I'm talking about, son? Is this real or am I –?"

Josh squeezed his wrist. "This is real. I promise. Shumacker came and got us."

"That son of a –"

"Yeah, him."

Carlton touched the soft sheets under his other hand. There were tubes stuck in his arm. But how come his chest didn't hurt anymore?

"So it's true?" Carlton whispered pulling the boy closer.

"About this?" Josh asked.

"No, what Maribel told me. About how you saved my life."

"Not me. Bekah and Maribel."

"And you son. I would have never survived without you."

Josh shook his head.

"How's the baby?" Carlton suddenly asked. He remembered that Bekah was pregnant.

Bekah pulled back and Josh gathered her in his sheltering arms.

"Carlton!" Maribel fluttered over them like a momma bird. "I'm so sorry. He doesn't know."

"We lost the baby." Josh hugged Bekah closer.

"Jesus!" Carlton felt wounded. Wounded for Josh. Wounded even for himself. "Josh, I don't know what to say."

"That's okay, we'll be fine." Bekah lifted her head clasping her arms about Josh's waist. Over Bekah's shoulders, Carlton saw Josh's eyes. They were full of self assurance and love.

"Josh?" he said awkwardly.

"Yes sir?"

"I suppose you're not going back to Standex after this are you?"

"I'm going straight back. Not giving up that easy."

"Hey that's good son. Well remember — don't let the bastards or the good life ever get you down."

Josh laughed. "No chance of that." He hugged Bekah again smiling into her face. "I guess we ought to pack up. We've got a flight to catch." Josh let go of his wife and moved closer to the bed. He shook hands with Joe and then turned to Carlton as Maribel and Bekah whispered at each other, hugging and kissing.

"Carlton." Josh extended his hand.

Carlton clasped the hand as hard as he could, now not wanting to let go. "Josh?" Damn what was he going to say? There was a sudden tug across his chest. He'd become connected to this boy, didn't want to let him go without telling him... But what could he say? He didn't want to seem the fool. He glanced over at his son. Joe was looking at him. Like he expected him to say something. But what? "Josh?" he said again, shifting uncomfortably in the bed. "You ever come Connecticut way?" He held his breath, goddammit, hoping the answer would be yes.